Fishplates
&
Frogs

by

Mag Cummings

**Grosvenor House
Publishing Limited**

This book is published by
Grosvenor House Publishing Ltd
28-30 High Street, Guildford, Surrey, GU1 3HY.
www.grosvenorhousepublishing.co.uk

A CIP record for this book
is available from the British Library

ISBN 1-905529-99-6

For Mum and Aunt Elizabeth,
It's done.

Acknowledgements

I wish to thank my brother, Des, for the stories that made this book possible. My husband, John, whose support and encouragement enabled me to work harder. Also my three grown-up children, Kit, Des and Geri. Without their faith and I.T. expertise, my computer screen would have remained blank.

I am a local author. If you enjoyed this story please contact me by email at mag.cummings@blueyonder.co.uk. I am NOT on social media. MC. x

Preface

The "Glory Days" of rail travel in Britain have gone forever. Gone are the busy branch lines that once criss-crossed our land, with trains calling at picturesque little stations. Nowadays, CCTV cameras are suspended overhead, replacing the wisteria of old that hung from station canopies.

So climb aboard right now, and we'll take a "glory" journey one more time. Put your feet up on the opposite seat (unless you see the guard coming) and enjoy the ride. The destination is back in time to the sixties, in the aftermath of the Beeching Cuts, when Britain's railways had to fight for survival against the growing trends in improved road travel to bring about the real "age of the train."

Prologue
1958

'I won't – eh, - I won't *see* anything, will I?'

Young Coley was looking worried and glanced at his colleague apprehensively.

'See anything? What d'ye mean?'

Frankie knew exactly what young Coley meant. He knew what was coming but affected nonchalance.

'Well, I mean, like - any bits and pieces left over, y'know? Big Oweny and Degsie were saying that sometimes – sometimes —'. The boy broke off, not knowing quite how to put his fears into words.

They had been walking along the side of the rail track towards Ayr sheds, where the engine that they were assigned to clean had been docked overnight. They were carrying the buckets and brushes that they would use on their gruesome task. Frankie stopped and gave the boy a steady look. There was no getting round it. He would have to level with the lad.

He laid a hand on the boy's shoulder.

'Look son,' he began, 'I won't kid you. This will not be a pleasant task. I've done it before and it's one of the worst jobs I've ever had to do and, sad to say, it happens far too often. But listen now. The police and the ambulance people will have done the best they can. They won't have been able to get everything, but they'll have done a good job – for the relatives, like, y'know? There might be a few nasty bits and pieces – in fact I'm sure there will be. Do you think you're up to it? Do you want me to get someone else? I'll be okay wi' that, son. I wouldnae wish this on my worst enemy, so if you're a bit squeamish —'

The boy's pallor had taken on a whitish tone, but he swallowed manfully a few times and then said, blustering, 'I'm no' squeamish, not at all! I'm here, see! I'll dae it!'

Frankie made a chomping sound with his lips. 'O.K, let's go!'

The two started forward again and Frankie said,

'We won't be on our own. There's a guy coming wi' a jet hose or whatever it's called. That should save us a bit of work, and the carriage cleaners will be there, so just think of it as a normal cleaning job.'

Frankie was thinking hard as they walked the rest of the way in silence. This suicide had been a particularly horrific incident even though it had taken place at a lonely siding and the only witnesses were the two train drivers involved. Fatalities of this sort were most likely to happen on crowded station platforms. Suddenly, without warning, someone would jump in front of an incoming train. That always puzzled Frankie; why anyone would want to end their life so publicly, in front of other people – young women, wee children and the like. Heaven knows what that does to them, or to the traumatised driver, who can do nothing. Nothing, that is, but go into deep shock. His nerves are then so shattered that his confidence in his ability to continue to do his job can be severely affected for months. Years, even.

One of Frankie's closest friends, Paddy Preston, had been driving the passenger train from Ayr to Glasgow. Paddy had been back on the job for only a few months after having been involved in two previous fatalities, and was struggling to come to terms with the fact that this was part of the job. They had never prepared him for this during training. Methods of dealing with fatalities were explained, and procedures hammered home and practiced, but the impression given was that these occurrences were rare. This evidently was not the case.

Now, Frankie was really concerned about Paddy. He had visited his friend at home last night and had learned some of the details of this latest tragedy.

'I had just come to that double bridge on to Kirkfield Junction,' Paddy told him. 'You know the one, Frankie? It's on a long bend, so I had no clear view ahead. As I emerged from the bridge, I saw a man on the track right in front of me, only a few yards away. When I spotted him he was staring at a slow moving freight train travelling in the opposite direction to me on the other side of the junction. I realise now that the man had been contemplating running across the tracks to throw himself in front of the freight train, but when my train suddenly appeared as if out of nowhere, on the very line on which he was already standing, he turned and looked straight at me, and I swear, Frankie, he looked positively relieved that I was coming right at him.'

'What makes you think that?' Frankie asked.

'Well I don't know for sure, of course, but he had an eerily gleeful look on his face that seemed to say 'You'll do.' It was as if he knew the freight train was moving too slowly for his purpose. In a split second, he stretched out his arms, and ran as fast as he could up the track towards me, his coat flapping behind him in the wind like the wings of a demented angel. I was already hammering on the brake for all I was worth, but I knew it was too late. I know I was shouting something but I can't remember what. It all happened in a few seconds – literally – a few seconds. The poor fellow disappeared beneath me. The freight train driver could see the whole thing. I will never forget the horrified look on his face as he witnessed what he and I were both powerless to stop.'

It was clear to Frankie that Paddy was deeply affected this time, and no amount of reassurance that he was not to blame was going to help right now. He left, knowing that his friend would suffer many nightmares before he could put all this aside. He kept these anxious thoughts to himself though, and turned his attention to the young lad beside him.

It was the first time that fifteen-year old Coley had been in the maintenance sheds. He was a trainee ticket clerk, but today he had been seconded to help Frankie and he had jumped at the chance to see some of the powerful locomotives up close. But when he learned the specifics of his assignment, he had balked a little. Intense teasing from some of his older workmates had added to his discomfiture, terrifying him with grisly stories of gory sights and ghostly apparitions.

From a long way off, he could hear the clanging of hammers on steel, and loud voices as men shouted to make themselves heard. Inside, the air was thick with smoke and ash and he could taste oil on the fumes that he breathed in. The acrid smell of the place assailed his nostrils and permeated his clothes and skin and hair in minutes. The gloom of the interior was not helped much by the many electric lights. Shafts of bright sunlight that streamed down through murky glass panes on the corrugated tin roof should have relieved the darkness, but only intensified the dusty, smoggy atmosphere, showing it up in visible, dancing spotlights.

Gaffer McGucken beckoned them over to where he was standing beside a Stanier Black '5' locomotive.

'Right lads, you know what to do.' In a quieter voice he said, 'Frankie, there's a wee covered basket there. It's for anything you find that might be transported to the funeral parlour to be interred with the remains.' Louder he said, 'that's all guys. It shouldn't take much more than an hour.'

His gaze took in young Coley, who was staring glassy-eyed at the front of the engine. McGucken darted forward just in time to catch the youngster as he swayed sideways. Coley tried to straighten his buckling knees.

'I'm okay. I'm fine,' he protested, but his voice was weak.

'Sure ye are, son.'

They supported him to an upturned crate and sat him down. Frankie rummaged in his kit bag for a tin cup and filled it with water from one of the taps that lined the cleaning shed.

'Here, drink this.'

Coley sipped very slowly, each swallow battling to stay down.

The welcome squeak of the carriage cleaners' trolley broke an awkward silence.

'Jean! Bridie!' Mr McGucken smiled with relief when he saw the women. Women were always better at this kind of thing. 'Here, take this lad with you. He's to sweep inside the train, okay? *INSIDE!*' He emphasised the last word. 'All the carriages, mind. You're always greeting for extra help, well you've got it today.'

'Aye. So ah see! Well, jump up, son. We've got at least six coaches tae dae afore the brek. Let's get on.' Jean said it all without once removing the cigarette that seemed to be attached to her bottom lip.

Bridie raised a pencilled eyebrow at the gaffer and chewed her gum at him, open-mouthed and unsmiling, but she did not speak.

In the event, it took two hours to do the job, but in that time Coley recovered his composure and set about his assignment with real heart. His relief at having been ordered inside was patent, and he wiped windows and swept up rubbish with such enthusiasm that Jean and Bridie both admonished him to slow down.

'If we work that fast, they'll expect all the more from us every time. Take yer time, laddie!'

When he joined Frankie again, the pair made their way back to the bothy for further instructions.

'How did you get on, Frankie? There was such a lot of blood! I couldnae look. I'm sorry.'

'Nae need to be, Coley, son. You'll be better prepared noo, for the next time.'

'Don't say that! I don't want a next time. I'll be happy to stick to sellin' tickets from now on. By the way, I never asked – do you know who was driving that train?'

'Paddy.'

Coley stopped and put down the bucket. He switched the long handled brush to his other shoulder and bent to pick up the bucket again.

'What? Paddy? This is no' the first time that this has happened to him. He was telling me only a wee while ago that if it happened again, he would give up train-driving.'

'I'm afraid you're right, Coley. He's already put in for a transfer. He will not drive a train again. What a waste! He was desperately keen to drive the new diesel electrics and the blue trains - that's if they ever get round to building them. Silly idea! Electric trains!' he smirked scornfully. 'Overhead cables! I never heard the like! People would be too scared to ride in them. They'd fear electrocution. People trust steam power. Anyway, Paddy believes in all that electric stuff. Progress, he calls it. But I think this business will finish him.'

Frankie took a tattered hanky from his trouser pocket and blew his nose noisily. 'I don't mean to sound insensitive, because, believe me, I'm not, but I wish that when people make that god-awful decision to end their life, they would choose another way. Something less messy, that doesn't traumatise other people and that doesn't disrupt the whole railway system for days. One incident like that causes untold chaos!' The hanky came into use again. 'Paddy and I trained together as signalmen y'know. He might go back to that. Who knows? I'm really sorry for him, though, because driving was what he always wanted to do.'

Part One

Paddy on the railway, picking up stones.
Along came an engine and broke Paddy's bones.
Oh, said Paddy, that's not fair!
Well, said the engineman, you shouldn't be there.

Children's Skipping Rhyme.

CHAPTER 1

About Time.
The Sixties.

He could hear her before he saw her. Paddy had approached the station via the path that rose up from Main Street. As he neared the ticket office, he stopped short, listening. Peeping cautiously into the archway that led out on to the station platform, where the voice was coming from, he could see her now - Mrs Gillan! If he could quietly tiptoe to the door of the ticket office, he might just manage to slip inside, unseen.

Mrs Gillan was giving forth about the stink of cigarette smoke in the waiting room; how something ought to be done about it, and how she herself never used the waiting room, but always stood outside on the platform no matter what the weather, because she didn't want to arrive at her destination with her clothes reeking of smelly pipe tobacco, or worse, coughing up clouds of nicotine laden smoke from her previously clean and healthy lungs.

'Mark my words,' she was telling the complete stranger beside her, 'there will come a time when smoking will be banned altogether. Dirty, filthy habit!' Her face screwed in disgust, and her nostrils flared contemptuously, as if they had become suddenly filled with the stench of rancid pipe dottle.

The fact that it was not quite six o'clock on a warm sunny morning in June, and that the waiting room wasn't even open yet, didn't stop her complaining about its deficiencies. Nor did the fact that at this very moment, far from foul-smelling, the air around her was heavy with the luscious scent of the vibrantly coloured sweet peas, lovingly planted long ago along the back wall of the platform in a former attempt to win the Best Kept Station award. Her captive audience shuffled his feet uncomfortably, and longingly fingered the unseen pack of Senior Service in his jacket pocket. He had arrived a bit early for the train that would take him to Hallside Steelworks and had just been about to light up when Mrs Gillan accosted him. During their mostly one-sided conversation, a few more of the regular early-morning commuters had gradually appeared, but on catching sight of Mrs Gillan they hung back, grouping together at the far end of the platform, keeping a safe distance.

At the big wooden door of the ticket office Paddy fumbled amongst the keys that hung from a small steel ring on his belt. Selecting the largest, he inserted it into the lock and turned it, but she spied him before he had time to open the door. Abandoning the man on the platform, who showed visible signs of relief, she honed in on Paddy.

'I've been waiting here for the past fifteen minutes to speak to you,' Mrs Gillan boomed in her large voice. Everything about Katie Gillan was large. She was certainly taller than Paddy, and *he* was five feet eight. And though nobody who knew her would dare to call her fat, she was definitely 'well filled out'.

Paddy consulted his pocket watch.

'Good morning, Mrs Gillan,' he said. 'It's just going on six now. The ticket office opens at six o'clock you know, so I'm not late.'

'*You* might not be late,' she barked, agitated. 'But *I've* been here since Jamsie jumped on the milk train quarter of an hour ago. I've got loads to do today and I'm not best pleased to be hanging around here.'

Paddy could see that. In his experience of Mrs Gillan, he had never known her to be 'best pleased' about anything. He could also see that she was wearing house slippers and had plastic curlers in her hair, imperfectly concealed beneath a slippy red head-square that she constantly had to yank forwards on to her forehead every time it slipped past her crown. She would not be wanting a ticket then. He tried to keep the weariness from his voice.

'What can I do for you, Mrs Gillan?'

'My sister Lily will be arriving here at three-fifteen, off the Lanark train. I want you to show her where my house is. She's never been before.'

Katie Gillan lived only a few hundred yards down the hill and was a regular visitor to the ticket office window. Apart from an occasional shopping trip into Glasgow, she rarely travelled, but she had four sons (also large) who worked on the railway and she was always leaving scribbled messages for them, or insisting that information be telephoned through to them. Due to the scarcity of public phones in the town, Mrs Gillan had quickly discovered that a short trip up the hill to the ticket office and getting someone to use the railway phones was a useful way of communicating with her sons. In this way she became well known, though not always well liked, by the station staff.

Paddy Preston had been assistant station manager here for two years now and had come to know Mrs Gillan and her sons, including Jamsie, very well. It occurred to him that, bearing in mind her close connections with railway shift work, Mrs Gillan should have known that Paddy would no longer be on duty at quarter past three.

'My shift finishes at two, Mrs Gillan,' he said. 'I won't be here when the three-fifteen gets in, but I'll tell Eddie to look out for your sister and point her in the right direction.'

Mrs Gillan pulled her mouth into a thin line. Realisation of her own stupidity slowly dawned on her. If only she'd thought it through properly, she could have organised her time a little better.

'Well I hope you remember to pass on the message. I don't want to have to come back at two o'clock to speak to Eddie myself. I've wasted enough time already. I could have had a washing out by now!' She gave Paddy a withering look as if somehow this was his fault.

'Er, - Mrs Gillan - ,' began Paddy tentatively, 'I'll be happy to pass on your message, but if you're free to come back at two o'clock when Eddie starts his shift, why don't you just wait until three fifteen? Then you can meet your sister yourself.'
Mrs Gillan rolled her eyes heavenward and leant forward, resting her fleshy arms on her hips.

'Bee-coz,' she enunciated slowly and deliberately, 'I'll have scones in the oven by then. I won't be able to leave them or they'll burn. They've got to be fresh out the oven as she walks in the door. She never could bake a scone, our Lily, and it's the one thing I can do better than her.'
With that she turned and lumbered off down the hill. Paddy thought he heard her say scathingly,

'*Men!*'
He was left feeling sorry for the unknown Lily and hoped that she liked scones.

❧❧ ❧❧

If Paddy thought that a dose of Mrs Gillan first thing on a Monday morning was a raw deal, he was soon to find that his troubles were only beginning. On the previous Friday, he had received a letter from the area manager informing him that the old station clock, due for replacement since the station was soon to be modernised, had been sold to one of those people who collect railway memorabilia - a Railway Enthusiast. The letter stated that men would arrive today and Paddy was to assist in every way possible with the dismantling and removal of the precious old clock. Paddy was looking forward to this job with mixed feelings. He would be sorry to see that old clock go. He'd have bought it himself if he'd had the money. It was a beautiful mahogany double-faced clock, built right into the ticket office woodwork. One face looked out on to the platform and the other was facing inside, into the office. It had served both the public and the railway staff for nearly a hundred years and was still keeping perfect time.

At least, it should have been. But when Paddy opened up the ticket office after Mrs Gillan had gone, a nasty shock awaited him. The beautiful clock had been smashed to smithereens and was dangling pathetically, bashed and broken, tilting inwards above the office floor.

A few stunned moments he stood there, his mouth open in disbelief, then anger broke the spell and he moved forward. Crunching his way through broken glass, coils and springs, he bent to pick up a half brick, obviously the instrument used for this horrific act of destruction. Incensed, he asked himself who would do such a thing? What kind of mind can think to destroy something so beautiful? More questions raced through his head, questions that will forever remain unanswered when it comes to trying to understand the stupidity of vandalism.

Why, Victorian gentlemen had consulted this clock and had adjusted their pocket watches accordingly! This same clock had seen mothers wave brave sons off to war, dreading each relentless tick as it brought the departure nearer. Countless lovers had rendezvoused under its face. It had seen many sad partings and many happy reunions. Paddy remembered being on duty in late summer evenings when tired parents returned from day excursions to the seaside. Carrying sleepy children who were still clutching buckets and spades, they would glance up at the clock, checking to see if they might still be in time to catch the last bus to the outlying, newly built housing schemes. Many passengers saw the clock as an old friend and quite a few had put in a bid to buy it when word got round that the station was to undergo refurbishment. Who could have guessed that on the very day that it was due to be carefully removed to a proud new home, mindless morons would strike? A voice behind him made him look up.

'Good God! What happened here?' It was the young station clerk arriving for work.

'Vandals,' was all Paddy could say in a hoarse voice.

Paddy was gradually becoming used to this new word 'vandalism'. As a young man he'd never heard the term, but these days vandalism was more than a word. It had become a sad fact, a sign not only of changing times but also of a changing society. It was an ordinary Monday, not much different to any other Monday among the thousands in a working life, but some days stand out to be remembered, and Paddy was to look back and remember that for him, the Monday that the clock was vandalised was the marking of the end of an era.

He was only thirty-eight, but he could remember the old days, the glory days, some said, when powerful steam locomotives hauled their passengers along busy branch lines and into picturesque little stations, each with their own Stationmaster. Stationmasters were being phased out now, and Paddy wondered how the powers-that-be who came to this decision could consider this progress. More recently, he had seen the arrival of the diesels. It seemed right that in a changing industrial world there should be progress. Already the electrification of Central Scottish lines was a reality and people looked forward to travelling on faster, cleaner transport. That's what people wanted, wasn't it? Then why did he feel a distinct sense of foreboding?

He guessed that more of these sad sights would follow in the coming years. The railway system was in the middle of the biggest decade of change in its entire history.

Even the passengers could sense it. The re-shaping plan for the modernisation of Britain's railways was well under-way, and he was already experiencing the greatest upheaval in working conditions and long held traditions. Massive changes lay just ahead and increased vandalism was just one of them. After a minute he got to his feet and said with a weary sigh, 'Get a brush and shovel, Sandy. I'll need to make a phone call.'

As his shift that day drew to a close he became aware of a gentle but insistent tapping sound under the ticket office window. He pulled up the glass shutter and leaned forward. He could just see the top of a little boy's head. Four fingers of each hand grasped the counter top. Two brown eyes peeped from a fair fringe, head tilted backwards as he strained to see.

'Ma Mammy wants to know,' said the wee lad, 'if the ten o'clock train on Thursday will be on time.'
If only he had a crystal ball!

∽⧫∾ ∽⧫∾

Paddy called at the Railway Inn on his way home. Squinting in the dark smoky interior, a sharp contrast to the bright sunshine outside, he made his way to the bar, nodding here and there to familiar faces. He ordered a pint and carried it to an empty table where he shook out his rolled up newspaper and began to scan the front page. He became aware of someone at his elbow and looking up, saw one of his colleagues, Johnny McEachen. Johnny's face wore a serious expression.

'Paddy, have you heard? Frankie Wilson is dead. Heart

attack, it's thought. Davey McCally brought the news to Glasgow Central this morning.'

Paddy put his paper down and shook his head. 'Aw naw! Are ye sure? Frankie?'

There was a pause while Johnny nodded sadly. Paddy was silent too.

'I'll find out about the funeral and let you know,' said Johnny.

'I'll be there.' Paddy said.

Johnny returned to where he'd been standing at the bar with some friends.

When Paddy had started his career on the railway Frankie had been his mentor. Paddy's mother had moved the family to Largs from Motherwell shortly after the death of her husband and soon afterwards Paddy, then aged fifteen, became a trainee clerk in Largs ticket office. Under Frankie's easy tutorage Paddy progressed rapidly, and eventually, they both became signalmen after training at the same time. Frankie was much older than Paddy but the two had become good friends. Though Paddy was now back living in the Lanarkshire area, he had kept in touch with Frankie over the years. Memories of his old friend's exploits came back as he slowly sipped his pint, his newspaper forgotten. Lump in throat, he remembered Frankie's concern over an injured seagull. In his mind's eye, he could see and hear the whole incident as if it were happening all over again.

It had been a clear summer evening and Paddy had arranged to meet Frankie for a quick pint in the railway club. 'Do you want another, Paddy?' Davey McCally had called over from the other end of the bar when he saw that Paddy had drained his glass. Davey was usually tight-fisted but yesterday a lovely daughter had at last been added to his four sons and he was still in celebratory mood.

'No thanks, Davey. I'm waiting for Frankie. I was only going to have one drink.'

'Come on man, ye'll have to help me wet the baby's heid. And anyhow, ye ken Frankie. He's aye at the coo's tail. Have another one while ye wait.'

Paddy was persuaded, but by the time he had downed this second pint there was still no sign of Frankie.

'I can't wait any longer,' said Paddy, getting to his feet. 'When Frankie gets here will ye tell him I had to go?'

Just then Frankie appeared in the doorway, out of breath and all apologies.

'I'm sorry man,' he gasped, 'there was this seagull with a twisted beak. I had to take it to the vet.'

Frankie, an ex-farmer, was already forty years old when he had joined the railway. His farm had been compulsory purchased to make way for the large nuclear power station that had been planned near his land, but that had been several years ago and politics and protests had delayed the action on the proposed power plant so that it was as yet unfinished and the promised jobs on the site were still awaited. He had a gentleness of speech that belied the real strength in his slight frame and steadfast character. His wife was a nurse at Irvine General Hospital but she treated many more patients in her own home than she ever did on the wards. Everybody with the least hint of a boil or a migraine used Effie and Frankie's house as their own personal surgery and no-one was ever turned away until Effie had listened to their complaint and given advice accordingly. She was particularly good with kiddies. Scraped knees, skelfs, sair bellies - Effie had the right remedy. And Frankie, having experience of livestock, was deemed to 'have a way' with animals, so as well as the sick and injured there was also a steady stream of ailing cats, dogs, pet rabbits, hamsters and even the odd tortoise who made their way, in the arms of their worried owners, to the couple's front door.

'Tell us about this seagull then,' a voice said, through the babble of chatter at the bar. A few interested heads looked up.

'Well, every day for weeks now this seagull has been coming to land on the wooden veranda around the outside of my signal box. It must have been in some kind of a fight or an accident or something, because the top part of its beak is twisted over the bottom part and it has real difficulty eating anything.' By way of illustration, Frankie raised his right hand high enough for everyone to see and stretched his middle finger over and across his index finger.

'Like that,' he said.

'I've been putting scraps of food out for it every day. It can manage to eat soft things – bread an' that. Eventually, it started to come right inside the box and I would give it a bit o' ma piece. Maybe give it a wee slice o' Spam an' the like. Sometimes I'd have to hook the food round the bottom part of its mouth to help it, like, on account of its twisted beak. Every now and again I bring some chips in wi' me at the start of my shift and I tell you, it can smell thae chips a mile away. Within minutes there it is. Mooching my meal. It loves chips.'

'Ye mean, you've been gein' it yer chips?' asked Davey incredulously. Why anyone would waste good chips on a ganneting big bird like a seagull was beyond him.

'It loves chips.' said Echo, the new trainee clerk at Saltcoats Station.

'I don't think it eats any place else. It's aye starvin'. It even drinks the tea out o' ma cup.'

'Tell it tae bugger aff!' said Big Oweny, taking a gulp of his beer. He turned away, having already lost interest and went in search of someone who would join him in a game of darts.

'Naw, I couldnae abandon it. They're moving me to West Kilbride tomorrow so I had to do something.'

'How did you get it to the vet's?'

'Well, it trusts me, and like I said, its been coming right inside the signal box now for days, so I brought in a big cardboard box and at the end of my shift I put some food in it and the bird hopped in as nice as you like. I put the lid on and carried it to the vet's house. He wasn't in, so I left the box in his front porch with a note inside. That's what kept me late.'

This was not the first time that Frankie had gone above and beyond the call of duty where animals were concerned. One day he had refused to change a signal to green until he had climbed down from his box and rescued a few sheep and their lambs that had strayed on to the line. He lifted each one over the wall to the safety of the field before climbing back up to the box and changing the signal. As Paddy remembered, he smiled to himself and wondered how Frankie had gotten away with keeping a whole trainload of passengers waiting. But Frankie would listen to no arguments on the subject and remained convinced in his belief that the passengers, had they ever found out the reason for the delay, would have applauded his actions. They never did find out, of course.

Reminiscing over, Paddy picked up his discarded paper, slung his haversack over his shoulder and headed for home. There was no sign of his wife in the house, although something was simmering away quietly on the stove and it smelled good. He hung up his jacket and went out into the close in search of Agnes. He found her in a disused washhouse in the backcourt. She was bending over a rusty old pram and she looked up, smiling excitedly when his shadow fell across the entrance. She held a little fluffy bundle up to her cheek.

'Oh Paddy look, the kittens are here! There are six of them. Six! Can you believe it? The poor wee thing's been in labour all day.'

Paddy stretched his neck forward and glanced reluctantly

inside the pram where he could make out some furry shapes snuggled into the dirty, cracked padding that lined what had once been a beautiful baby carriage.

'Agnes.' He drew his brows down, 'I told you days ago to chase that stray cat away. You don't know what kind of germs it could be carrying. Put that kitten down. You'll catch something! And what's this old pram still doing here? I told the boys to take it back where it came from. Does nobody ever listen to me in this house?'

Agnes fondly nestled the fluffy bundle back beside its mother.

'Aw, Paddy. I couldn't turn her away. She just needed a place to have her kittens and she climbed inside the pram. You know the boys are going to use the wheels to make a go-cart just as soon as the kittens are old enough to leave their mother. Then we can get rid of the pram.'

'Aye, and we'll be getting rid of the kittens as well, Agnes.' Paddy said determinedly. 'They've got six weeks for you to find them a home.'

She looked at him, crestfallen.

'I mean it Aggie. These wee cats are no' staying here. We're still feeding that bloody mongrel that Danny brought home six weeks ago. That was only supposed to stay until its paw healed, but it's still here, and don't you try and tell me its still got a sore paw, because the paw is fine. I had a look at it and there's not a thing wrong wi' it, so if you think these cats are here for keeps, you've got another think coming!'

'Oh, I know we cannae keep them all, Paddy. I was thinking that when they're old enough we could maybe send them through to Frankie. He'd find homes for them out there in the country!'

'Aggie love, that's what I came out here to tell you.'

And he told her.

CHAPTER 2

Once I Caught a Fish Alive

'Just two pieces of dressed haddock Lily, that's all I want. Medium sized, mind. No' too big,' said Mrs McHattie, shuffling up to the counter when her turn came.

Lily nodded and weighed out the fish. She noticed that Mrs McHattie wasn't using her stick today.

'How's your hip, Mrs McHattie?'

'No' too bad lass,' the old lady said cheerfully. 'This good weather helps a lot, and I can carry two bags of messages if I don't need to bring my stick.'

'Aye, well, just you watch that you don't overdo it,' said Lily, dipping the fish into the tray of breadcrumbs.

Mrs McHattie could see that Lily's black eye was subsiding now. It was still very bloodshot but the bruising was now a dull canvas of blue and yellow on her thin face, compared to a week ago when it was black and red and so badly swollen that the eye was actually shut. She wondered if she should mention it again today, but decided not to. Why embarrass the lassie any more?

Walked into the coal cellar door, indeed! Aye, that will be right!

She'll only babble some excuse, and I'll be helping her to sin her soul. Better not mention! But if I had any right to interfere, that man o' hers would be clapped in the jail.

'That'll be two and six, Mrs McHattie,' said Lily, wrapping up the fish.

'My God, lassie, half a crown for two wee bits o' fish! What's the world coming to?'

'It'll be worse if we get decimalisation. Prices will go sky-high then.' Lily said, taking the ten-shilling note held out to her.

'It'll never happen, hen. No' in my lifetime anyway. I cannae see anybody standing for that.'

Mrs McHattie took her seven shillings and sixpence change and after depositing the money in a wee black purse, she lifted her parcel from the counter and with her usual shuffling gait, made her way to the door.

'See ye next week, Lily.'

It was on the tip of Lily's tongue to say that she wouldn't be here next week but she bit back the words just in time. 'Cheerio,' was all she said. She watched the old woman hobble past the plate glass window and sighed. She would miss Mrs McHattie. She turned her attention to the queue.

'Next please!'

Only one person knew of Lily's secret plan and that was her boss, Mr McGregor. He had every right to know, she reasoned. He had been very fair with her over the years and she couldn't leave him in the lurch, without a word. He had always been very tolerant of his 'accident prone' employee. Like the time when Lily's arm had been in a sling and she really was no use at all in the shop. Who can wrap up a parcel of slippery lemon sole using just one hand? He had let her go home early on full pay. Now, how many other employers would do that? she had asked herself. And he had been pretty generous in giving her and the other staff a few unsold fishcakes or the odd bit of whiting at the end of the day. When she had made up her mind that she was leaving, she knew that she couldn't just 'not turn up'. She would have to give proper notice.

He would be sorry to lose her, he had said when she told

him, and would respect her wish for wanting to keep her leaving a secret. He did not ask why she was going or where, but wished her well, adding that he hoped she would be very happy.

She tidied a tray of herrings and thought that only a short time ago they had been swimming busily in the sea, free and happy. Now, here they were on a tray, smoked, glassy-eyed and dead. Catching sight of her own bruised eye reflected in the shiny chrome of the weighing scales, she knew she had to escape from her own net while she felt she was still alive. Apart from Mr McGregor, she hadn't told another soul that on Monday, when the fish shop was shut, she would be on a train to take her away from here, away from Charlie, never to return. Charlie Dunne had lifted his fists to her for the last time. She had been planning this all week and Charlie must not get wind of it until she was well and truly gone.

She had already set up an interview for a job in the new MacFisheries, in Glasgow's Union Street. She had written to her older sister Katie to say that she'd like to come and stay for a day or two and see her new house since the good weather was holding. Now would come the tricky part. She would have to ask for Katie's help, and in all her married life she had never done that. She knew she would have to tell Katie everything, all about Charlie's physical abuse of her, and how she'd left him and how she would need a place to stay until she got a job and could afford a wee place of her own. Lily worried that her sister might not be on her side. Katie Gillan was loud and bossy and self-righteous and liked to call a spade a great big shovel. Would she send her packing, back to Charlie, with one of her favourite sayings like, she'd made her bed and she'd have to lie in it? Sometimes Lily thought she was more afraid of Katie than she was of Charlie. One thing was certain, if Katie did lash out at her, at least it would only be with her tongue. She could take that. Hadn't she taken a lot worse these last few years?

Whatever Katie Gillan had thought when she read her sister's letter, she didn't say, not even to Jamsie, the only one of her four sons still living at home, but she replied via the fish shop like Lily had asked. Lily had scribbled something about the fish shop getting mail delivered early, but it had sounded lame even to herself as she wrote it, and Katie was no fool. Katie told Jamsie only that his Aunt Lily was coming to stay for a while and she'd appreciate it if he didn't sit about in his vest when she was here, or play those terrible rock 'n' roll records. She had invited Lily to her home several times since she'd moved there nearly a year ago, but for one reason or another, Lily hadn't yet been able to come, so Katie was very surprised at this sudden decision on Lily's part, and she began to think there may be a more pressing reason than just the good weather for her proposed visit.

'I hope *he's* not been up to his old tricks again,' she said to her reflection in the mirror as she dusted the dressing table that morning.

⌘⌘ ⌘⌘

On Monday afternoon when the Glasgow bound train steamed into Lanark station, Lily was already on the platform. No one would have guessed from her calm exterior that her heart was thumping hard in her chest and that her brain was in turmoil. She paid no attention to the inward turbulence. That was the old Lily, still shaking and afraid. The new Lily was calmly opening the door of the first empty compartment and placing her case inside. A last minute panic swept over her as she climbed in after it, and for an awful moment Lily thought she would burst into tears, but no tears came. Perhaps she was all cried out. She realised that she hadn't actually cried in a long time.

Not even to cry herself to sleep, which she vowed she would never do again. When she'd made her decision to leave she knew that the time was right. The children had lives of their own now and she was due hers. She hadn't even left her husband a note. As far as she was concerned, the marriage was over. There was nothing to say that she had not already said many times to no avail. But the children; they were a different matter. They would need to know she was safe and that she would meet with them soon; she would write to her daughter Barbara as soon as she was settled.

She would miss her friends of course. They would be flabbergasted at her disappearance. 'Not before time!' they would probably say. Lily was always so amiable, so eager to please. Everybody loved Lily. Everybody that is, except the husband who should have loved her more than all the others. Oh, aye. That man, who praised her worth in the pub on Saturday and praised the Lord in the Kirk on Sunday, was the same man who ladled into her whenever it suited him. Mostly, the bruises didn't show and Lily could keep her self-respect. When the kids were young, and Lily sported a particularly bloody nose, she would smile and tell folk that young Charles' cricket ball had rolled off the top shelf in the cupboard just as she opened the door. She became adept at making up new stories. Occasionally the look on people's faces made her wonder if they believed her. Sometimes she got the feeling that they knew, and that she sat in church a liar, as big a hypocrite as Charlie.

Waiting for the train to move off, Lily allowed herself to think of Charlie just for a moment. She tried to remember the Charlie she had married, but she could not conjure him up in her memory. There must have been a young, even handsome Charlie, the man she had fallen in love with. There must have been! Why couldn't she remember him? Funny, but she just couldn't bring him to mind. She couldn't even remember being in love. She did remember that this was not the first time she had run away. Twenty- five years ago she had run away *to* Charlie, not away *from* him.

When he first set eyes on Lily Anne Hanley, Charlie Dunne was a thirty-year-old widower, a miner who had been left with two young children to bring up. Lily had been serving behind the counter of her parents' corner shop where he called in every morning to buy an ounce of War Horse tobacco on his way to Hatton Pit. It did not take him long to see that the Hanley girls, unlike his first wife, who had had a sickly constitution, were hard-working, strong women, any one of whom would be just the type who could cook, clean and look after his two children. (Their grandmother was presently looking after them while he worked, so that when his shift was over he always had to collect his girls, and he was never free to go off and enjoy himself.) The idea of marrying again had been in his head for a while now.

He surveyed the Hanley women. Katie, the eldest, didn't count of course, because she was already married to Dan Gillan and had two boys of her own and by the looks of her, there was another on the way. Anyway, she was brash and officious, a bit too tetchy for his taste. She would often show her disapproval when people asked for tobacco or cigarettes.

'Don't you miners suffer enough damage to your lungs?' she would say, but she sold them the stuff nonetheless. Rosie, the next sister, though more polite than Katie, was disinclined to chat with him and had proved impervious to his flirting banter. That left Lily. She was certainly a looker, but at sixteen, a bit too young for courting. 'However,' he pondered, as he studied her through the shop window, 'Give me time, give me time!'

His careful seduction of the lovely Lily began, and within a year Lily had fallen for his charms. (Or at least the charms of his two motherless little daughters, Meg and May, who could captivate anyone's heart.) What made it easier for him was the fact that Lily had left off working in her father's store and had gone to work in Boots the Chemist at the corner of Argyll Street in Glasgow and he was sometimes able to meet her on the train or to walk her to and from the station when his shift permitted.

After another year, when Lily eventually told her parents that she was 'walking out' with Charlie Dunne, Patrick Hanley nearly had an apoplexy. Long and bitter arguments ensued. Night after night, tears, tantrums and slamming of doors were commonplace. In calmer moments her father tried listing all the reasons why such a match was unthinkable.

'For Pity's sake, Lily! He's thirteen years older than you. He's a widower with a family already. How are you to cope with those two little girls of his? Tell me that! You're barely eighteen yourself. And another thing, the Hatton Pit is to close soon. Did you know that? Naw, he never told you that, did he? He'll be unemployed. How will he support you? And let's not even mention the fact that the man's a Protestant! A Protestant, Lily! Have your brains gone begging, girl?'

'See sense, lassie, see sense! You know your father's right!' Her mother pleaded, wringing her hands.

Lily never saw sense. Instead, she and Charlie planned their elopement.

Two days after her eighteenth birthday, Lily dressed for work wearing three pairs of knickers, two bras, two blouses and a jumper and cardigan. She wore a light skirt under her heavy tweed one. She managed to stuff some stockings and a pair of shoes into a shopping bag. She topped this all off with a roomy raincoat and hoped that nobody in the house would notice how bulky she looked. They didn't. Soon she was behind the counter at Boots, flushed and agitated, trying to appear normal. Charlie was to meet her after work, and they would be off to start their new life together. He had found work as a farm labourer near Lanark, and they would be married tomorrow in Lanark Registry Office.

The day dragged slowly with Lily becoming more distracted and jumpy by the minute. She half expected to see her mother appear before her, having noticed the lack of clothes in her wardrobe. She would be discovered. She knew it. She felt her Supervisor's eyes on her and tried to calm down.

❧❧ ❧❧

Mr Ferguson the store manager called the staff supervisor into the office.

'We'll go ahead with our plan as arranged, Miss Wylie,' he said. 'This pilfering has to stop, and I'm sure we'll get a result if we carry out a search, this being Friday, which seems to be the favourite day for stuff going missing. Have you any idea who the culprit is?'

'No sir. I've tried to watch them as closely as I can but I've nothing concrete to go on. Mind you, that girl, Lily, has been acting very strangely today. She seems agitated and has asked permission to go to the toilet several times.'

'Lily? Which one is she?'

'Lily Hanley; the one at the Combs and Hair Colorants counter.

Just before closing time, Lily, along with others, was subjected to a spot check. Though innocent of any pilfering, she had been forced to tearfully explain to a bemused Miss Wylie why she was wearing so many articles of clothing and why she had been so nervous all day. The store detective who was present said that since Lily's plans were none of their business, she was free to go. A traumatised Lily fled out of Boot's back door and straight into Charlie's arms.

Patrick and Maggie Hanley had been frantic with worry when Lily did not return home that Friday evening. The police were alerted and an all night search began. When morning came, Patrick travelled into Boots the Chemist to trace Lily's movements and was told what they knew. Because of the spot check, Lily's plan had been discovered and her father and mother came to know that she was not lying murdered in some ditch somewhere, she had not been sold into slavery, she was not lying in a hospital ward suffering from amnesia, but, every bit as devastating, she had run off to marry a Protestant and to live forever outside the safety and the sanctity of the Catholic Church.

Apppalled at what Mr Ferguson and Miss Wylie had been able to disclose, Patrick immediately set out again, this time for Lanark Registry Office, a tediously slow journey on the number 240 bus. He arrived too late to stop the marriage and met the couple as they emerged arm in arm on the steps outside. His dignity would not allow him to look at Charlie Dunne. He knew that if he did, he'd punch him, and he'd be guilty of causing a brawl in a public place. Instead he pleaded with Lily not to break her mother's heart and to come home now. His entreaties fell on deaf ears. Lily clung to her new husband and refused to let go. She broke her father's heart too, that day. He returned home without her.

'Lost,' was all he said to his distraught wife, and all contact was severed.

Through various means they got to know that by the age of twenty-three Lily had become mother to five children - three of her own, and the two from Charlie's first marriage. Patrick and Maggie both died several years later without ever seeing their youngest daughter's offspring. In the wider span of the family, it was rumoured that they never really got over Lily's defection.

Contact was not re-established until some twenty years later when Rosie, who by that time was married with a growing family of her own, had to go into Law Hospital to have a hysterectomy. Who should be in the same ward but Lily, the sister she hadn't seen for all those years. Lily had suffered a broken pelvis after 'falling downstairs'. Though their first conversation was a little strained, it wasn't long before they were hugging each other and laughing through tears.

When they left hospital the sisters kept in touch through Rosie's phone and the occasional letter. Lily was gradually introduced back into the family and slowly she became part of their lives again. Little by little, forgiveness took the place of hurt. Times had changed and they were all aware of it. The happy united family that they used to be, eventually made its return. Though Lily's pride (and also her shame), could never allow her to admit that it hadn't taken her long to realise what a great mistake she had made all those years ago, her astute brothers and sisters began, after a while, to piece together a pretty accurate picture of her life with Mister Dunne.

Charlie had no idea that Lily had been reclaimed by her family. She had never told him, and her sisters had expressed no desire ever to lay eyes on *him*. Lily had been able to hide her correspondence from Charlie. Being a farm labourer, he always left the house very early, before the post arrived. Now that she had her sisters again, Lily felt that she had gained a safety net, somewhere to run to, and last week's trouncing had decided it. She would throw herself on Katie's mercy, and tell all.

The train jolted slightly and her reverie came to an end. Jerked into the present, she asked herself another question. What happened to the spunky teenager who defied her parents and her Church - the girl who was afraid of nothing - not even everlasting damnation? It had taken a great deal of courage, twenty odd years ago, to execute the daring plan that she and Charlie had devised. What had happened to that steely resolve, that determination?

A brief glance at her pinched face, reflected in the grimy window, and she realised that she knew the answer to her own questions. The love she thought she'd had for Charlie had been beaten out of her. And while the children depended on her, she had little choice. But now it was different. The kids were adults now and her courage had returned. It had never really left her, she realised. It was just lying dormant, waiting to surface when the time was right. She could build a new life again. Of course she could! People were doing it all the time nowadays. This was the sixties, for God's sake! A few moments she spent, wondering what it will be like to wake up without fear clutching at her, and she felt heartened as she imagined it. Out on the platform, a whistle blew and she saw the guard wave his green flag. A chug or two and the train began to move. She turned her head and stared straight ahead at the little picture on the opposite wall. A highland scene. The Cairngorms. Concentrate. Think about the Cairngorms. Don't think of anything else. Don't even look out of the window. She would only look ahead from now on.

∝∂∾ ∝∂∾

Paddy had told Eddie, his opposite number on the later shift, all about Mrs Gillan's early visit to the ticket office, so when the Lanark train arrived, Eddie was looking out for a replica of Mrs Gillan and was preparing to have his nose bitten off, should he say or do the wrong thing. Instead, the only woman to alight from the train was a tall, slim lady who looked to be about his own age. She was wearing a print dress of some light floaty material and a pale straw hat with the brim drawn down over one eye, sort of Bette Davis-y, he thought. She looked about her a little hesitantly. A person more unlike Mrs Gillan would be hard to find. Still wary in case the resemblance to her sister, though not visual, might be in her tongue, he approached and asked her if she might be the sister of Katie Gillan. Trying to hide her bruised eye, Lily glanced up briefly and nodded shyly, ducking her head again almost immediately and clutching at the brim of her hat. He lifted the heavy case and took her through the arch to the path that led to the road, and was pointing out the way to her when he was surprised to see Mrs Gillan herself come puffing up the hill. She too was wearing a print dress and her usually frizzy hair was even frizzier which made her head look twice its real size. And was that lipstick the old battleaxe was wearing?

'Mrs Gillan,' he said, surprised. 'What about your scones?'

'Bugger the scones! Where's our Lily?'

She took one look at Lily, saw the bruise inexpertly concealed with make-up, noticed the bulging, large sized suitcase and knew right away that Lily intended to stay for more than just a few days. She hurried towards her and frightened the life out of her sister by engulfing her in a fierce hug.

'Aye, ye'll be fine now, Lily. It took ye long enough.'

She pushed back the sleeves of her new summer frock, revealing strong chubby arms and grabbed Lily's case from Eddie's grasp. As she was led off down the hill, Lily turned to offer a whispered thank you to Eddie.

'Well, well, well,' thought a very surprised Eddie, lifting his cap to scratch his head. 'What's the story here? Wait till I tell this to Paddy!'

Lily did actually cry herself to sleep again that night. But they were different tears, not her accustomed tears of pain and heartache, but tears of relief and hope. Tears that washed away some of the hurt and left her refreshed and ready to ask Katie, in the morning, how to make scones.

CHAPTER 3

Frankie of Assisi, R.I.P.

Frankie's funeral was mobbed. Afterwards, his former workmates joined relatives and friends and crammed themselves into Effie's little cottage. The women were in 'the good room,' which was what Effie called the largest room, made over into a living room. It contained the most presentable furniture and was only used on special occasions. The large sofa and two brown leather armchairs were groaning under the unaccustomed weight of several large bums whose owners sipped sherry or tea, nodding or shaking their heads sympathetically towards Effie whenever she spoke.

One woman sat on a hard chair by the window. She held a damp hankie to her eyes and was sobbing away quietly. From across the room Mrs Lynn Brown nudged her neighbour, Miss Susan Leggate, and cocked her head towards the crying woman.

'It's Doreen,' she said knowingly. 'It's devastating for her. I don't think she'll live much longer. Not now that Frankie's gone!'

Susan Leggate's heartstrings were wrung just watching such grief. 'Who is that lady?' she asked.

'Oh, that's Frankie's sister. I thought you knew.'

'No, I've never met her. She looks so sad.' Susan decided she would try to comfort the lonely looking soul, and later, when she chanced to be nearby, she reached out and stroked the woman's shoulder.

'I'm so sorry about Frankie,' she said, in what she hoped was a consoling voice. 'At least when his time came, it was sudden and short; he would have wanted it that way. But you know, he would have wanted you to live on. He's in a good place now, but he would not want you to join him yet. We must make the most of whatever time we have; that's all we can do. So come on now, Doreen, dry your eyes and live for Frankie.'
The woman brought her head up at that and stared uncomprehendingly at Susan.

'I'm not Doreen,' she said. 'I'm Cissie. Doreen is my cat and Frankie was treating her. The vet can do nothing. He says she's old and will die soon, but she was showing great signs of improvement with Frankie's massages and his tonic mixture. Now there's no hope; she'll dwindle away now. I'm gutted, because I'll miss Doreen, but believe me, I've no plans to join her or Frankie.'

'Oh. Oh. That's good. I'm sorry. I got mixed up.' Susan quickly retreated to the other side of the room and gulped down the last of her sherry. Then she accepted a large refill from Effie and gulped that down too, thinking to herself, 'Funerals! Why does the word begin with 'f-u-n'? There's nuthin' *fun* about funerals. They give me the creeps!'

Most of the men were in the kitchen, grouped around the table where the talk   focused on the newly departed Frankie. Big Oweny was remembering when he and Frankie were signalmen at West Kilbride.

'I used to tell him he'd be late for his own funeral', Oweny said, 'but I was wrong. Everything went like clockwork today.'

'Surely he was never late? He always set out on time.' The voice spoke concernedly from behind them.

They turned and saw that Effie was standing in the doorway,

a large teapot in her hand, which she had come to refill. The men looked embarrassed. They hadn't realised she was there.

'Well - never quite *late*, exactly,' Oweny replied falteringly, 'though he did seem to have his own notion of time.'

'Whatever do you mean?' asked Effie, looking puzzled. Oweny stuttered and coughed into his hand and did his best to explain what he meant by Frankie's own notion of time.

'He was never late to start work, Effie. Oh no. Don't think that. But sometimes he was late to finish, if you get my meaning.'

Effie continued to look enquiringly at him, her sad little eyes blinking.

Oweny's eyes darted expectantly at the faces around the kitchen table, hoping for some support. Paddy came to his rescue.

'What about the time that Frankie didn't know his shift was over?'

Oweny remembered, shot Paddy a grateful look, and embarked on his explanation.

It had been a bitterly cold January night and Oweny had breenged into the signal box bringing an icy blast in with him.

'Gad, it'd freeze the bollocks aff ye oot there!' Oweny shouted, kicking the snow off his boots. He shivered noisily and heaved the door shut against the biting wind. Frankie visibly jumped and the newspaper he had been reading slipped off his knees and blew into different corners as the pages separated in the draught. He had been toasting his feet on the stove, quietly munching a cheese sandwich, and he looked up at Oweny now, his nerves all a-jangle.

'What are you doing here?'

Oweny was cold and in no mood for Frankie's vagueness tonight.

'What do you think I'm here for, Frankie?' he said, grumpily. 'I'm here to start ma shift and to relieve you of yours.'

Frankie glanced up at the big clock.

'I didnae realise that was the time,' he said. 'I didn't even hear you mount the stairs.'

'Aye, well the stairs are all covered in sna'. It's like walkin' on cushions.'

Oweny hung both his cap and his old kit bag on a hook by the door.

'You're aye at the coo's tail, Frankie. I cannae understand that in a railwayman.'

He took Frankie's cap down from the rack above the coat-hooks and threw it towards him. 'Nobody would ever need to tell *me* when it was lousin' time.'

Frankie made no attempt to catch the cap, and allowed it to fall at his feet as he began to wrap up the remaining sandwiches in the waxed paper from the end of the loaf that Effie always used to parcel up his piece. He gathered his belongings methodically and slowly shrugged himself into his railway greatcoat.

'Well, I'll be off now,' he said as he stooped eventually to retrieve his cap, and placing it on the back of his head, he slung on his own kit bag. 'The 9.15 was running ten minutes late, but there's been no other problems which is a mercy, considering the weather. It's all logged in the train register.'

'O.K. Frankie. See you tomorrow.'

Oweny watched Frankie climb down the wooden stairs and wondered. Railwaymen live by the clock. If you're a railwayman, your whole life is governed by time. Minute by minute you know what time it is. You have either just belled the two-fifteen into West Kilbride station or you're waiting to pull lever Number 7 to send the three-thirty-five straight through to Dalry, by-passing Kilwinning.

'How can you not know your shift is over?' mused Oweny to himself. 'Every other man is packed and ready, waiting for your foot on the stair, to rush past you on the way to The Railway Bar for a pint before it shuts. But not Frankie. Sitting there, munching away as if it was lunchtime and not 10 p.m. It must be the farmer in him. Maybe farmers have a different outlook on time. Aye, that must be it!' thought Oweny.

That was the night that Frankie plodded homeward sighing. It was not that he didn't like his job as signalman on the Glasgow to Largs line, stationed just outside West Kilbride. He had always loved trains and railways so when he had to give up the farm, training for a job with British Railways was a natural choice. Yes, he *did* view time somewhat differently from his colleagues. Time is just as important to the farmer but it was a different kind of clock watching. When he had been out in the fields with his tractor, he would hear the whistle of the four o'clock express to Largs as it steamed towards Fairlie tunnel and he would know that the lads would have brought the cows into the sheds, so he would turn the tractor for home and set about helping with the milking. He did own a pocket watch but the comings and goings of the trains saved him from consulting it too often. In the summertime, the whistle of the last mail train usually sent him homewards.

He missed all that. It had been hard work, sometimes in extreme conditions, but it was satisfying at the end of the summer to see the harvest brought in. The harvest you had nearly lost and had laboured so hard to save from crop mite or the effects of a dripping, sunless Scottish summer. In those days Frankie would feel a great sense of accomplishment, as if he'd just won an enormous battle and after the harvest he often experienced a deep feeling of elation that he would never have known how to put into words. But those days were over. The farm had had to be sold and he must make the best of it. He thought of Oweny, stuck in that signal box all night and a tired look came over his face as he remembered that it was his turn on night shift next week. He had never told anyone that he dreaded night shift. He just couldn't be doing with sleeping during the day. He decided to talk to Effie soon. Maybe it was time for another change.

Oweny knew nothing of these thoughts, of course, but it wasn't the first time that he wondered if Frankie was happy. He told Effie now that he wasn't surprised that Frankie left the railway soon after that.

'Tell Effie about the lost train, Paddy,' somebody said.

'Aye, that's got to be Frankie at his best, that is!'

Effie handed the teapot to her niece, who had come into the kitchen to see what was keeping her, and settled herself at the table. She didn't want them to stop. The more they talked about Frankie, the closer he seemed. Listening to his friends' cheery laughter, she could almost believe that he would walk in the door at any minute, demanding to know why every light in the house was burning in the middle of a summer after-noon, and who was paying for all this whisky. She couldn't bear to think of him lying out there in the graveyard where she'd had to turn away and leave him today, so she poured another whisky into Paddy's glass and nodded for him to begin.

'I was at work in Largs signal box,' said Paddy. ' In between duties, I filled in the train register or read the paper. At around three o'clock I listened for the 'Is Line Clear?' bell that would tell me that the passenger train from Glasgow Central, having already gone through Paisley Gilmour Street and the rest of its destinations on time, had now passed West Kilbride signal box and was heading towards Fairlie, where it was due to pass my box on its way into Largs station in a few minutes. No bell came. It's not unusual for this train to be a bit late, so I waited. And waited. After five minutes I rang through to Frankie's box at West Kilbride. There was no answer. I began to wonder why I hadn't heard from Frankie'.

He turned to Effie to explain. 'A train's journey is tracked all the way by a system of bells, and each signalman knows when it is about to enter his section.'

Again Effie nodded.

'I decided to call Holm Junction. *"Where's 2T 25?"* I asked. *"Frankie hasn't belled it on to me."*

'Well we know it's gone past here so it must be in Frankie's section. Give him another minute or two. You know Frankie. He's aye at the coo's tail. Maybe he's in the toilet - or he's feeding wounded gulls again.' After five more minutes we knew something was wrong. We guessed that the signal before Frankie's box must still be at red and that the train was standing somewhere between Ardrossan and West Kilbride. Frankie should have belled by now with the reason for the delay. Maybe he had taken ill or had had an accident.'

'It was me they sent out.' This came from Duncan Brewer. He spoke from his wheelchair in the corner of the room. 'I was at West Kilbride that day and I was really pissed off because I had to go and discover what was wrong. The quickest way was to ride my bicycle alongside the track from the station to the signal box; it's a distance of about half a mile.' He went silent for a moment as the memory came back, and he digressed a little. 'God, I wish I could ride a bike today. Ye wouldnae hear me greetin' aboot it noo, I can tell ye. Anyway, there was me, puffin' an' pantin' and by the time I got to the box I was really worried because I didn't know what to expect. Frankie was nowhere to be seen. The box was empty. The signal was at red and I could see the steam from the waiting train rising above the trees a few yards down the track. I called Largs and reported that Frankie was not there. Just then a car pulled up on the road outside and Frankie's boss appeared. He hurried in and changed the signal. Soon the long delayed train came slowly into view. The driver stared up at me as he passed. He hunched his shoulders up to his ears and the palms of his hands were turned upwards as if he was asking what was wrong, but I could only shake my head.'

'Where was Frankie, then?' asked Effie.

'Well, just then I noticed a railway cap bobbing about just above the wall of the nearby field. I went to investigate and there was Frankie, beaming all over his face, a baby calf nestling in his arms. It had just left its mother's belly. The cow was lowing contentedly now that her difficult labour was over.

"She could never have managed on her own. I could see her, strug-gling, from the box." Frankie said when he saw me. *"She was in trouble, man"*

'No' in half as much trouble as you're in, Frankie!' said I, shaking my head in disbelief.

I returned to the signal box and reported all was now well. Frankie was safe and sound. He was just at the coo's tail again. Literally, this time.'

There was a great deal of laughter.

'That sounds just like my Frankie,' Effie said, wiping away a tear.

⚘⚘

It was after 7 o'clock but still daylight when Paddy Preston, Duncan Brewer, Davey McCally and Joe and Danny Gillan waited at West Kilbride station for the train back to Glasgow. Joe lived in nearby Saltcoats, and would not be travelling on the train, but had come to the station to help lift Duncan Brewer's wheelchair on board and to see his brother off. Duncan would be helped off at Kilwinning, where he lived in special accommodation that catered to his handicap.

'Effie seemed to have cheered up a bit by the time we left

her,' said Joe Gillan. 'I thought she was going to pass out earlier, at the graveside. Did you see how pale she was?'

'She's no' the woman she used to be, I can tell ye that,' Duncan said. 'I haven't seen her in years, and I got quite a shock. She's awfu' wee, and frail getting.'

'Effie'll be fine. Think of all the people she's had to lift and lay in her time as a nurse. She's made of good tough stuff. It's a great sadness that Frankie has gone. She'll miss him badly. We all will. But she'll cope, if I know Effie.' Paddy said.

'They say death comes in threes.' Duncan observed. 'I wonder who'll be next!'

'Away ye go, man! What rubbish is that you're talking? Folks are living and dying by the hundreds every day. We just don't think aboot it till it hits somebody we know. Have less of these auld wives' tales!'

'It's nae auld wives tale,' Duncan muttered ominously. 'Just you wait and see. There'll be two more afore a year has passed. Mark ma words.'

The noise of the approaching train saved them from having to reply. As they lifted Duncan, chair and all, up on to the guards van, they made wry faces at each other above his head.

'Aye, just wait and see.' Duncan said again.

LETTERS

My Dear Barbara,

How are you, my darling girl? I hope you are not working too hard and that you are taking care of yourself. I am very proud of your being a staff nurse now after all the difficulties you have had to overcome. I hope you are still happy working in the Royal Infirmary. It is a very busy hospital, I know, and you must be run off your feet, so make sure you take time to relax when you are off duty. Do you know that your grandmother was a nurse in the Royal too? That was years ago, before you were born. I wonder what conditions must have been like then?

But this is not why I am writing to you. I have something to tell you. I have finally done what we have often discussed. I have left your father. This may come as a surprise to you, since you have urged me to do so time and time again without success. He had another temper outburst last week, which was the last straw for me. Funnily enough, he had been very well behaved over the last few months - in fact, ever since your visit home at Easter when you stood up to him, (brave wee girl that you are.) I thought he'd go for you, he was that mad! But your stern words to him must have had some effect, because he did seem to be making a big effort to control his temper. However, one day last week I was making soup and I wrapped up all the vegetable peel from the sink in a newspaper, not realising that it was that day's paper and your father hadn't read it yet. He went crazy, and before I knew it, I was picking myself up off the kitchen floor.

I knew right away, even before I saw the lovely keeker of a black eye he had given me, that it was the last time I would take this. I won't go on about it Barbara love, as you know the story inside out, but I *started planning my getaway right there and then. Now, I have not put an address on here, as I want to protect you should your father come to ask you where I am. You can honestly tell him that you don't know. But I want you to tell Charles and Benny that I'm safe and well, and that they'll hear from me soon. You don't need to tell Meg and May; I will write to Canada and tell them myself, but not right now. I want to see how things work out first.*

I will be in Fuller's teashop in Buchanan Street on Wednesday at 11a.m. If you are not on duty, maybe you could meet me there and we'll have a long talk about my plans. I'll wait there until 12 o'clock. Hope you can make it as I'm dying to see you. Take good care your-self till then,

Your ever loving
Mum xxx

CHAPTER 4

Magic in the Air – Or Coal Dust?

There were four small boys in the station. They were sitting happily huddled together on the steps of the bridge, laughing and jostling each other. They had been there for over an hour and Eddie had been keeping a discreet eye on them. They had not caused any trouble, but it was becoming obvious that they were not here to catch a train. Eddie decided it was time to approach them. The railway station can be a dangerous place and it was policy to discourage kids from hanging around. He didn't want to appear confrontational, like he'd come to throw them out, so he got a broom from the supply cupboard and began to sweep the platform, working his way towards the boys. He was trying to think what he might say that would cause least offence when one of the boys called out to him.

'Hey, Mister! When is the next Blue Train due in?'

'There'll be no Blue Trains today, lad.' Eddie said. 'Where is it you want to go?'

'We're no' goin' anywhere. We just came up to see the new Blue Trains. Is this line no' electrified?'

'Aye, it's electrified, but the Blue trains are not running this week. They've developed a problem.'

'What kind o' problem?' was the next question.

Eddie saw that one boy had pulled up his jumper and had produced a notebook and pencil.

'Oh, you're train spotting!'

'Aye.'

'Well it seems that there's been some instances of fire breaking out in the traction equipment, so we've had to revert to steam haulage till they sort it out.'

The boy licked the tip of his pencil and wrote in his little book.

'Ach! When will the Blue Trains be back, then?'

'It might take a week or two. I really don't know. Maybe Mr Preston could tell you. He's the station manager. He's off this weekend, but he'll be here on Monday, if you want to come back then and have a word with him.'

'We go back to school on Monday. The summer holidays are over now.' The boy who said this chucked his pencil over the fence in his disappointment.

'I'm sorry, lads.' Eddie commiserated.

Hands in pockets, the boys wandered away disconsolately.

A few minutes later on the opposite platform, Lily Dunne alighted from the Motherwell bound train from Glasgow. Eddie noticed her and had put his broom away and had straightened his tie by the time she had crossed the bridge.

'Good afternoon, Mrs Dunne,' he greeted her.

She handed him her ticket. 'Hello Eddie. Nice again today, I see. Even nicer, because I've been taken on full time now at my job and that means more money. Isn't that good?'

'I'm glad to hear that.' Eddie smiled and touched his cap as she passed through the archway. He watched her progress down the hill. She was wearing a smart grey suit and was carrying a black and white checked bag. Her brown hair was blowing softly in the light breeze. He found it hard to believe that she had just finished work in a fish shop. He wondered if the rumours about her were true. Had she really left her husband? And how long might she stay with her sister? Then he wondered at himself wondering such a thing and told himself sharply that it was none of his business. What on earth had come over him? In all his forty- six years he'd never been nosey about anyone! He wondered instead how Paddy had got on at his interview.

৵৵৵ ৵৵৵

Paddy Preston had applied for a job as guard on the Glasgow to Largs line. His real love of trains had made him grow tired of being station-bound all day. He had been offered his present job, acting station manager at Bellside Station, in the aftermath of a horrendous spate of fatalities when he was a train driver and he had reluctantly accepted. At the time, though there was no blame attached to Paddy, he felt his train driving days were over. He knew it would take more courage than he could muster to get back behind the controls of a train again. But lately Paddy felt he wanted to be mobile again. If not *upwardly*, at least he could be *westerly* mobile, travelling to and fro and hearing that noisy clickety-click in his ears that was music to him.

He made his way home now, feeling confident that he had been successful, although he would not know officially for a day or two yet. He had been a guard on that same route many years ago and he hoped that this would stand in his favour. That was before he had trained as a signalman, then as a driver. He must be the only man employed on the railways who had tried out every job. He passed the Caley Row, where he had been born. Nobody lived there now. The houses, a long row of terraced two-roomed cottages, due for demolition soon, had been built in the last century to house Caledonian Railway workers. One of them had been turned into a shop. The sign above the window, formerly somebody's sitting room window, said

'O.K. Geordie.'

Geordie was an immigrant who spoke with a thick Polish accent. He sold everything and anything in his little shop. He was chatty and friendly, always anxious to please his customers, and he was very popular with the townsfolk. If he didn't have what you needed, he would get it for you. (I have eet for you by Fry-day, O.K? You leeve eet with Geordie, O.K? I get some for you.) Clothes pegs, dog biscuits, firelighters, fruit, vegetables, second hand clothes, sweeties and flypaper. You name it, O.K. Geordie had it. All stacked around the shop with no attention to order or hygiene.

Being optimistic about his interview, Paddy felt like celebrating so he went inside and bought two plastic toy aeroplanes for the boys and a pink fluffy purse for Debbie. These were handed to him in a brown paper bag, which he put in his pocket as he turned towards Hatton Close, the tenement where he lived. His thoughts were on buying a car. It would mean that wherever they sent him, no matter how late the shift, he could always drive home. What would Agnes think?

As he neared the close, he heard loud caterwauling and raised voices coming through the open window of his own house. He ran up the flight of stairs to the first floor and hurried inside to find five-year old Tommy sitting on the draining board in the tiny scullery, which was the flat's kitchen area, bawling his head off. Agnes was dabbing Dettol and kisses on a badly scraped knee.

'What's all the hullabaloo?'

'He fell off the wall near the dustbins again. I don't know how many times I've told him not to climb.'

Agnes moved over a bit to allow Paddy to squeeze into the small space between the sink and the cooker to inspect the injuries.

'Oh dear, oh dear,' he said drawing in his breath sharply and shaking his head. 'This might mean an amputation.'

Tommy stopped crying. 'What's an am-poo-tay-shun?'

'It's very serious,' Paddy said grimly. 'I'd better take a closer look at this. Wait till I take my jacket off.'

He went into the lobby and hung up his jacket, removing the brown paper bag of toys from the pocket and hiding it in the coalscuttle, which was outside the front door, on the landing. Rolling up his sleeves, he returned to the scullery where Tommy had begun crying again even louder now that he had good reason. Danny and Debbie hovered in the background, waiting to see if a trip to Casualty in an ambulance would be wee brother's lucky fate. Paddy manipulated the little knee carefully.

'Will I still be able to start school on Monday?' Tommy asked, fearful that this tragedy might prevent him being among the new August intake, an event he had looked forward to all summer.

'I think you're lucky this time, wee man. No need for an ambulance. You'll live.'

Danny and Debbie were disappointed. Tommy was disappointed too and decided to cry for a little longer just in case anyone got the idea that his injuries were trivial.

It was then, by way of a diversion, that Paddy revealed his long kept secret.

He was a *MAGIC* Daddy!

'Naw!'

Oh yes he was!

Tommy's crying abated to a soft whimper as he pondered this awesome news. He was lifted down from the sink and joined his siblings on the settee to hear more.

'Could you do some magic now?' they wanted to know.

'Well, you might just be in luck. I haven't used my powers in a long time, but as it's Friday, I'll give it a try.'

'Why have you never told us about this before?'

'Up till now, you've been too young, but I think the time has come to tell you all about it.'

They listened intently as Paddy swore them to secrecy. The magic powers about to be used could only come once a week, on a Friday, and had not to be used more often or the spell would weaken and the magic could disappear forever. They pledged allegiance, and Paddy began his spell.

'Abracadabra, look in my eyes, Magic these children a lovely surprise.'

Then he held his hand to his forehead, eyes shut as if concentrating hard.

'It's coming to me,' he said. 'Yes. I see it now. It's a dark and dusty place - a small area! It could be – um – it looks like - the inside of a coalscuttle. Tommy, go and look in the coalscuttle and see if there is anything inside it.'

Without even a trace of a limp, the badly injured Tommy jumped up and ran outside to the landing, followed closely by his brother and sister. Agnes leant against the scullery door drying her hands on a kitchen towel that smelled strongly of Dettol. She was shaking her head in disbelief as she once again marvelled at her husband's ability to change the whole mood of the house.

The kids were full of wonder at what they found in the coalscuttle. They dropped the brown paper bag on the floor and held the treasure aloft with grubby blackened hands. Agnes could see that the Dettol would be needed again before bedtime, but the kids were ecstatic and cared little for coal dust. Imagine! Their very own daddy having such a wonderful secret gift. And they never knew till now!

And so began the pattern for several Fridays to come. The surprises would vary each week and they were never hidden in the same place twice, so the children couldn't catch Paddy out. Their excitement would heighten as each Friday approached and they wondered what they would receive when daddy worked his magic. Sometimes it was a bag of their favourite sweets. Debbie loved it when she got her favourite Fruit Gums, ("Threepence a tube they were, in Coia's café up the road, if you actually had to *buy* them.") Sometimes it would be a comic for each of them, magically appearing under the cushions of the very settee on which they were sitting. How could this be? They never felt a thing! Danny loved 'The Eagle' where he could read about the adventures of his namesake, Dan Dare, Pilot of the Future.

The fun lasted until Debbie was pressured into exposing the secret. One Friday the school bully, who had the very inapt name of Jesse Rogers, decided to pick on her. She warned him that he had better watch what he was doing because her dad was a magician and he could banish Jesse and his family from the face of the earth. She had no actual proof that her father had this ability, but reasoned that a man who could make things appear could surely make things disappear, including people, if the cause was just. When asked to explain, Debbie blabbed it all; how her father didn't need to buy sweets or toys or comics or anything for them; he just magiced them. Soon a crowd gathered, some sceptical and scathing, others incredulous but willing to be convinced. Debbie was the centre of attention as arguments abounded in the playground as to whether this revelation was true or not. Just then, verification personified came along in the form of wee brother.

'She says your da's magic and he can magic sweets and banish people. Is that true?' Jesse Rogers demanded.

Wee brother gasped and looked at her accusingly.

'You're not supposed to tell!' he hissed.

No more proof was needed. All of a sudden Debbie was everyone's pal. She basked in this newfound popularity and invited any sceptics to come and watch her father in action this very home-time. Some were being picked up after school by their parents so they couldn't take up the offer, but three boys, including Jesse, and two girls accompanied her home at four o'clock.

Paddy was puzzled to see this delegation. Debbie explained in a halting way why they were here. They had come to see the magic for themselves. Paddy turned a little pale. He put them all in the living room while he had a whispered chat with Agnes in the lobby.

'It's all very well bamboozling your own kids, but some folks just might take offence if we try it on their kids.' Paddy whispered.

'Ach, it's only a bit of fun, Paddy. Who could possibly take offence?' Agnes said, pulling on her coat. 'Besides, we can't let Debbie lose face. Do you see the size o' that big Jesse guy? I'll away to O.K. Geordie's and get something for all of them. I'll put it in the coalscuttle. You keep them busy till I get back.' With that she hurried off.

Paddy re-entered the living room, where Debbie and her friends had been joined by Danny and Tommy, and explained that to work five extra magics at short notice needed a wee bit more time for the power to penetrate, so they would need to wait a few minutes. A total of eight pairs of eyes told him they didn't mind. When Agnes returned she signalled to him that all was ready and Paddy did his stuff. The wonder was awesome as the trick was performed. Eight toffee apples were discovered in the coalscuttle when they were told to look. Everyone went home happy and Debbie experienced the rare joy of being 'Most popular Girl.'

However, at bedtime that night Paddy broke the sad news to his kids that he had overstretched his magic powers and that his 'gift' was gone. They begged and pleaded, and promised to lay off the magic for as long as it takes, but he was adamant. His powers had been unexpectedly stretched (and also the house cash flow, though he didn't mention this) and they'd have to tell their pals at school that the magic was over. It certainly was for Debbie! The whole school had heard the story of her magic daddy over the weekend and by Monday morning dozens of kids were ready to accompany her home any time she said the word. Disappointed, they shunned and disparaged her when she explained that the magic had dried up. Her daddy was no longer a magic daddy, but just an ordinary daddy now, just like theirs.

An unhappy choice of word.

Bitter jibes were targeted at her throughout the day, and several vociferous kids assured her that their dad was no ordinary dad either. Various tales of fatherly daring-do were recited in her face. These included some unlikely acts of heroism during the war, and being able to drink a whole pint of beer without taking a breath once. But the story that puzzled her most was the one wee Petey Miller told her. She decided she'd tell her dad about it later and ask his opinion of it.

༺༻ ༺༻

Agnes had gone shopping in Glasgow and Paddy was dozing on the couch, having just driven home from Irvine in his new car. He was enjoying his new job as guard but the extra travelling was making him extra tired. A sudden urgent pounding on the door awakened him. He staggered sleepily to his feet but before he could open the door an angry voice yelled.

'Open up! I know fine ye're in there! I see your car parked outside.'

'What in the name of god is it?' He tried to de-fuddle his brain as he opened the door and stared blankly at the big fellow who was standing on his doormat.

'Who are you?'

'You're about to find out, pal. My name is Jesse Rogers. Jesse Rogers *senior,* that is! My son says your kids have been terrorising him.'

'*My* kids? *My* kids are terrorising *your* Jesse? Ah don't think so!'

'They've been telling him that you are some sort of wicked wizard and you're gonnae banish him from the face of the earth. He's scared oot his heid.'

'No, no,' Paddy began to understand and thought he'd try to diffuse the man's anger by using a light-hearted laugh that he was far from feeling.

'Think it's funny, d'ye?' insisted Jesse Senior. 'My boy says you worked some magic right here in your house. Now he's terrified, and he thinks he'll have to keep on your good side now in case you work some magic on him.'

'He wasnae terrified when he tucked into the toffee apple we gave him.' Paddy countered, getting into his stride. 'It was only a bit of fun.'

'Bit of fun, eh? Is that how you get your kicks? Scaring the shit oot o' weans for a bit o' fun! Think because you own a car you're better than the rest of us, do ye? What have ye got to say for yourself? Tell me now, or you'll get your teeth to play with.' Paddy was wide-awake now. The man couldn't have roared any louder if he'd been at Hampden.

'Look, Mr Rogers, you've got it all wrong. It didn't happen like that.'

He was aware that his neighbour's door across the landing had opened just a crack. Auld Granny Park must be having a field day.

'Come in Mr Rogers. I'll explain –

'NAW. *I'LL* EXPLAIN! YOU LISTEN!'

By this time, Paddy knew, the whole Close was listening.

'You leave ma boy alone. O.K?'

Jesse senior suddenly bent down and seized the coalscuttle and held it aloft. He emptied the contents all over the landing. Dross and coal dust billowed everywhere, even down the stairs to ground floor!

'Think yourself lucky I'm in a good mood. I should have emptied that all over your fancy car!'

A moment later he was gone. A quiet click from the door opposite told Paddy that Granny Park had heard enough.

It took Paddy a whole hour to clean up the mess but by the time Agnes came home, the stair-head, landing and ground floor were spick and span and the children had had their tea and were ready for bed. She didn't suspect a thing. He would pick his moment, but he knew he had to tell her about Jesse Rogers' visit before she heard it from a dozen different sources in the co-op tomorrow. Granny Park's tongue would not be idle.

'Daddy,' Debbie said when he tucked her into bed later that evening, 'Wee Petey Miller says he understands why you don't want to work any more magic. He says his dad has a brilliant secret too. He whispered to me today that his dad can dress up exactly like a woman. He says he's even got a wig an' every-thing, and when he puts on his mam's clothes and lipstick, you could never tell he was really a man. I don't think there's anything very brilliant about that! Do *you*, dad? Emmdy could do that!'

CHAPTER 5

Hiccups and Hogmanay

'It's no' fair, Joe Gillan. It's just no' fair!'

Joe's wife was furious. She slapped the dishcloth she had been using down into the sink and stormed out of the kitchen. Joe followed her into the living room and through into the hall, a pleading note in his voice.

'I cannae help it Julie. I've got to take my turn.'

'Aw, don't give me that! You worked the last two Hogmanays *and* you worked Christmas Day this year as well. You won't stand up to that Railway, that's all it is. You said you'd make sure you got Hogmanay off this year and you've done nuthin' about it. Nuthin'! What about the party? I've been looking forward to the party! It's the only time we don't need a baby-sitter and we can have a wee drink without having to worry about the kids. Am I to be there on my own again this year?'

She changed direction several times, confused in her agitation, not knowing where to go. He followed.

'Come on, Julie, you'll not be on your own. You'll have the kids, and the family will all be there.'

Julie stopped her erratic meandering and looked at him in astonishment. Standing in front of her in his simmit and railway trousers, braces hanging off his shoulders, was the love of her life. Seven years come April they'll have been married.

Was she only discovering now that he was *thick*? Did he really not understand? Of course she'd bloody well be on her own if *he* wasn't there! She couldn't trust herself to speak so she stared at him for a long time, thoughts racing through her mind.

Like the American goes home for Thanksgiving, the Scot goes home for Hogmanay. Everybody knows this. *Everybody knows this!* But obviously not her Joe. Any self-respecting Scot will do his best to be home in time for the bells.

'Be reasonable, Julie… ' But he got no further.

'Reasonable? *Reasonable?*' She heard her voice getting shrill so she took a deep breath and tried to calm down. Her breath came in short gasps when she spoke next.

'I know you work for a public service industry, Joe, and I do my best to put up with it. The unsocial hours. The delays when you never get home on time. The lousy pay. And I'm prepared to accept that you often have to work on Public Holidays. All this I can put up with. What really gets me is that I know there's a rota in place. It's supposed to be a fair rota, so that everyone takes a turn at working on special days. So how come you're the one that's working again?'

He opened his mouth to speak and then shut it again. Faced with Julie in one of these moods, it was usually better to play dumb. Silence took over for a while. All Julie could think of was that now, two days before the event, he was telling her that he would be working the late shift on New Year's Eve. Angry disappointment swirled inside her head and brought a dangerous colour to her cheeks. She knew that Joe had not put his foot down hard enough at work when the rota was being made up. There is always someone with a sob story and soft Josey always falls for it.

'What was it this time, eh? Somebody's maw breathing her last; won't live to see New Year's Day, was that it? Somebody's grandson emigrating to Australia and this is their last Hogmanay together? Could that be it? Or maybe a dog has died? Aye, that must be it! Somebody else's dead dog! That's always worth missing a long-planned family party for!' Julie couldn't keep the sarcasm from her voice. She reached the bedroom and went in, slamming the door behind her. Three years ago at this time she was in the maternity, having just given birth to Holly, their youngest, and Joe had been on duty for the following two Hogmanays. This would be the fourth year in a row that Joe and Julie would not be together for the bells. But this time he had promised. *He had promised*!

'I'll make it up to you, Julie.' Joe's voice came from the other side of the door. 'I'll be off duty by one o'clock and I should be at Poackets before two so you'll hardly miss me at all – *and* I'm off the whole of New Year's Day."

'Aye, and all you'll do is sleep! I've eaten apples off that cart before,' came the snarled reply.

Julie's family took it in turn each year to celebrate Hogmanay at each other's house. This year it was Poackets' turn to be host. Poackets was Julie's younger brother and he had a spacious four-apartment tenement in Stevenson, a mile or two along the seafront from Saltcoats, where Joe and Julie lived. Aunties, uncles, cousins, in-laws, would all get together a week or so before the party to decide who will contribute what. Allocations such as who will bring the steak pie, peas and potatoes etc, are usually the same every year because each branch of the family took a pride in being the best at something different. Maureen, Julie's sister, made delicious trifle, with chocolate pieces and a secret flavouring: Aunt Gussie made great shortbread, and Auntie Nellie always made the clootie dumpling. It was really good clootie dumpling. The men folk attended to the booze.

The 'big room' at Poackets' house would be converted into a makeshift dormitory to sleep all the wee cousins. There was no official bedtime for the kids on Hogmanay. They would never have gone to bed willingly anyway, and there was always so much excitement among them that pandemonium would reign in the big room, so the rule was that they were allowed to stay up, listening to the adults singing, wandering in and out, stuffing their faces with cakes and jelly and Irn-bru and occasionally entertaining the adults with a song, or a poem they'd learned at school. Eventually, one by one, they would fall asleep on somebody's knee and the appropriate mother would lift her exhausted offspring and head off down the hall to tuck the child up in the first available sleeping bag. The muffled sound of Uncle Gerry's voice yodelling his way through the lyrics of 'Ain't Misbehaving' would likely be heard coming from the living-room, or maybe it would be Aunt Cathie's rendering of 'The Heilan' Chorus.' Adults didn't go to sleep at all. They stayed awake partying and welcoming First Footers and maybe doing some First Footing themselves, which often involved bringing somebody else's party back to your party. Julie loved this yearly gathering and was deeply hurt that Joe had decided to work that night. Her sense of disappointment and consequent bad temper did not subside any during the next two days.

∽∾∾ ∽∾∾

Around the time that Julie and the kids arrived at Poackets' house on New Year's Eve, Joe was about to drive the last train out of Glasgow Central, bound for Largs. He was miserable. Julie had hardly said a word for the last two days and to cap it all, he was feeling guilty. It was true that he hadn't tried very hard to get off duty tonight. He had never really enjoyed Julie's family gatherings as much as she did. He would have liked to have spent the bells at Julie's side and be the first to kiss her and wish her a Happy New Year, but he was not overly fond of

Julie's brother, though he tried hard to hide this from his wife. The man was not called 'Poackets' for nothing. The guy simply never took his hands out of his pockets. Never bought a round in the pub. Never lifted a stick of furniture to help at a flitting. Never wielded a paintbrush to help a mate with the decorating. Where was the man's pride? Joe didn't have much respect for idlers like Poackets. He and his three brothers lived by a different code. You don't have to ask for help when you're a Gillan! As soon as you mentioned that the hall needed decorating, the boys were there on their next day off with ladders, scrapers and dungarees. Even young Jamsie, who still lived wi' Ma, and didn't even have his own house would turn up with trowel, hoe or paintbrush, depending on the job in hand.

The Gillan brothers always tackled major chores with a team effort. The idea was that they could take the hard slog out of any task by doing it together as a family. In that way, fences got painted, gardens got dug, huts were creosoted or kitchens got tiled while they bantered and laughed and drank beer. (Though, on occasion, it had been known for an argument to break out and more turpentine would be needed to wash off paint from slapped faces than was ever needed to clean accidental drips, but that's another story and certainly not one to tell to Poackets.) Yes, thought Joe. That was the measure of a man. Help out where you can and, most important, stand your round. Joe would never understand Poackets, and only tolerated him for Julie's sake. Poackets' wife could be sarcastic too. A right nippy sweetie was Big Liz.

Glasgow Central was almost deserted when Joe heard the whistle and set the wheels in motion. He was due in at Largs at twelve-forty-five in the morning. Then, because this was the last train, he would have to drive the empty carriages back to the siding at Ardrossan Harbour to put the train to bed. It was going to be a long lonely night. Not many people on the train, only some last minute stragglers. Most people would be home by now enjoying their pre-bells bevvie. Joe wondered how his ma and his brothers were doing out in Lanarkshire. Joe had come to live in Ayrshire shortly after his marriage and was happy enough with a visit home every now and then, but occasionally he wished that Julie might consider moving nearer *his* folks. He missed his brothers, particularly at this time of year.

It was lonely in the cabin. Maybe he *should* have got the night off and joined Julie at the party. Too late now. By the time they left Paisley Gilmour Street, there were only half a dozen people on the train. Joe caught sight of himself, reflected in the glass by the darkness outside. He realised he had a face like a wet Friday. *Ach, cheer up, man,* he told himself. *It's Hogmanay!* Paddy Preston was the guard tonight. Paddy was good fun and would lift his spirits, and he was coning home with Joe to Saltcoats tonight anyway. He'd summon Paddy for a blether.

In the guards van, Paddy heard the bell: three rings followed by another three rings; that meant - 'guard required by driver.' He made his way through the nearly empty train to the driver's cab.

Joe asked 'What's the passenger situation?' as soon as Paddy's head appeared.

'There's only five people and they are all going to Ardrossan. Even Wee Hughie. No one is going as far as Largs."

'What? They're all going to Ardrossan? Must be some party there!' Joe pulled out a half bottle of whisky from his pocket. 'Would ye like a wee half?'

'Happy New Year to you,' said Paddy, filling the cork and downing the golden contents in one go.

'Here, how about a nip of mine.' Paddy poured Joe a measure from his own bottle which he pulled from the inside pocket of his railway jacket.

Then a passenger appeared at the cabin door. 'Would ye like a wee half, boys?'

They both recognised Wee Hughie from Fairlie, a regular passenger. He had been a champion boxer in his youth and his great claim to fame was that he had gone a few rounds with no less a person than the great Benny Lynch himself.

'That's very kind of you, Hughie!' Joe and Paddy were deferential to this local minor celebrity.

Another two passengers appeared at the door of the cab, opening bottles and claiming acquaintanceship with Wee Hughie. Soon, as if by magic, all five passengers, including Mr and Mrs Forsythe, who owned a fruit shop in Dalry, but were getting off the train at Ardrossan to attend a Hogmanay party, were all crammed into the little space beside the driver and the guard, sharing their bottles and talking away like budgies.

After a little while, a glow of appreciation seemed to seep over Hughie's Acquaintance No 1. Turning to Paddy and Joe he smiled warmly and said,

'You guys are champions, so you are. Champions!' He poured whisky into the cork of his bottle till it overflowed onto his shaking fingers. 'Working through the bells an' all. Where would we be if it wisnae for you? Stranded at Glasgow Central, that's where! We should have been home hours ago, but we kept missing the train, so we passed the time by having another drink each time. Didn't we, Archie?' He looked towards Hughie's acquaintance No 2, who nodded happily. He passed the brimming cork carefully over to Mr Forsythe, who savoured the contents slowly and delectably before passing the cork back to be refilled for someone else.

Paddy, delighted that he was a champion, and basking in his own warm glow, was moved to tell them that he wished all passengers were as appreciative as this lot. He held the company in a beatific gaze, and launching into one of the tales he was renowned among his colleagues for, told them of the two silly lassies he had met only yesterday.

'It was at Glasgow Central,' he began. 'I'm getting ready to give the signal to depart and these two lassies came running up to me.

Wait, mister. Wait! They shouts. *Does this train go to Saltcoats?* They were about fifteen. You know the type - all mini-skirt and chewin' gum.

Yes, says I, it does.

Does it go to Irvine? they asked.

No, I says, it doesn't go to Irvine.

How no'? they says. *It's on the same line, in't it?*

No, says I, it's not the same line at all. And I explained that the line diverts at Kilwinning. It goes one way to Saltcoats and another way to Irvine.

Oh is that right? they says, thoughtful like.

They thought this over, and then one of them said slowly

Oh, aye. Right. Right. Well, does it go to Fairlie?

Yes, I said. It goes to Fairlie.

Oh, that's good, they said, *Cos we're going to West Kilbride.*

And they jumped on the train. You wouldnae believe that, would ye? Could they no' just have asked that in the first place?' Gales of laughter ensued and cigarettes were produced and passed round, along with more corkfuls of whisky, though by this time Joe felt he'd had enough and refused to take any more.

'Nae mair for me,' he said sadly. 'Three corkfuls is the limit. I've got a train to drive.'

The train slowed to a halt at Cowden signal box. The signal-man gave them all a wave.

'Happy New Year,' he called down.

Joe pulled down the window. 'Would ye take a wee dram?' he called up to the signalman.

'Aye. Bring it up.'

Paddy jumped down and began to ascend the steps to the box. The happy passengers obviously felt that they had been invited too and when Paddy turned round, six people, including Joe, were following him up the stairs. Mrs Forsythe's upward progress was carefully and politely assisted by calls of 'Watch your step there, Missus Forsythe!' And 'Mind your foot, Missus Forsythe.' and 'You're all right, I've got you!' The blushing Mrs Forsythe thanked, giggled and protested. The chunky beads that adorned her ample chest glistened in the moonlight. She had never had such an adventure in her hitherto well-ordered life and her rosy cheeks showed that she was enjoying herself immensely. They all bundled into the signal box and all, except Joe who had a drink of Irn-Bru, had another wee half with the signalman, and then they all trundled merrily down the stairs again and back on board the abandoned train.

'I'll tell ye another,' began Paddy, taking up where he left off as Joe set the wheels in motion again. They headed for Kilwinning.

'It was a few years ago now but I've never forgotten. I was on platform thirteen talking to Robert the postman. You mind Robert, Joe?' Joe nodded, and everyone else nodded too as if they were first cousins of Robert. 'He was in his postman's uniform, wi' the wee horn on his cap and Royal Mail on his shoulders, and there was me with my uniform with British Railways on my lapels and on the badge in my cap. Up comes this wee woman. She looked at me, then she looked at Robert, and she says to Robert *Excuse me, is this the train for Glengarnock?* Now I was just about to take the train out, as I was the guard. We were just waiting for the mail to be loaded. So Robert looks at me, and I says No, this train doesn't stop at Glengarnock. So Robert turns to the woman and says No. She said to the postman, Aye *it does.* So the postman looked at me and we both laughed. So I addressed her myself, and I said   No, lady. I'm sorry, but this train does not stop at Glengarnock. Well, she looked at me as if to say, "Who asked you?" and she said *Yes it does! I get this train every day!*

'It must be another train you're thinking of, madam, I says. This train does NOT stop at Glengarnock. All this time, people are walking up the platform and getting on the train. So the woman turned from us and stopped a man who was about to board the train, just an ordinary punter, like, you know? She says to him *Excuse me, but does this train stop at Glengarnock?* And this passenger says Yes. So she turned to me and she says   *See, there ye are!   It does stop at Glengarnock!* So away she went, up the platform and settled herself in a seat by the window. It was one of the High Density trains, the kind where the seats are like long couches facing each other and there is always a door right at every window.' (Paddy explained this for the benefit of his enrapt audience, who all nodded knowingly.) 'So I thought, *what do I do now? If she's going to Glengarnock, she's on the wrong train.* I waited for a minute and then I thought, I better try again to help her, so I went up and opened the door right beside her and I said

"Excuse *me madam, you're the lady who wants to go to Glengarnock. I'm afraid you are on the wrong train. The train you want leaves from platform ten in twenty minutes. This train does not stop at Glengarnock"*

Well, she nearly snapped my head off. *YES IT DOES!* she said, in no uncertain terms.

So I said, *Suit yourself, madam,* and closed the door.

By this time the mail was all loaded up and it was time to go. Ding, ding and away we went. Sure enough we went straight through Glengarnock without stopping. The next stop was Dalry. So at Dalry, I put my head out and I see her get out. Her face was furious. She came marching right up to me and the funny thing is, she didn't seem to recognise me for she said, in a fierce temper, *I was told that this train stopped at Glengarnock.* I leant down and put my face real close to hers and I pointed at my face and I said, LOOK AT THIS FACE! THIS IS THE FACE THAT TOLD YOU AT GLASGOW CENTRAL THAT THIS TRAIN DID NOT STOP AT GLENGARNOCK. A thunderstruck expression crossed her face as recognition dawned on her. She backed away and began to hurry off down the platform.

"AND YOU'RE LUCKY I DON'T CHARGE YOU THE FARE TO DALRY!" I called after her.'

Amid the guffaws and applause that followed, Mrs Forsythe became helpless with laughter and spluttered so much that she was offered more whisky to soothe her throat in case she choked. Paddy was praised for his wit and for his tolerance of the public in general. The journey continued until Joe suddenly said 'Right lads, that's us at Ardrossan.'

They all looked surprised. 'Aw naw, no' already! I'll tell ye what! Where do ye go from here?' asked Mr Forsythe, a bright idea forming in his brain.

'We go straight through to Largs, but we come back to Ardrossan Harbour with empty carriages to stable the train. Then we're off home'

'But there's nobody goin' tae Largs.'

'I know but I still have to go there.'

'We could come back via the Harbour. It would be just as easy for us to get off at the Harbour. Right,' he said decisively. 'Florrie and me will stay on just for the run. We'll get off on the way back. I'm enjoying myself and I don't want to get off just now. Is that O.K with you Florrie?' He looked enquiringly at his wife. Florrie's beaming smile said it all. She had never been so proud of her husband. What a brilliant plan!

The others agreed that this was a great idea. So Joe started up the train once more. Nobody noticed the cold clear moonlight reflected on the dark waters of the sea at Fairlie, or the white horses lapping beyond the Pencil as they approached Largs, one of the jewel towns on the west coast of Scotland. They were so engrossed in each other's company.

Passing Largs box, they saw Boyd Johnson the signalman. 'Do you want a wee half, Boydie?' they called up. Sure enough, Boydie wanted a half and seven bodies trundled up the wooden steps. The fire was burning brightly and the signal box was warm and cosy. Boydie shared out his ma's clootie dumpling. His mother had given him a whole dumpling because he had to work nightshift over Hogmanay.

'This is the best dumplin' I've ever tasted,' said Joe.

'Have a few more slices. Here, wrap this bit up and take it away with you,' said Boydie.

They were tempted to stay longer in the signal box, but reluctantly the cheery, chattering bunch got back on the train, waving goodbye to Boydie, (the best signalman in the whole wide world,) and headed into Largs station. The station was completely deserted. All the staff were long gone. Hughie got out first and sang a song about the towns on the Clyde coast to the darkened station buildings. They all joined in at the bits they knew and Mrs Forsythe demonstrated a few steps of the Highland fling on the empty platform.

'C'mon lads!' Paddy shouted. 'We've got to go to the back of the train. Follow me.' He began to walk towards the other end of the train. Mrs Forsythe was secretly delighted at being one of the lads, and she teetered along the platform with the others in Paddy's wake, laughing and stumbling.

'Why are we going to the back of the train?' Hughie's acquaintance No2 wanted to know.

'Because the back of the train is now the front of the train.' said Paddy.

The man tried hard to focus on this information and was clearly baffled.

'Well! If that's no' clever! These new fangled diesels!' he marvelled. 'You couldnae do this on a steam train!'

They all got into the driver's cab at the other end, which was facing the way they had to go. Boydie gave them a wave as they passed him for the second time. Ardrossan Harbour was reached just as the whisky ran out in the last bottle. All the passengers got out, singing merrily and slurring 'A Happy New Year to y'all' and swearing allegiance forever to railway staff in general, and train drivers and guards in particular. Joe and Paddy watched them until the last wave of a hand disappeared.

❧❦ ❧❦

It had begun to snow quite heavily by the time Joe and Paddy made it to Poackets' house in the wee small hours. Woozy, pie-eyed relatives immediately surrounded them.

'Happy New Year! Happy New Year!' They chorused.

'Joe's here, Julie,' they called. 'You're our first foot! What have you brung?'

Joe put his hand in his pocket and pulled out Boydie's ma's clootie dumpling, wrapped in its greaseproof paper.

'Daddy! Daddy!' Holly's small voice shouted, not a trace of sleep in her bright eyes. 'We've been waiting for you. Look at me! I'm wearing a new nightie. Auntie Maureen got it for my birthday.'

Joe lifted her into his arms and kissed her sticky face.

'Happy New Year, and Happy Birthday ma wee princess! You look brilliant. I can taste you've been having a good time.' Julie came out of the kitchen when she heard him arrive, a glass in her hand, and waited to give him a kiss.

'Happy New Year, darlin',' she said. A few vodkas had made her forget she was supposed to be mad at him. 'Was it lonely and boring in that driver's cabin all by yourself at the bells?'

'It was dead boring,' he lied, winking at Paddy.

'Where did you get this dumpling?' Auntie Nellie was examining the contents of Joe's parcel carefully.

'One of the guys at work brought it, but it's no' as good as yours, Auntie Nellie,' he lied again.

'*What a way to start the New Year,*' thought Joe. '*Two lies in already!*'

CHAPTER 6

It Always Comes in Threes

Duncan Brewer pulled the Ayrshire Gazette out of the letterbox and backed his wheelchair away from the front door. He then manoeuvred his way into the living room, turned his gas fire up a notch, and removed the shawl from his knees. Sometimes, in spite of the cost, he preferred to heat up the whole room rather than sit huddled in blankets. It certainly needed warming up today. The temperature outside was below freezing and had been since New Year's Day. Snow was still lying in hardened, dirtying mounds on either side of his pathway where his neighbour had shovelled it some days ago. This winter was the coldest he could remember. His was the only house in the street so far that had not suffered from burst pipes and he was grateful for that. The cost of extra heating was at least offset by that benefit.

He looked around for his glasses. There they were, on the arm of the sofa. He wheeled himself nearer and reached out for them, but they eluded his grasp and somehow managed to fall on the floor.

'Bugger!' Duncan said. He reached for the little home-made gadget he had devised to help him. It was a simple long cane with a hook screwed into one end, amply sticky-taped for good measure. An invaluable little tool. He began fishing with it, but instead of curling itself round the leg of the specs, it pushed them further under the sofa. The more he tried, the further away he managed to push his glasses.

'Damn. Bugger tae Hell!' he called out, irritation flaring. 'How can I read the damn paper with no bloody glasses?'

He made another half-hearted attempt, but cruel experience had taught him to know when he was beaten, so he gave up, tossing his hooked stick on to the couch.

'Another wee job for the home help when she comes in at five o'clock,' he muttered, defeated.

He opened up the folded newspaper and with narrowed eyes scrutinised the headline. 'TRAGIC INCIDENT AT NORTH BEACH STATION' and underneath in slightly smaller lettering, 'Railwayman hit by Train.' He could see that clearly enough. Instantly alert now, he tried to follow the ensuing article but couldn't make out the small print. Who was hurt? How seriously? He panicked a little, holding the paper closer and screwing up his eyes. He made out a name – William Gallagher.

William Gallagher? William Gallagher? Who was that?

He knew all the railway staff at North Beach. In fact, he knew them all from Largs to Dalry, but he could not recall a William Gallagher.

Wait a minute! Wait a *wee* minute! Of course! Wullie. Wullie Gallagher! That's Rice Krispie. Aye, that's Rice Krispie's proper name! Rice Krispie has been hurt. He made another attempt to make out the story, but it only hurt his eyes.

'I can't walk and now I can't even read. Useless big lump!' He tossed the paper aside angrily. It was at moments like this, fuelled by frustration, that he became most depressed. He remembered the conversation he'd had just after Frankie Wilson's funeral about Death always coming in threes.

'Aye, they laughed at me. I know they did. But I'll be proved right yet. I know I will. Could Rice Krispie be death Number Two?' He

drummed his fingers impatiently on the arm of his wheelchair and knew he'd have at least four hours to wait before he could find out.

∞⊰∞ ∞⊰∞

Rice Krispie, station clerk on the Glasgow to Largs line, had made his way in the early morning darkness to open up North Beach Station. Day shift was all right in the summer, but on a bitingly cold pitch-black January morning, Rice Krispie could see it far enough. An icy wind was blowing in from the sea and the pale whiteness of the snow, which had been lying all night, gave off an eerie, reflective half-light as he slithered along, keeping his feet with difficulty. He trudged into the dark station onto the westbound platform, knowing he would have to cross the track to get to the ticket office on the opposite side.

A wooden walkway had been built into the sleepers on the track at the far end of the platform to enable railwaymen to take wheelbarrows across the line from one side to the other, a practice later outlawed when passenger trains would no longer carry mail or parcels. Rice Krispie shuffled precariously towards the walkway, digging deep into the pocket of his railway uniform for the station keys. Maybe it was his woolly winter muffler, huddled up around his ears, that dulled his hearing, or maybe it was just that it was so damn cold, making him want to hurry into the station and get the fire lit in the big grate that caused him to be less cautious, but as he stepped on to the walkway, keys in hand, the early morning mail train returning from Largs to Ayr, suddenly loomed upon him out of the darkness. Rice Krispie could only raise his arms as if to protect himself, in the second before it hit him.

The mail train, A16, just one wagon and an engine, carried on its journey, the driver totally unaware of the catastrophe. He had delivered the mail at Largs as he did every morning and was soon due in at Ayr Sheds for reloading. Big Alec had travelled this route a million times, and with signals at green all the way, this was a straight-through, non-stop run and Alec was looking forward to his break and a quiet read at the paper.

While A16 was thundering on towards Ayr, the other members of staff arrived at North Beach and were surprised to find the station still in darkness.

'It's no' like Rice Krispie to be late,' said young Dougie, as he waited with Echo at the locked door of the ticket office. He blew into cupped hands. 'He's usually got the fire goin' b'noo. Ah wish he'd hurry up. Ah'm freezing.' Dougie was stamping his feet and swinging his arms around himself in an effort to keep warm.

'Ah wish he'd hurry up. Ah'm freezing.' Echo repeated.

They waited.

'What do you call him Rice Krispie for? That cannae be his real name.' asked Dougie. His fresh little face showed glowing cheeks. Echo showed a trace of a grin, too cold to actually smile.

'Don't you call him that to his face. He doesn't know we call him Rice Krispie. Some people earn themselves a nickname. You might too, if you're liked enough – or maybe *not* liked enough!'

Echo was about to add more when he suddenly noticed what looked like blood, trailing bright red in the snow at the far end of the platform. He blinked in the gathering dawn light, hoping he had been mistaken. Then he grabbed at Dougie's sleeve and pointed.

They found him a few yards beyond the walkway, just under the bridge. He was unconscious but breathing and with a very weak pulse.

'Find the keys! Find the keys!' Dougie shouted, trying to

think quickly. 'We need to get into the office to phone an ambulance!'

'Find the keys. Find the keys.' cried Echo. 'Phone an ambulance.'

A frantic search of Rice Krispie's pockets and of the surrounding area revealed nothing. Echo removed his heavy, railway-issue greatcoat and carefully covered Rice Krispie's motionless frame. There was an involuntary twitch.

'He's in shock.' Dougie said.

'Shock.' Echo said.

Young Dougie was in shock too. His colour turned ashen. Although basic training had taught him what to do in an emergency, he was unprepared for the retching sensation in his stomach and the panicky feeling of seeing a casualty so soon into his first job. The horror of it all was clearly to be seen on his soft baby face.

'What do you think happened?' His voice was almost a whisper.

Echo lifted his cap and ran his hand wildly through his hair.

'I think he must have been hit by A16. You know? - Big Alec's train. You stay with him. Try to find the keys. I'll go get help.' He ran out into the street and hammered on the door of the nearest house.

Dougie continued to search around, feeling in the snow for the keys. If Rice Krispie had been hit while on the walkway, the keys must be here somewhere nearby.

Oh God, where the hell are they?

The sound of a faint moan came from the still figure on the track and Dougie went to kneel by his friend's side. *Surely if he's moaning, that's a good sign.* He groped under Echo's big coat with frozen fingers, trying to feel for a pulse through the numbness.

'Echo's gone for help, big man,' he whispered to the unconscious form. 'You hang on now. O.K?'

After a few minutes Echo came back, half running, half stumbling, to report that the ambulance was on its way.

'The people living above the pub had a phone,' he panted.

Rice Krispie was removed to Irvine General. As daylight increased the scene became alive. Police, medical examiners and rail authorities buzzed around. They gained access to the ticket office with a spare set of keys. The business of cancelling and diverting services began. Rice Krispie's keys, however, were still nowhere to be found.

∽∾∽ ∽∾∽

When A16 arrived at Ayr Sheds, Big Alec lifted his Daily Record and his piece-box and climbed down from his engine. As he did so, a glint of shiny metal on the engine's step caught his eye. *What's this?* He thought. *A set of keys? Where did they come from?* He noticed the gaffer hurrying towards him.

'Alec! Alec, are you all right, man?'

Alec was puzzled. The gaffer was usually a brusque and irritable little man who never showed the least concern for his staff's personal welfare, so this obvious change of demeanour was certainly out of character.

'Aye. Ah'm O.K. Ah'm fine,' Alec said slowly, and a little suspiciously. 'But I've just found these keys on the step o' ma engine and ah cannae think how they got there.'

Mr Mc Guckin stopped short and stared at the keys in Big Alec's hand.

'Oh, my God! They cannae be!' He clasped a chubby hand over his mouth, which had fallen open in disbelief, as realisation dawned on him. 'They cannae be North Beach's keys!'

'North Beach's keys?' Alec began to suspect Mr Mc Guckin had been drinking.

'Have they reported them missing? How did they get on the step of my engine?'

'Come into the bothy, Alec, an' ah'll tell ye.'

෯෬ඣ ෯෬ඣ

Rice Krispie's injuries were severe. His arms had been forced right back into his body, breaking both shoulders and several other bones. Whatever miracle had occurred to knock him clear as the train caught his arms will never accurately be known, but he made a remarkable recovery. After several months in hospital and a long recuperation at home, he eventually returned to work. His workmates and the regular passengers, though glad that Rice Krispie's accident had not been fatal, were indifferent when they saw his face appear at the ticket office window again, for they soon realised that some things never change. In no time at all, there he was, *snapping* at customers, *crackling* with indignation if he had to interrupt his cuppa to answer a query, and even taking a *pop* at anyone who upset him.

It became known that he had been awarded an undisclosed sum in compensation, and rumours abounded as to how much this might be. His mates tried in vain to wrangle the secret out of him but he never revealed it.

'Just suffice it to say,' he answered to their queries in his deceptively soft Ayrshire accent, 'that instead of *Rice* Krispie, maybe ye should be calling me *Rich* Krispie.'

෯෬ඣ ෯෬ඣ

Duncan Brewer was another who had accepted Rice Krispie's recovery with mixed feelings. It became apparent by the middle of February that Rice Krispie was not going to die from his injuries and Duncan felt cheated. It had been eight months now since Frankie Wilson died, and there were still two more deaths to come. Injuries and accidents aside, who was going to be the next to actually die? He just knew that somebody would go soon and he wished they'd hurry and get on with it, if only to prove that what he'd believed all his life was true. Death came in threes. Paddy Preston and Joe Gillan had called his theory an auld wives tale and he wanted to look them in the eye and say -

'See, I told ye!'

⁓⁓

The big freeze continued without let-up right into March. Frozen points and frozen signals were commonplace, causing long delays and cancellations. Irate passengers bombarded ticket office windows demanding information about re-scheduled services and calling for refunds for cancelled journeys. Phone lines were kept busy as people moaned, and queried, and complained, and doled out general earache to whoever was on the receiving end of their particular grievance.

Being a signalman, Big Oweny was spared direct contact with the travelling public but he had his own misery to contend with. Oweny was a massive eighteen stones in weight and there were fifty steps up to Grangehall box, where he was relief signalman. Snow and ice made this climb even harder, although there was some compensation in that the exertion tended to warm him up a bit as his inner central heating system was forced into action. This, however, went largely unappreciated by Oweny when he reached the top step, wheezing and spluttering.

The real cause of Oweny's misery, though, came in human form. His opposite number in the Grangehall box was a crabbit, mean-spirited wee man by the name of Mr Kynd, a misnomer if ever there was one. Nobody ever knew his first name and it would have made no difference if they did because he always insisted on being called 'Mister' Kynd. He had no intention of allowing any old Tom, Dick or Harry to be on first name terms with him. The men, of course had their own name for him. At first they called him Un-Kynd, because he was. This soon became Spiteful, which was then shortened to

Spit. This came about because somebody once said, 'If you were on fire, he wouldnae spit on you to put out the flames!' That had caused a lot of laughter and more character traits were added.

– He wouldnae gie ye daylight in a dark corner.
– When he was a clerk at Johnsfield, he used to give people the wrong information just to cause them hassle. It fairly makes his day if he can do somebody a disservice. I think he's got a cloven hoof, myself.
– I never knew a man wi' more bitterness in him!
– Who? Old Spiteful Spit, are ye talking about? He'd take the eyes oot yer heid, and come back for the blinkers!

An opportunity to cause unnecessary trouble for someone had presented itself to Spit during the previous autumn. Building had at last started on the nuclear power station. This required blasting into the rock-face along the coast near the railway line, so the track between West Kilbride and Largs was closed while explosives were being used. This dangerous and lengthy procedure amounted to several days lost revenue for the railways and had caused widespread disruption to services and the rail authorities were determined to get things back to normal as soon as possible. When the line eventually re-opened, the men were served explicit instructions to make up for lost time and each man understood, on threat of severe penalties, that there could be no more delays, so every effort was being made to keep the line open and the traffic moving.

Big Oweny was waiting in his box for Des Blackwood to relieve him. To avoid a long walk when he finished work, Oweny always hopped on a passing freight wagon that took him into Largs. It was due to pass the box every day just after Des started his shift and Oweny finished his, so usually, Oweny only had time to say 'Hello, Cheerio,' to Des before jumping on board.

Des Blackwood was already two minutes late. Oweny could see him in the distance, hurrying alongside the track towards the box. Oweny's taxi, the freight train, lumbered into sight and slowed down to await its passenger. Oweny leaned out of the window and shouted at Des, who was nearing the box now, to hurry up. Just then a bell sounded inside the box with the 'Is line clear?' signal. Oweny knew that this was the signalman at West Kilbride letting him know that the Paisley / Largs passenger express was on its way through to his stretch. Instead of sending the 'Line is clear' acceptance signal, Oweny, who was technically off duty, decided to phone through to West Kilbride.

'The line is clear,' he said. 'Keep the train moving. I'll accept it on my stretch, but it can't go any further until Des gets here. I'll need to go, my shift's over and my taxi's waiting. Des is coming towards the box now. He'll take over in a minute.'

'Ah cannae send it through if there's nobody in your box,' came Spit's voice.

'*O, God! It would be him!*' thought Oweny. '*Piggin' Malice Aforethought!*' Aloud he said,

'Aye ye can. We've to keep things moving. You know that. I can see Des now. He'll be here in less than a minute.'

Oweny hung up the phone and belled in the signal to accept the train and waving to Des, who was only a couple of yards away, he jumped on the first wagon of the freight train. He saw Des climb the stairs and enter the box as he moved off.

Back at West Kilbride station, Spit seized the moment. Here was his chance to get Oweny and Des! Why would he want to 'get' Oweny? What was his reason? Oweny was fat and fat people deserve all they get. What other reason do you need? And Des? Well, Des was young, good-looking and too cock-sure of himself. He needed sorting. That was a good enough reason. Spit sent out the most serious signal; the six bells, emergency, 'SHUT DOWN ALL TRAFFIC' signal. All traffic in the vicinity, freight and passenger, was halted. Lines went dead. Nothing moved. Des phoned through to West Kilbride.

'Where's the express? Did you not get the acceptance bell? What's the emergency?'

'You're the bloody emergency!' Spit snarled. 'You were late. You caused the delay. I couldn't send the train through when I knew the box was empty.'

'For God's sake, do you realise what you've done? The box was only empty for a second. Otherwise Oweny would have missed his train.' Des said exasperatedly.

'Too bad.' The phone at Des's ear went dead.

The resultant delay caused chaos and the rail bosses were not amused. Technically, 'right' was on Mr Kynd's side, and Des and Oweny were severely reprimanded. When their colleagues discussed it, the predominant feeling was that sometimes, such intransigence was more stupid than right, because they felt that the delay to the already beleaguered passengers could have been avoided with a little bit of common sense, so there was a great deal of sympathy for Oweny and Des. Spit was not in the least phased by the bad feeling that grew up around him in the days that followed the incident but slept soundly at night, pleased with his work.

Spiteful Spit had a large cosy armchair that he brought into the signal box to relax in during quiet times. But such was his cantankerous nature that every time his shift was over, he carried this heavy armchair down the fifty steps and locked it in a store cupboard under the signal box and took the key away with him. This was to prevent anyone else, particularly eighteen stone Oweny enjoying a comfortable doze on *his* armchair.

During the really bad weather that had continued right into

the middle of March, Oweny approached the box, and caught sight of old Spit struggling downstairs with his precious armchair. He stopped and watched the pantomime for a while thinking, *'It must be three below zero, and that mean old git is still determined to hide his stupid chair'*. Unaware of Oweny's presence, Spit manipulated his cargo carefully down each step. With a great effort he eventually got it locked up, pocketed the key and trundled back up the steps. Oweny followed a minute later, shaking his head.

The changeover took place and Oweny was left alone in the box. He soon discovered that there was a problem with signal twenty-one. It was a heavy nine-inch pull at the best of times, but today it was totally immovable.

'The signal must be frozen. I cannae budge it,' he reported on the phone to his boss, Bomber Bell.

In complete contrast to the disgruntled and disobliging Mr Kynd, there was Big Bomber Bell. Bomber was the gaffer on Oweny's stretch and he was well liked by the men. He was a 'hand's on' kind of boss and never asked the men to do anything he was not prepared to do himself. He mucked in and helped when he could and providing the men got the job done, they had nothing to fear from Big Bomber. He had that enviable quality, too, of knowing when to turn a blind eye, if opening it would cause more bother than it was worth. Like the time Andy Taggart was caught.

Andy was a line walker. He walked up the down line, and down the up line all day with his spanner and hammer checking the fishplates and frogs that kept the rails in alignment, and tightening all the loose spikes and wedges. It was a lonely job and he often paid a quick visit to each signal box to beat the boredom and to catch up on the latest gossip. He also liked a beer and he would plank a couple of cans here and there along the route. Early one morning he was passing by Fairlie box and he saw young Des Blackwood pull up the window.

'Hey, Andy,' Des yelled down, 'I'm a daddy. Mary had our baby yesterday. A wee boy! We're going to call him Andrew!'

'Aw, that's brilliant, Des! You couldn't have picked a better name.'

'Aye, I thought *you'd* like it.' Des laughed.

'Haud on a wee meenit, I'll be right up. I'm feenished ma shift noo.'

Andy darted back down the line to one of the recesses inside a tunnel. He groped around for a while and unearthed two dusty cans of Guinness that he'd planked there some time ago. Joining Des in the box a few minutes later, he opened a can and placed it on the work panel in front of Des.

'Tae wet the baby's heid,' he said.

Des looked guiltily at the can of beer. 'I don't think I should, Andy. I've still an hour to go till my shift ends. What if I get caught?'

'Away, man! Who's going to know? Get it down ye!'

Des took a few gulps from the can. 'To Andrew Desmond Blackwood!' He lifted the can in a toast. Andy Taggart did the same and finished the can in one long swig. He tossed it into the litterbin, licking his lips and belching noisily. Suddenly the door flew open and in came Bomber Bell.

'How's it going, Des?' he boomed. Immediately his eye caught the can of beer on the board and his face fell. Des's face reddened in alarm. Quick as a flash, Andy jumped up and grabbed the can.

'Oh, that's mine, Mr Bell,' he said. 'I've just finished for the day and I came up to see Des and drink my Guinness. It's no' his beer, I can assure you.' And Andy raised the can to his lips and finished off the contents just to prove it.

Bomber eyed them both for a moment.

'You may be finished Andy,' he said, 'but you cannae bring

booze up to the signal box. If I see you in possession of another can on railway property, I'll report you. O.K?'

'Aye. Aye. Mr Bell. Sorry. I'll no' do it again,' Andy spluttered.

Bomber checked the train register, asked Des a few questions and made for the door.

'I hear you've just become a daddy,' he said to the still blushing Des.

'Aye, Mr Bell. A wee boy.'

Bomber opened the door and pulled on his cap.

'A wee word of advice, Daddy Blackwood. Don't be letting anybody coax ye into wetting the baby's heid while you're still on duty. O.K? Good Luck to you and the wee bairn.' He was gone.

Des blew out a long whistle and looked with relief at Andy Taggart.

'Bomber's right,' Des said.

'Aye. Bomber's right,' said Andy.

They sat in silence for a while and then Des said 'He's a good sort is Bomber. Tam McCulloch told me the other day that he was trying to tie two engines together at the shunting yard. He just couldn't do it. The hoses were too short and it was taking all his strength. Along came Bomber to see what was causing the delay and he rolled up his sleeves and pushed and pulled at the hoses along wi' Tam until between the pair o' them, they got those two engines tied up.'

'Aye, that's Bomber all right,' said Andy.

⁂

That was the kind of attitude that endeared Bomber to his men, and it was no different today when he visited Oweny in Grangehall box.

'What's the problem, Oweny?'

'Could you get someone to look after the box for a while, Mr Bell? I'll need to go and chip the ice off signal twenty-one. It's frozen solid.'

'Look, you stay in the box,' said Bomber. 'I'll see to it.' He was wearing only a jacket because he'd come by car. There was a large spare coat in the box, known as the mufti coat. He shrugged himself into it, grabbed a couple of tools and was off.

At the foot of the stairs, Bomber pulled his cap down over his face and hauled the wide collar of the mufti coat up around his ears. Oweny saw him battle his way through the deep snow until he disappeared into the darkening gloom of late afternoon.

It was about half a mile to signal twenty-one and there was no other way to reach it except on foot. Frozen signals were not uncommon in a Scottish winter and Oweny had done his fair share of hacking the ice off semaphores in his time, but the single life and a diet of beer and fish suppers had taken its toll. He was no longer the twelve stone Adonis who had wowed the girls on the seafront at Largs several years ago. Oweny was really grateful to Bomber for taking care of this thankless task for him.

Bomber meanwhile trudged on, head down, cursing this hellish weather. It took him well over half an hour to reach the signal and another ten minutes to climb the slippery ladder. He hacked away until the signal was cleared. His fingers had become so numb that he couldn't even separate them. 'It will take a number nine black lever to prise them apart!' he said aloud. He slid thankfully down the pole, glad that his task was over. Looking around he noticed that the signal on the up line was clogged too. He stood for a long cold minute and stared at the signal. For a weary moment he thought he could just ignore it. His shift was over now, anyway! Leave it to somebody else. But he knew that in a few minutes that signal would be useless too.

'C'mon Bomber. You know you cannae just walk away. You're here now. May as well do it while you're here.'

He crossed the line and painstakingly clawed his way up the footholds and hacked away at the ice, which had formed around the signal on the up line. After a while the job was done and with a sigh of relief he slid down the pole, jumping the last few feet to land on the piles of soft snow below. The fingers of both hands were stiff and white. He struggled to drop the hammer and chisel into the big pocket of the mufti coat, and made to cross the line. He knew that the mail express was due soon but he just could not bring himself to fumble about with his frozen hands to get his watch out of his inside pocket. He listened carefully. No sound. The mail train was surely not due for another ten minutes. But Bomber had underestimated the time it had taken to get the job done, and the conditions in which he had been working. Soft lying snow had somewhat muffled the sound of the approaching train, and when Bomber stepped on to the line, the second part of Duncan Brewer's prediction became fulfilled.

୭ଈ୬ ୭ଈ୬

Back at Grangehall box, all the signals were operating well now and Oweny knew that Bomber had done a good job. He put the kettle on. Bomber would need to thaw out with a good hot mug of tea when he got back. Oweny waited quite a while, watching through the gloom until it got too dark to see. He listened for the sound of Bomber's foot on the stair and when time passed and still no sound came he became increasingly concerned. He could see that Bomber's car was still parked in the clearing by the road outside, so he had not returned to it. Eventually Oweny got worried enough to raise the alarm and the tragedy came to light. For days a gloom much darker than the weather surrounded the men. Long after the funeral, just the mention of Big Bomber Bell brought tears to even the most hardened wee ganger. Bomber left a great big hole and most of the men were aware of the emptiness.

Some weeks later, long after the snow had disappeared and there was a light promise of spring in the air, Oweny came along the road towards the signal box and again saw Spit struggling to carry his precious armchair down to the store cupboard. It took only a second for disgust to rise in his throat. The idea that this miserable, mean, greedy old bugger could expend energy every day, lugging that chair up and down fifty stairs, keeping all his comfort to himself made Oweny see red. He remembered kind-hearted happy Bomber, who lost his life because of his willingness to help and to be of use, and he looked at this greetin' faced old sod who wouldn't give you a nod if he was a rocking horse, and yet there *he* was, alive and well. It was too much for the normally placid Oweny. He ran forward taking the steps two at a time.

'Let me help you there, Mr Kynd,' he said, smiling sweetly but with a great deal of sarcasm in his voice. He lifted the armchair easily out of Spiteful Spit's arms and with a mighty heave, he tossed it over the side. It fell with a heavy crash on the gravel thirty feet below and split apart. Spit was speechless with shock.

'Oh dear,' said Oweny, in mock dismay. 'Look what's happened. But wait, I've got an idea!'

He jumped down the steps and ran inside the store cupboard, emerging a few seconds later with an axe. Before Spit could move, he jumped on to the offending lump of armchair, the armchair that, at that moment, epitomised for Oweny all that was wrong in the world. He raised the axe high and chopped and chopped again and again until it was just a mess of wood, springs and stuffing.

'There now,' said Oweny, his face sweaty and wreathed in smiles. 'You'll be able to carry it up and down much easier now. I've cut it into manageable chunks.'

Spiteful Spit found his voice. 'What the hell do you think —?' But he lost his voice again as Oweny's hands grasped the wee man's whinging throat.

'NOT ANOTHER WORD! NOT ANOTHER FUCKING WORD!'

Spit's eyes goggled and he clawed ineffectively at Oweny's large hands.

'You miserable, craw-faced old codger! You're a poor excuse for a man. When I think that Bomber's gone and we get stuck wi' the likes o' you! There cannae be a God, man! That's how you make me feel.' Words just tumbled out of him in anger and frustration. A moment more Oweny held his crushing grip, then he flung the little man away from him with a contemptuous gesture.

Spit fell backwards, grasping and clutching at his bruised throat.

'You'll - you'll - p-pay for that chair,' he croaked weakly when at last he found his voice.

Oweny lifted the axe again and wielded it higher.

'Do you want me to use this on you? You greetin' faced wee bastard! Get away off duty! Get out of my sight. Now!'

Eighteen stone Oweny actually ran up the fifty steps to the box and grabbed Spit's belongings and tossed them over the banister. They landed at the wee man's feet with a thud. A sloshing sound told Mr Kynd that his flask was broken.

'And here's yer hat,' Oweny said, throwing that too. 'And if ye want to take this further, it won't be just your flask that gets broken, believe me! I'll fucking finish the job wi' this axe, so ah will! It'd be your word against mine anyway, and I wonder how many o' the lads would blame me.'

Oweny went inside and slammed the door. He paced up and down the length of the signal box several times, thumping his fist angrily into his palm and breathing hard. He knew he was raging, but he felt great. He couldn't believe he'd just run up fifty steps without feeling it. He felt better than he'd felt in days. He decided to brew some tea and eat his piece early, and he enjoyed every mouthful. The tomato sandwiches tasted great! Or was it revenge? Aye, something tasted good today!

LETTERS

Room 10
Nurses Quarters
Royal Infirmary
Glasgow

Dear Mum,

I'm glad you caught your train on Wednesday and got home safely. I have still not recovered from our late night sprint down Renfield Street to Central Station so you could catch the last train. Neither have my new stiletto heels – they will never be the same – but I don't care. We had a brilliant day, didn't we?

I can't believe we had such fun in the shops without spending much money. I blush every time I think of you dropping all your parcels on the escalator in Lewis's and all the fuss it caused. There was me, running down the 'up' escalator frantically chasing brown paper bags like some kind of lunatic, while you stood watching from your lofty position at the top, shaking with laughter. When I landed on my bum, it was nipped several times by the moving slats and if it hadn't been for that nice floor manager coming to my rescue, I could have lost a few inches off my backside, which might have been no bad thing. I didn't mention it at the time because you had enough to laugh at. He was very polite about it all and was not the least bit bothered about all the people who complained when he had to switch the escalator off while he extracted the paper bag that had got caught in between the treads. And you managed to eat two sausage rolls and chips for your tea even after that great big cream puff thing that we both ate in Fuller's earlier. I don't know why you're not the size of a small house.

Actually, you looked great, mum, and I really do believe you've done the right thing. The boys think so too. Charles wonders why you put up with dad's violent temper for so long, but you know Charles! He hasn't got a clue about how hard it can be for a woman to just up and go. It was easy for him, having no commitments. He buggered off to the R.A.F. as soon as he could. He had no one else to think about. You had us. Benny said he knew it would happen one day, and he's glad you're out of harm's way. He says he used to worry about you after he left home because he was the last one of us to leave and he felt we had all abandoned you. He says he will still keep in touch with dad, though.

Talking of dad, you were right. He did phone me here at the nurses home and I told him that I couldn't tell him where you were but that you were all right. He said to tell you 'Good riddance.' And then he asked me where the rent book was and where his life insurance papers were, so he could continue to pay the bills. I can hardly believe he didn't know that all the papers and bills and such are kept in the big biscuit tin in the press. You looked after him too well.

He seems to be managing fine on his own, although I don't know why we should care. But I do care, mum. I know you had to leave and that you did the right thing for you, but I feel so divided. Like I've been cut in half, even though I'm an adult now and live my own life.

One thing I do know is that it was good to see the change in you. You seemed so carefree and you laughed so readily when I told you stories of my troublesome patients. I remember at home, whenever you laughed, you always used to glance at the clock, as if the time for laughing was limited. And so it was, I suppose. You laughed less as the time approached when dad would be home.

Anyway, whatever the boys think, we will all get through this. I'm glad you got the job in MacFisheries. At least it's a wage and it will help pay for a place of your own when one turns up. Give my regards to Auntie Katie. I'll call in at MacFisheries next week on my day off and we'll go for lunch together.

All my love,
Barbara xxx

(P.S. That nice young floor manager in Lewis's is called Douglas Birrell. I was in Lewis's the other day looking for new shoes and I bumped into him. He asked if we were both all right after our ordeal. Ordeal! I was mortified and utterly embarrassed that he'd even recognised me! It is an episode I would rather forget. Remind me not to go shopping with you ever again.)

That small postscript was all Lily had to go on, but like any astute mother, she knew in her bones that there was probably a lot more that Barbara could have told her. She had not told her mother everything. What young girl ever does?

Part Two

Choo choo train, puffing down the line
Taking all the people to work on time
But there's something on the line and the train's got to wait.
Now all the passengers are going to be late.

Children's Skipping Rhyme

CHAPTER 7

Lost!

L ily was right. Barbara had not told her mother every-thing that had occurred on the day she re-entered Lewis's department store in search of new shoes. The escalators took her up to the second floor, but as she neared the top, a couple of old ladies who had been a few steps ahead of her, stood still after reaching the top. They looked around them, considering where to go, not realising that if they didn't move forward, out of the way, there was imminent danger of collision from those coming behind.

'Excuse me!' Barbara called out as she moved unavoidably closer. They didn't hear and didn't budge.

'Excuse me! Please get out of the way!' Barbara repeated. Her pleas fell on deaf ears as the old dears dithered at the top of the escalator

Barbara held her breath as the inevitable happened. She careered into both their backsides, pushing them forward. They stumbled a few steps on to the shop floor and turned on Barbara.

'What on earth?' said one, gasping in shock.

'Wait your turn! You nearly knocked us over!' said the other, angrily.

'You young people have no respect. Just push your elders out of the way, why don't you? Rush, rush, rush and going nowhere fast. You're all the same!'

Barbara managed to keep her feet, but only just.

'You were blocking the exit. I couldn't help but bang into you. I called out but you didn't hear me.' She moved aside to make room for others to pass as they ascended behind her.

'If we didn't hear you, you should have waited until we did,' came back the reply.

'I was on a *moving staircase*,' said Barbara, her voice beginning to rise. 'Where was I supposed to wait?'

'Is there a problem?' asked a man's voice at her ear. She turned and saw with utter dismay that it was the same young man who had had to turn off the escalator last Wednesday when she was going down as it was going up.

'This girl pushed us!' exclaimed one of the old ladies.

'Check your purse, Henrietta,' said the other one. 'She may be one of those pick-pockets who pretend to bump into you and then make off with your wallet.'

'I didn't mean it,' Barbara protested to the young man.

'Are you all right, madam?' the man asked them both as he steered them out of harm's way by taking an elbow each.

'Aye. Yes. We're okay.' Then, after checking inside her shopping bag, 'My purse is still here.'

'So's mine,' Henrietta declared, snapping her handbag shut. 'Let's go to the tearoom now, Elsie. I've had such a fright.'

'It'll need to be the Ladies' room first for me,' said Elsie.

They stomped off arm in arm, drawing Barbara a haughty look.

'I think I'll have to ban you from using the escalators here,' said the young man, looking severely at Barbara. 'It looks like you don't know how to use them. May I suggest that you use the lifts? They are located by the far wall, over there.' He pointed towards the elevators. 'They are operated by staff, so you don't need to do a thing. Just alight at the floor you want.'

Barbara got the impression that he was making fun of her, and felt humiliated. She tried to draw her own haughty look.

'Of course I know how to use the escalators. It was those two old biddies. They stopped for a chat right at the top, but I can see you don't believe me. You think because of last Wednesday, I'm the one at fault. Well, you think what you like, but maybe I will use the lifts in future. Too many old ladies clogging up the system here, and causing innocent people all kinds of embarrassment. My own mother included!'

He saw her discomfiture and laughed. 'I'm sorry. I couldn't help teasing you; you looked so chagrined. I was only joking. You are welcome to use any means you like to visit all our floors.'

A half smile fleeted across Barbara's lips. She dusted her skirt with her gloved hands.

'H'mm,' she said.

'My name is Douglas Birrell. I'm the manager on this floor. I hope you came to no harm – on both occasions,' he added with a twinkle in his eye. Then he said, 'Is your mother all right after her ordeal on Wednesday, - and her parcels, did they survive unscathed?'

Barbara eyed him with renewed hostility. '*Her* ordeal? I seem to remember it was *me* who had the ordeal! It was *me* who tried to rescue the stuff that *she* had dropped and it was me who got the red face and, I might add, the red bottom, trying to fetch them for her. And it was *you*,' she pointed a finger at him accusingly, '*you* who got all the thanks and all the glory, and all *you* did was push a button!'

'At your service, ma'm!' He bowed ever so slightly and walked away, leaving Barbara fuming.

She made it to the shoe department, though she had no idea how she got there. She tried to choose a pair, but couldn't concentrate She decided to go to the cafeteria on the sixth floor for a cup of tea and a ciggie to calm her nerves. She carried her tray past several tables, heading for one at the back when she saw him.

'Oh no, not him again! That bloody floor manager! It must be his tea break. I'd better sit somewhere else.' She whirled round quickly to change direction and bumped into a man coming behind. Their trays collided and hers dropped to the floor, spilling hot tea and a jug of milk everywhere. The man's tray tipped up, causing his coffee to slop about, soaking his caramel wafer. Barbara was so embarrassed that she couldn't even apologise. She was bereft of speech, and to crown it all, there *he* was, leading the man back to the cash desk and calling for another cup of coffee and another caramel wafer for him, while motioning to a girl in a nylon overall and a net hat to clean up the spillage. The man was soon disposed of and Douglas turned to Barbara. 'Are you accident prone, or what?' She cast him a withering look. 'I notice you didn't offer to re-place *my* tea.'

'I was just about to, but on condition that you join me at my table over there.' He turned to the girl behind the counter. 'Two more pots of tea, Rita,' he said, 'and could you bring them over, please. I don't think this lady can manage a tray.'

Barbara found herself seated at his table while he poured her tea for her.

'Don't you have to be back on duty?' she asked hopefully.

'I am on duty. I'm seeing to an accident-prone customer. All part of the job.'

He lit her cigarette, and they shared an ashtray. After a few puffs Barbara's jangling nerves calmed down a bit and they managed to have a normal conversation, and she began to see the funny side that had so far eluded her. They talked for a while exchanging information about each other.

'You're a nurse?' he repeated incredulously, when she told

him. 'I wouldn't like to be ill on your ward. Do any of your patients ever make it safely home?'

'A *staff* nurse actually,' she corrected. 'And yes, it might surprise you to know that I'm a very good nurse and my patients do get home safe and well.'

Before she'd finished her tea, he had asked her out and it wasn't long before they were dating regularly. It could be said that that first 'date' in the cafeteria at Lewis's formed the pattern of their relationship over the next few months. He teasing her, and she parrying with just a raised finger, to symbolise that he never solved any problems himself. He either pushed a button, or summoned someone else to clear things up.

She hadn't failed to notice how good looking he was though, and amazed all her colleagues one day in the staff room when they were all saying how they were positively intent on marrying a doctor, by declaring that she wouldn't have a doctor if they were being given away free with soap powder. Give her a store manager any day!

❦❦❦

'I don't want to move house. I'm not going!' Danny.

'I'm not going either!' Debbie.

Tears from the wee man.

Agnes and Paddy looked exasperatedly at the glum faces of their offspring.

'I've not said it's definite,' Paddy said. 'We might *not* move. I only want to know what you think of the idea.'

'We don't like the idea!' Three voices, petulantly.

'Would you not like to live in a nice new house with your own room and a bathroom?' asked Agnes, trying to inflect great enthusiasm into her voice.

They were seated around the dinner table in what Agnes liked to call the dining area; in fact, it was the space that used to be a bed recess in former years.

'We can't move house now, mam! I've been picked for the Easter Pageant. I'm to be Mary Magdalene!' The distress in Debbie's voice was pitiful.

'Sparky would get lost if we moved house,' Tommy wailed. 'He'll not know his way home.'

Paddy was losing patience with all this negativity.

'That's another thing we have to discuss.' He continued in a severe tone. 'If we move house, Sparky will not be coming. Neither will the cat, so you can get that notion out of your heads immediately. I warned you at the time that that dog was not to become part of the family but nobody would listen to me. Same with the cat. You all insisted on keeping the last kitten from that litter, even though I told you not to.' His voice softened a little as he surveyed the panic in the three small faces.

'Don't worry, we'll find a good home for them before we go, I promise. But we're not taking those strays to a nice new clean house and that's final!'

There were horrified gasps followed by a stunned silence.

Beneath the table, Agnes gave Paddy a hard kick on the shins. She whispered under her breath, 'So much for breaking it gently!'

Then the wee fella let out a scream, left his chair and made a bolt for the door. The dog was at his heels instantly.

'Tommy! Get back here! Get back here now!' shouted Paddy.

'Sparky and me are never coming back. We're going into hiding. You'll never find us!'

'I'm warning you, Tommy. If you don't come back now, the only hiding you're headed for is the one I'll give you. I mean it, wee man!'

But the front door had slammed and the wee man's sobs could be heard along with his footsteps as he ran through the close, the dog yelping at his heels.

'I'd better go after him.' Agnes got up and made to follow him but Paddy caught her wrist.

'You'll do nothing of the kind,' he said. 'We're in the middle of a discussion here. He'll no' go far. He'll be back when he's hungry. He's not even touched his dinner.'

'Aye, thanks to you!' But she sat back down.

Danny and Debbie toyed with the food on their plates desultorily, eyeing their parents from under bowed heads.

'Eat your dinner, you two!' Agnes snapped. 'At least some of us can get it while it's hot!'

'We can't move to a new house. We'd have to leave all our friends.' Danny said sadly.

'Look.' Paddy tried a softer approach. 'I've had to do a lot of driving since I changed my job, and its not been as easy as I'd hoped. You don't want me to be tired all the time, do you? Danny, you were disappointed when I didn't come to the swimming baths with you last Saturday, weren't you?'

A sullen look was his only reply.

Debbie put tomato sauce on her chips. 'Dad, could you not just get your old job back again? Then we could stay here.' It seemed to her like the perfect solution.

'Your father and I haven't made any firm decision about it yet. We just wanted to know how you might feel about it, to help us make up our minds. I know it's a big step and that it would be hard for you kids at first. But give it some thought, eh? There are lots good things about moving house that you haven't even considered yet.'

'What good things?' Danny chewed on a chip.

'Well, we'd be near the seaside. You'd like that, wouldn't you?' Agnes lifted the teapot and poured herself a cup of tea.

93

'What else?' A half-chewed piece of sausage somehow managed to stay inside Debbie's mouth.

Agnes looked towards Paddy who was giving full attention to his dinner. No help there, then! What happened to the 'discussion'?

'If Sparky isn't coming with us, and Misty isn't coming, then there *are* no good things, and we're not moving and that's THAT!' Danny said the words unhesitatingly, braving up to his father's displeasure.

'Look, kids, I think your father was a wee bit hasty there. I don't think he really meant that. Of course we would take Sparky and Misty. That's if we *do* move.'

Paddy had a bottle of brown sauce in his hand. He had been holding it over his plate, battering the backside out of it for the last two minutes, but the sauce was staying put. He turned the sauce right way up and stared into the neck of the bottle, then he turned it upside down again and began to shake it.

Danny decided to push his luck further. 'You're only pretending to ask our opinion. We know that whenever dad gets a bee in his bonnet, nobody has any say. If he decides we're moving, then we'll be moving! It's obvious he's thought it all out already. He's made up his mind that Sparky and Misty are not to go with us, so I don't know why you're even bothering to ask us.'

That was it! Paddy's anger flared. 'That is cheek, young man. I will not stand for cheek! I am your father and I will be respected.' He thumped the sauce bottle down hard on the table. At that moment the previously reluctant sauce decided to come out of the bottle. With the force of the thump, sauce shot up in the air and come down on Paddy's head with a splash. The children stared into Paddy's angry eyes and watched as the murky brown fluid streamed down his face, covering his nose and ending up dripping from his chin.

'I WILL BE RESPECTED!' shouted Paddy, and raising his voice even louder, 'DO YOU HEAR ME?'

He received no answer. 'DO YOU HEAR ME?' he repeated, his face red with anger. Well, red with lots of brown.

Still he received no answer. The other three were helpless with laughter.

∞∞ ∞∞

Lily was going to the pictures again tonight. Lately she felt she had seen just about every movie ever screened. Sometimes she stayed in Town and went with some of her new friends from work, but since she was shy by nature and wasn't one for socialising, she usually went on her own to the local cinema. She did this as often as she could to give Katie and Jamsie some time in their own home without her being there. Although they both insisted she was welcome, a natural instinct told Lily to make herself scarce occasionally, and get out from under Katie's feet. Katie had a love affair with cleaning. Her vacuum cleaner, or her ironing board, were always in use and that made Lily uneasy at times, since all offers of help were refused with 'Not at all. You sit down. You've been working all day! I'm happy doing this, truly I am!'

She had been trying hard to find a place of her own, so far without much success. She was very happy at Katie's, but she did not want to impose any longer than was necessary. The first weeks after her arrival had been so good. Katie had been, and still was, a great support. Young Jamsie too was always joking around and had kept her amused with his playful banter and unlikely tales of his prowess with the girls. This made her feel young again and involved. She was less nervy and she laughed a lot, something she hadn't done in a long time.

Tonight Lily was actually looking forward to the film. It was 'Young At Heart' with Doris Day and Frank Sinatra. She had missed it first time round and she was really pleased that the

George Cinema had brought it back for a repeat showing. She knew she would get lost for a while in a world of catchy love songs and pretty dresses. A couple of hours of pure escapism. And she needed some escapism tonight. She had had an extremely trying day.

It had been her day off and she had spent the morning with a solicitor arguing about the terms of her divorce from Charlie. This, he assured her, was going to be costly, long-drawn out and harrowing, unless she took his advice and got the police involved and charged Charlie with assault. That, he insisted, would certainly speed up proceedings and would be far quicker than the 'irretrievable breakdown' version that Lily favoured. He was very insistent, long-winded, and not a good listener. Her efforts to make him realise that she could not bear a public linen-washing session in court fell on unresponsive ears. Neither did he understand that she did not want Charlie to know her whereabouts. Ever. She did not want to see his face again, particularly in court.

In the end, she left without anything being properly resolved.

'I'm a little tired now, Mr Cochrane,' she said. 'And I have another appointment so I really must go. We'll talk again.' It would mean another costly session at a later date, but she'd had enough and she left.

She went straight to the housing department where she had lodged an application form several weeks ago. She had had a letter telling her that they were in receipt of her application and she would hear from them in due course. Since then, nothing. After waiting for over an hour in a stuffy waiting area, which looked more like an anti-natal clinic with the amount of prams and go-chairs that crammed the place, her turn eventually came. She was told by a stony-faced individual with dark horn rimmed glasses copied from Buddy Holly, that she had not lived in the area long enough to qualify for a council house. There was a long waiting list and in the absence of any extenuating circumstances, for example, were she to become pregnant, she might have to wait up to two years before even being considered.

Another dead end.

She bought the local paper on her way home like she did every Thursday in the hope that she might find somewhere cheap to rent. She trod wearily up the path and let herself in softly. Hanging up her coat and scarf in the hall, she heard Jamsie's voice from the kitchen.

'All I asked, mam, was how much longer do you think Aunt Lily is going to stay? I like Aunt Lily. I do. It's just that I would really like to have my room back. I miss sleeping in a proper bed.'

Katie's voice said, 'Try to be patient a while longer, son. Your aunt Lily's been through a lot.'

Lily was mortified. Jamsie had given up his room to her when she came, and he slept on a sofa bed in the living room, but obviously this was becoming a strain. She had to do something quickly about this terrible situation, but what? In that moment, she decided to take the first house that was available for rent, no matter what its condition or its cost. She took her coat and quietly went outside, re-entering again noisily and closing the door with a loud snap.

'Hello,' she called out. 'I'm home!'

They came out of the kitchen, all smiles, to greet her.

꧁꧂ ꧁꧂

She followed the light of the usherette's torch and was shown to a seat at the end of a row. Trailers for forthcoming movies were being shown on the screen so the lights had already gone down. Lily removed her coat and placed it across her knees. When her eyes became accustomed to the darkness, she glanced around and was surprised to see Eddie, from the railway station, sitting in the same row. There was one empty seat between them. He saw her at the same time and they smiled and nodded to each other then both faced the screen again immediately. She felt a little awkward. She spoke to Eddie nearly every day on her way to work; yet somehow he looked different, out of uniform and sitting in the cinema like an ordinary person. She tried to glance round unobtrusively to see if he was with anyone. He didn't appear to be as the seat on the other side of him was empty.

The 'B' movie started and neither looked in the other's direction for the whole of its duration. It was a war movie and Lily was totally bored. They must have made a million of these after the war and they were still doing the rounds. She was glad when it ended and the lights went up. Eddie leaned across the empty seat.

Hello, Mrs Dunne,' he said in a loudish whisper. 'I wouldn't have thought you liked war movies.'

'I don't. I came to see Doris Day. I wouldn't have taken you for a Doris Day fan,' she replied in the same loudish whisper. Adverts were appearing on the screen now.

'I'm not, particularly. I came to see the war movie, but I've paid for the lot so I'll stay for the rest.' He did not add that this was a sudden decision.

A voice behind them said 'Sssh!'

The ice-cream girls carried their trays to the front of the stage.

'Would you like a choc ice?' Eddie asked.

Being shy, Lily would normally have answered no to such a question, but she totally surprised herself by saying 'Yes, please.'

'Sssh!' said the voice behind.

When he returned with the ices, Eddie pointed to the empty seat between them.

'Do you mind if I sit there?' he said. 'We could talk more quietly without disturbing anyone.'

She nodded, and took the choc-ice. 'Thank you.'

But they didn't talk, more quietly or otherwise. They ate the choc-ices in silence and then watched the whole movie in silence too, because neither could think of anything to say.

෨෨෯෨

Paddy and Agnes were arguing as, together, they cleared the table and washed up.

'Hell, you really messed that one up, didn't you?' Agnes said as she turned on the gas and put Tommy's plate in the oven to keep it warm. 'Ploughed right in there with two big feet, didn't you? Telling them their pets would not be coming to the new house! Sometimes I wonder at you, Paddy Preston, I really do. How could you expect to win them over, dropping a bombshell like that? You know they'll use that as a bargaining tool now, don't you? You're going to have to give in on this one. The pets will have to come, if we move. I thought we were going to take it gently. Sort of sell them on the idea!'

'Just remember, it *is* still only an idea.' Paddy pointed out. 'And as for the animals, if I've said it once, I've said it a thousand…'

'Don't start that again Paddy,' she interrupted. ' I don't want to hear it!' Agnes looked at the clock. 'It's after seven. Where is that wee man? He's been gone an hour now.'

Paddy reached for his jacket, which was hanging over the back of a chair. 'I'll go and get him. He'll be in wee Petey Miller's house.'

'C'mere,' Agnes said, before he got to the door. She used a damp dishcloth to lift a spot of brown sauce from the back of his neck. 'You missed a bit,' she said.

Half an hour later Paddy returned. 'Is he here?' he asked.

'No. Have you not got him?'

'I've been everywhere. He's not in Petey Miller's. He's not down at the sandpit. He's not up at the rope swing. I've tried most of his pals. I don't know where else to look. I even went to your sister Sadie's house. He's not there either.'

'Oh, Paddy, no! You didn't let our Sadie know we've lost the wee man! What is she going to think?'

'I don't care what she thinks. I'm too worried. At least I know he's not there.'

'I'll never hear the end of this. She'll be up here tomorrow with her Bible, letting me know I've failed in my duty as a good Christian mother, letting Tommy out of my sight.'

In spite of his highly concerned state, Paddy paused and looked at Agnes.

'If she utters one word – *one* word – of criticism, she and her Bible will find themselves at the bottom of the stairs P.D.Q. She wants to keep her own daughter in her sights! She's hanging round the boys up at the café right now, giggling away and crackin' gum! But it's my own wee lad I'm worried about at the moment. I can't think where he can be.'

A slow fear crept into Agnes's heart. 'Did you try up the street, by the chip shop? Sometimes boys gather there when it gets dark.' She grabbed her coat from the hall.

'No, Agnes, you stay here in case he comes back. Somebody's got to stay with Danny and Debbie. I'll go. I'll get Walter Samson from downstairs to help. I'll be back as soon as we've got him. You keep the kids busy.' He was gone in an instant.

Paddy and Walter searched the whole of the main street. A small gang of kids was loitering outside the chip shop, just as Agnes had said. Walter approached. 'Have you seen wee Tommy Preston?' he asked.

'Aye, Mister. Ah saw him about an hour ago, up by Coia's café. He had the dug wi' him.'

'Thanks. We're heading up there now. If you see him, will you tell him to go home immediately? His mam and dad are worried sick.'

'Right-ye-are, Mister.'

Paddy and Walter headed off towards the café. The gang of boys became excited and shouted to another group that wee Tommy was missing. They caused a stir by running up and down the closes calling out for Tommy and Sparky.

It was dark now and Paddy was frantic. There was no sign of Tommy at the café. Walter and Paddy separated and searched different areas. Paddy returned home again in the hope that the wee man had come back, but one look at Agnes's face told him it had been a vain hope. Danny and Debbie were subdued and they all hugged each other.

'I'll have to go to the police, Agnes. We've got half the town out looking for him and nobody's seen him.'

Debbie burst into tears and Danny chewed the collar of his school shirt. After Paddy left, Agnes tried to finish washing the dishes, but her fingers were like butter. She gave up and sat on the sofa, rocking backwards and forwards, holding the tea towel to her face.

'This is all Paddy's fault,' she thought. 'He wouldn't let me go after him.' Then she thought, 'No. It's my own fault. I should have gone after him in spite of Paddy. I'll never forgive myself if anything has happened to my wee man.' She began to sob. The children came and hugged her. They could hear distant cries rising up from the street. 'Tommy! Sparky!' It was the eeriest sound Agnes had ever heard.

∼∙∙∽ ∼∙∙∽

At ten-thirty the picture was over and people spilled out on to the street. Eddie stood outside the cinema and waited while Lily buttoned her coat. He noticed there were more police about than was usual and a sizeable group of people was talking to one of them. He asked a woman if there was anything amiss and she told him that a wee boy had gone missing and people were helping to look for him. While she spoke, she looked Lily up and down and then looked Eddie up and down. Then she hurried off in the direction of the crowd with a sly looking grin on her face.

'Good Lord,' said Lily, 'did you see the look on her face? She probably knows my sister, so she'll know who I am and she'll put two and two together and make five.'

Eddie smiled. 'I wouldn't worry about it. People will be more interested in the wee boy who's gone missing, than in petty gossip. I hope they find him.' And since he lived near the station, not far from Lily, he walked home with her. They talked about the missing boy and wondered who he was. They talked about movies and he told her his wife had died twelve years ago and that she had loved going to the pictures too. Bette Davis and Glen Ford, they were her favourites. They talked about rented accommodation, Lily having mentioned that she was looking for a place. He said he'd let her know if he heard of anything. After having been silent all through the movie, it was as if they'd suddenly found their tongues and they talked about everything. Soon Eddie had dropped the 'Mrs Dunne,' and was calling her Lily. They were still talking when they reached Katie Gillan's gate and they stayed there for another ten minutes.

❧❧ ❧❧

Paddy was hoarse with shouting and exhausted with fear and worry but he kept on, praying all the time. *Please God, help me find him. Please God. I'm sorry, God. I'm so sorry I frightened him.* Tears rolled unchecked down his cheeks. *Where is he? Where, in the name of God, is he?* He was alone on the very edge of town now, walking alongside the railings that surrounded the Duchess Park, which was all locked up for the night. Beyond the park, the street lighting finished, and it was just dark country roads with fields on either side. He stood still and listened. There was not a sound. The others were far behind, searching alleys and outhouses. He leant against the railings and tried to think. His eyes scanned the road ahead, trying to see into the darkness. *Surely the lad would not have gone this far? Should I go on, or should I turn back and try the town again with the others? Please God, let me know what to do!* He decided to give one last shout along the dark road. He cupped his hands around his mouth and yelled as loudly as he could.

'TOMMY!' His voice broke on a sob. He did it again.

'TOM-MEE!' No answer. Nothing. Once more.

'SPARKY.' He listened again. A sound. What was that? Was that a muffled bark he heard?

'SPAR-KEE!' He shouted so loud this time, it pained his throat. Through the silence, came the definite sound of a bark. He knew that bark! Hope leapt into Paddy's heart. He called again.

'SPARKY, SPAR-KEE! HERE, BOY!' The answer came. Bark, bark!

'It's him. It's him. It's that bloody mongrel!' The barking was coming from inside the park.

'Sparky. Sparky! You brilliant wee dog! Where are you, boy?'

Out of the darkness a white furry shape appeared and pushed its nose through the railings.

'Sparky,' Paddy said on a sob. 'Good boy! Where's Tommy, Sparky?'

Paddy was excited now, daring to hope. Sparky ran off into the darkness of the park again then re-appeared a moment later. Paddy ran to the park gate, but it was chained and padlocked. He rattled the gate angrily.

'Get Tommy, Sparky. Good boy! Go get Tommy.'

A police car arrived and Paddy almost pulled the officer from the car.

'I think Tommy is in there,' he said. 'I've found the dog!'

The officer shone his torch into the park. A small figure emerged slowly into the beam. He was shivering and rubbing his eyes.

'I was asleep. Sparky woke me up with his barking.'

⁓⁓

Agnes heard the triumphant shouts and knew at once that they'd found him. Still clutching the tea towel that she'd wrung through her hands throughout, she ran to the window. Even in the dim lights of the street lamps, she could see the crowd was jubilant. In the centre was Paddy with Tommy hoisted high on his shoulders. He looked up as he neared the close and blew her a kiss.

'You are going to get it from your mum, young man!' he said to Tommy.

Agnes had put Danny and Debbie to bed some time after nine o'clock because that had seemed the best thing to do, but suddenly they were with her at the window.

'He's mucky, ma! Look at him!' Danny said.

'He's for it!' Debbie said. 'He's went out without his coat.'

Agnes laughed and kissed them both.

Debbie thought about the cosy bed she had just left and shivered in her nightie.

'I'm away back to bed,' she said, 'I'm frozen!' And off she went, followed by a yawning Danny. Wee man's antics were always so boring.

Tommy was ushered in. He approached a little sheepishly, expecting a tirade from his mum. Agnes threw down the tea towel and held out her arms.

'Come and get a big hug, my wee darling.'

Tommy was amazed at not having had his backside tanned, and while he wolfed down toasted cheese, his proper dinner having been spoiled long ago, he explained that he'd gone into the park and made a den in the bushes. When he saw the park-keeper lock the gates, he thought it was a good idea. Nobody would find him now.

'Me and Sparky stayed hid in our den until he'd gone. I told Sparky we would have the swings and the roundabout and the chute all to ourselves. We would play on them all night long. But when we sneaked into the swing park bit, all the swings were chained up and the roundabout was locked with a big iron bar. The chute had chains on it too. I was mad at that mean old park-keeper. Then Sparky and me got hungry but we couldn't get out of the park. I sat down on the roundabout and then I fell asleep until Sparky started barking and woke me up. Then I saw the policeman's torch.'

Paddy was stroking Sparky's fur. He looked at the little mongrel and gave a grudging laugh.

'We couldn't leave you behind now, could we? I'll bet this was all your idea, you mangy mutt!'

CHAPTER 8

—and Found

Katie looked in the butcher's shop window. A plastic ticket displayed the words, Gigot Chops, Two and Six a pound. Her eyes travelled along to Lean Steak Mince, One Shilling and Ninepence a pound. She was shopping for Saturday's tea. Today being Friday, she had already prepared fish for tonight's meal.

'Mm,' she pondered for a minute. 'It looks good mince. And it'll go further.' She looked back at the chops. ' I think I'll get the chops, though. Jamsie deserves a wee treat and Lily could do with a bit of good meat on her bones. And I've got all that fresh mint in the garden, I could make a nice sauce. Besides, I fancy a tasty wee chop myself. O.K then, lamb gigots it is.'

The bell jingled as she entered and the butcher looked up.

'I'll have three good sized gigot chops, please, Mr McKean,' she said.

'Certainly Mrs Gillan.' He selected them from the tray in the window and held them out for her inspection. 'These O.K?'

'Yes, they look fine.'

As he weighed and wrapped them he said, 'Did you hear all the commotion last night?'

The bell jingled again and Katie turned to see that old Granny Park from Hatton Close had come in. They all nodded to each other.

'No, I never heard anything Mr McKean. What happened?' said Katie, turning back to the counter.

'It seems wee Tommy Preston went missing for a good few hours last night. Had the whole town out looking. Even the police. But he was found safe and well.'

'Oh, I know the family. They must have been out of their minds with worry. I hadn't heard, but I'm glad the wee lad's O.K.'

Katie put her parcel of meat into her shopper and was about to leave when old Granny Park detained her with a conspiratorial hand on her sleeve.

Granny Park was neither old nor a granny. She had earned the nickname because she dressed in the frumpiest of clothes that were at least a decade out of date, and she frequently ventured out without her dentures, giving her a gumsy, aged look. She was a known gossipmonger and complainant, always calling the police for the flimsiest of reasons. If a child played with a ball in her close, or a dog barked too loudly, she was up at Sergeant Conner's desk within the hour.

'I see your sister's having a good old time to herself, then.'

Katie's hackles went up. She had no time for this meddlesome old madam.

'What?'

'Your sister. Is she staying with you permanently now? I would have thought her husband would be wanting her home, you know how helpless men are!' She rolled her eyes and gave a titter. 'Of course, he might be doing the same up in Lanark. It *is* Lanark they come from, isn't it? Well, I'm sure he'll be having a good old time to himself, too.'

'I've got no idea what you're talking about, Mrs Park.'

Granny Park laughed and dunted Katie with her elbow. 'Your sister. I'm talking about your sister and her friend.'

Katie still looked blank.

'Her friend from the station. You know! Mr McKenna.

Eddie!' Granny Park was enjoying this. She just loved it when she caught people off their guard.

Katie was conscious of Roy McKean eavesdropping on every word while he busied himself with the display trays of sausages.

'I'm sure I don't know what you mean, Mrs Park,' she said tersely.

'My, my! You don't seem to know anything of what's happening around you, do you?' She smiled benignly, as if she was happy to be enlightening her. 'I would have thought Lily would have told you about the wee Preston boy when she got home from her date at the pictures with Eddie McKenna.'

'I can assure you, you are very much mistaken, Mrs Park, and I'd be very careful what kind of stories that I'm tittle-tattling around the place, if I were you!'

Katie stormed out of the shop, holding her head and her dignity high. As she closed the door, she saw Granny Park and Roy McKean lean their heads together over the counter top.

'Two gossipy old sweetie wives,' she muttered. ' *Having a good time to herself!* Indeed! What could she mean, that trouble making old crow? I'll get the story right from Lily.'

But Katie was unhinged. She had not liked that encounter at all. Not one bit. With a great effort, she pulled herself together and scanned her shopping list. 'Where to, next? Oh, yes, corn plasters!' She made her way towards the Chemist. Lizzie Crilly worked in the chemist shop. She was a pert teenager who chewed gum all the time and was Agnes Preston's niece. She was on the pavement outside the shop with a bucket and a long-handled brush, engaged in washing the large plate glass window when Katie got there.

'Hello, Lizzie,' Katie said, more lightly than she felt. 'I hear wee Tommy had a bit of an adventure last night. Is he all right?'

'He's fine, Mrs Gillan. The wee rascal had us all up to high doh. More to the point, how's Mrs Dunne?' This she added with a coquettish tilt of her head.

'My sister? She's fine. Why do you ask?'

'I heard she was at the pictures last night with a gentleman. Sitting eating choc-ices together, they were, sweet as pie. Good for her, I say!'

Katie felt faint.

Oh, my God! It's all over town! What has our Lily been up to? She forgot the corn plasters and whatever else was on her list, and hurried home immediately, keeping her head down so that she did not catch anyone else's eye. She managed to get home without another encounter.

When she reached her front door she was shaking so much that she could hardly get her key in the lock. Mrs Gillan was well known for the righteous stand she took on everything. Never one to keep her mouth shut, she had often opened it loudly to disparage what she considered to be immoral behaviour in others. In the Woman's Guild she was always at the forefront of any scheme to halt the decline in moral standards among the young parishioners of her church. Always first in line, she was, with advice for them on common decency, and her pet topic, good manners. And if these efforts sometimes spilled out to other members of the community, so much the better. Now, to think that she, or anyone of *her* household, should be the subject of common gossip was the most humiliating thing that could happen to her.

She closed the door behind her and leant against it for a full two minutes before her shaking legs would let her take her shopping through to the kitchen. She tidied away her coat and hat and gave her attention to the shopping. She put the gigot chops on a clean dinner plate and covered them with another. A sudden loud knock on the door made her jump. She hurried to open the door, but tried to bang it shut again immediately. Standing there, large as life on her doorstep, was Charlie Dunne. He had the element of surprise and his foot was in the door in a trice.

'Where is she?' he hissed at her.

Katie could smell alcohol. He was unshaven and his appearance was grubby and dishevelled. Katie gathered her courage.

'You mean you don't know? Now I wonder why a wife would not tell her husband where she is?'

'I don't want to make any trouble for you. Just tell me where she is!'

'She's at work. Now get your foot out of my door before I get the police.'

'She'll have to come home sometime,' he said. 'I'll be watching and I'll be back.'

He removed his foot and Katie slammed the door shut in his face.

She immediately scurried through the house, making sure all the windows were shut and both doors were bolted. Not because she was afraid of Charlie Dunne. She was much more afraid of him causing a scene at her house. She could not bear scandal and by closing all the doors and windows she somehow felt she could keep it on the outside, away from her. She peeped through the curtains and saw him disappear down the street in the direction of the Tipper Davey pub.

The thought occurred to her that she could nip up the hill to the station and get a message sent to Jamsie to come home right away, but she realised that Eddie McKenna might be on duty and she did not want to face him at the moment. Not until Lily got home and they could clear up this whole mess. She decided to do the only thing she could do just then. Her legs were still shaking as she filled the kettle.

⤙⤚ ⤙⤚

Eddie McKenna awoke that morning from the best night's sleep he'd had in a long time. He felt unaccountably refreshed and light-hearted and he was aware as soon as he opened his eyes that the catchy tunes from the movie he had seen last night were still playing in his head. At forty-six he was still a very handsome man, though he had no idea of this. He had long ago lost interest in how he looked. Always quiet and reserved, he had become even more so since his wife's death twelve years ago, concentrating only on bringing up his two children and keeping a roof over their heads.

This he had done very successfully and he was privately very proud of their achievements. His daughter Helena, now twenty-two, was a teacher at the local primary school and had recently become engaged to another teacher there. His son John was at Aberdeen University and would graduate next year. These great strides on his children's part had brought him real satisfaction because it had not been easy on a rail-wayman's pay. He was whistling Doris Day songs as he washed and dressed and went downstairs.

'You're in a good mood this morning.' Helena said. She was leaning her back against the sink in the small kitchen, eating cereal from a bowl.

'Why don't you sit down to eat? You'll get an ulcer.'

'No time, dad.' She shovelled the last spoonful into her mouth. 'Must go, I'm running late. It's rehearsals for the Easter pageant today, and it'll be the usual nightmare. If any of the kids ever manage to get it right, there'll be another Easter miracle to go on record.'

She struggled into her jacket, grabbed a bag and headed for the front door. She was back a second later with the paper which had just been delivered.

'You ain't gonna like what it says in there!' She tossed the paper on to the Formica table, kissed his cheek and a moment later, the door banged behind her.

Eddie looked at the headline. MORE STATIONS TO CLOSE AS RAIL RESTRUCTURING CONTINUES.

'This is crazy!' he thought as he read of plans to close St Enoch station and Buchanan Street station. 'They've already closed the old caley line from Maryhill to Stobcross along with countless others. When is it going to end?' His eyes scanned the list of other proposed closures: branch lines such as the Bridgeton to Coatbridge. This was all bad news, but even so, it still did not have the power to dampen his spirits.

Later, on his way to work he thought of Lily Dunne and he knew that she was the reason for the spring in his step. She was a real nice lady, Lily Dunne. A married lady. Eddie had no improper notions in his head. He just knew that he had enjoyed talking to a woman for the first time in years, and that it had changed him in some subtle way. He realised that he had devoted all of the last twelve years to his children and none at all to himself. This had never bothered him before, but the thought that there might yet be a life out there for him filled him with a new energy. In a way he had a lot in common with Lily. She was trying to build a new life too. Maybe they could help each other.

There was an application form in the office for the job of station manager. The job that Paddy Preston had recently vacated. Yesterday Eddie had no intention of applying. Today he filled in the form and posted it.

Already he was a changed man.

෴෴෴෴

By the time Lily got home, Katie was in such a state that as soon as she saw her, she burst into tears.

'Katie! What on earth is the matter?' Lily cried, real concern in her eyes.

Between sobs, Katie managed to blurt out, – 'Did you see him? Is he out there?'

'Who, Katie? Is who out there?'

'Charlie.'

Lily went white. 'What?'

'Charlie! Your Charlie! He was here.'

It was Lily's legs that shook now. She steadied herself by holding on to a chair, then she sank down in it.

'Tell me, Katie. Tell me what happened. Why are you crying? Did he hit you?'

This made Katie stop crying. She cocked her head sideways and looked at her sister.

'Ha!' she said with a short laugh. 'If only! I'd have had him in jail if he'd done that!'

'Aye, right Katie. Okay. We know you wouldn't put up with anything like what I've had to. You're so smart. You know just what to do all the time. Nobody ever gets the better of you.'

Lily hadn't meant to sound off at Katie, but she was tired because Friday is always such a busy day in the fish shop, and the news that Charlie had been here had shocked her and she was more than a little afraid. But her comment turned the conversation.

Katie was tired too. She had spent all day in a tizzy, alternating between shame and fear.

'Don't be funny, Lily. There's no need to take that tone. Especially when it's you the whole town's talking about!'

'What are you on about? What has Charlie done?'

'Oh you can leave Charlie out of this for once, Lily. This is all your own doing. The whole town knows you were at the pictures last night with Eddie McKenna.'

Lily, already pale, went completely ashen. She didn't say a word. She couldn't. She just stared at Katie in horrified silence.

'You better tell me Katie,' she said very quietly.

Katie recounted the day's events and Lily listened in growing dismay.

'You know there's not a word of truth in all this, don't you?'

'Well I'd certainly like to hear your version.' Katie said, belligerently.

'I hardly know the man.' Lily's voice got a little louder. 'He was right next to me in the cinema. We had to make conversation. I speak to him every day up at the station. It was awkward for both of us. And we walked home together because he only lives up the road.'

'Lily, you were seen! Talking for hours!'

'I don't believe this! Come on, Katie! It was hardly hours! I was home here at ten to eleven. You must have heard me come in. I was in his company for about twenty minutes. That's all.'

'That's if you don't count the time you were in the pictures. You were seen eating choc-ices together, for God's sake!'

'Katie, you're my sister. You know me better than that. I can't believe you're siding with the gossips here.'

'I can't ignore talk that concerns my house. You need to be more careful, Lily. Your behaviour last night was obviously attracting the wrong kind of attention.'

'My *behaviour*? The man wanted a choc-ice and he offered me one too. What's wrong with that? It would have been bad manners not to ask me if I wanted one. Do you think I should have accused him of insulting me, slapped his face and called for the manager? For God's sake!'

'You could have said 'No thanks' to the choc-ice. You have to remember you are living here and your behaviour affects us all. And don't say "for God's sake" in this house.'

'You just did.'

'No I did not!'

Lily was flabbergasted. She stared at Katie for some time and saw how like their mother she had suddenly become. The years seemed to float away. It was like history repeating itself. Katie was using the very same words their parents had used all those years ago. Their voices came back clearly.

'*While you're under this roof, you'll do as your told!*'

'Think of what you're doing to the family. Don't be so selfish!'

'It's not just your reputation at stake, here! You'll bring shame and embarrassment to all of us.'

This was so unfair! How could Katie let that kind of malicious tittle-tattle get to her?   'Well, I suppose we all have our tolerance levels in different things. Look what I allowed Charlie to do to me.' Lily thought.

The thought of Charlie reminded her.

'Tell me about Charlie, Katie. What happened?'

'He came to the door and asked for you. I told him you were at work and he said he'd come back later.'

'How did he find me?'

'I didn't ask. I was only too glad to see the back of him. I've been petrified with worry all day.'

'I'm sorry, Katie. I don't know what to do, but I'll try to think of something. The last thing I want is for this to involve you or Jamsie.'

'It's a bit late for that now.'

Lily felt terrible. A long silence fell, each sister shocked by the other's inability to understand. Katie was the first to get up. 'I better get the tea going.'

Lily put away her things and changed out of her working clothes, all the while listening for Charlie's knock on the door. She set the table while Katie cut potatoes into chips. They both jumped at every unusual sound, but they did not speak to each other. Silence reigned until Jamsie came home. He bundled in brightly, sniffing into the air and saying, 'Fish and chips! How did I know?'

'Because it always is on a Friday, Sherlock!' Katie said, and gave him a weak smile.

He looked at them both for a minute, but said nothing.

❧❧❧

Lily switched on the bedside light, again, and looked at the clock, again! It was ten to two in the morning. Only ten minutes had passed since she last looked at it. She put out the light and faced the other way, tucking the bedclothes around her shoulders. Still sleep refused to come.

After their meal, Katie had told Jamsie about Charlie's visit while Lily sat silent. She mentioned nothing at all about *'the other business.'* (Surely the gossip would die down and Jamsie need never know that his aunt had been the subject of such unhealthy interest?)

Jamsie had been planning to go to the Speedway but insisted on staying home now to await the return of Charlie Dunne and to protect the two ladies. The young man, now that he understood why his mother and aunt had looked so fraught when he got home, said 'Don't worry, aunt Lil – I'll knock the living daylights out of him if he tries anything.' - Just the words his mother didn't want to hear. It set her off again.

'No, No, Jamsie. Please! We'll just sit quiet and not open the door. He'll think we're not in and he'll go away.'

Jamsie had tried hard to distract them all evening by playing Elvis Presley and Beatles songs for them on his new record player while they waited nervously for that dreaded knock on the door. In the event, Charlie did not re-appear. Lily was inclined to wish he had, so that she could get the whole nasty business over with. By midnight, Jamsie was convinced that Charlie was not going to show and persuaded the two ladies to go to bed.

Lily lay there in the darkness thinking about her life. She was afraid of Charlie, she knew, but not in a cowardly sense.

She just did not like to be punched around. Who would? That was very painful, to put it simply. In the early years of her marriage, she had put up with Charlie because she'd had no choice. Where could she go with five young children and no money? But she had not been devoid of *some* spunk. She remembered the time when Charlie had clouted her for being late with his dinner. She had been so mad she crushed up six laxative tablets and stirred them into his stew. He was off work for three days with *that* 'bug'. He was so weak, he wasn't fit to punch his way out of a wet paper bag, never mind take a swipe at Lily. Poor Charlie, he didn't suspect a thing.

Another time, when he insisted on taking the only few coppers there were in the house to buy tobacco for his pipe, she snipped a hole in the pocket of his trousers before he got dressed so he would lose the money on his way to work. She went out later and retrieved most of it on the path behind the house and the kids got French toast for breakfast. She was not proud of having had to behave in such an underhand way, but with Charlie, it could never be a fair fight. He won every time with his fists. Besides, she had to feel that she wasn't just a dopey old punch bag, and thinking up little tricks like these helped to keep her sane, keep her functioning, through those miserable years, until she devised her master plan.

What master plan? Where was she now? All she'd done was run away. Where was the glorious triumph in that? She hadn't even thought it through far enough to know what she'd do if Charlie came looking for her. The real truth was that she never thought for one moment that he'd even bother to look for her. She had escaped, only to bring heartache and shame to poor Katie, who had taken her in without a moment's hesitation. She had never intended this. This agony was just as painful as a beating. She felt crushed. And afraid. Because now he knew where she was, he could turn up at any time, causing more trouble. She put on the light and checked the time again. It was two fifteen. Eventually she fell into an erratic, restless sleep.

Katie tossed around in her bed too. Mother and Father had been good to her all through her life. They had allowed her to carry on working in the shop and had paid her a decent wage. Dan had been a good, hard-working husband who had left her well provided for when he died of emphysema. Even the tragedy of his death had been easier to bear because he'd left her with four stalwart sons to help her through it.

'What a self-righteous old crab I've been,' she thought. It was easy to bleat about morals and standards when they've never been tested. Lily had never had one iota of help all those years. Katie had been so distraught by all that had happened today that she totally forgot that Lily was terrified too, and with more reason. This man had committed actual bodily harm on her sister, not just once, but all her married life, and here *she* was, worried about her standing in the community! Who gives a damn about the community? A community peopled with the likes of old Granny Park and silly Lizzie Crilly? Katie scolded herself. Where was her heart? Where was her loyalty? She was ashamed of herself, and realised that Lily had more gumption than she would ever have. She, on the other hand, had been the coward. She had offered her sister sanctuary and at the first sign of trouble, had turned yellow. She would apologise to Lily first thing in the morning.

Jamsie slept like a baby.

At six o'clock, Lily heard Katie's slippers shuffling past her bedroom door in the direction of the kitchen. She immediately got up and draped a faded pink cardigan that she used for a dressing gown over her shoulders and followed. Katie was filling the kettle at the sink and did not hear Lily approach because of the noise of the gushing water. She turned to put the kettle on the stove and nearly jumped out of her skin when she caught sight of Lily, standing there quietly, her nightgown hugging her thin legs and her tangled hair falling over her face. She looked like an apparition. Katie let out a strangled scream. 'You gave me the fright of my life!'

Lily's hand shot up to cover her mouth. 'Oh, I didn't mean to startle you.'

'It's okay. My nerves are all to pot.'

'Mine too. It's all my fault.'

'No, no. mine.'

There was silence for a moment as they looked at each other and then slowly they both began to laugh.

'Bloody fool! You look like a ghost. Scared the B'Jesus out of me.' Katie said, smiling.

'Sorry. I need to talk to you, Katie.'

'No you don't. It's me who needs to talk to you. But first, wait a minute,' she whispered, and went into the hall to make sure the living room door was shut tight.

'Don't want to wake Jamsie,' she said.

They sat down and after two cups of tea and two slices of toast each, all was well again with the sisters.

Lily told Katie that she was trying as hard as she could to get a place. Katie said not to fret, everything would work out all right. Lily got up to get ready for work.

'What will you do if Charlie comes back today?'

'Don't worry. I'll be ready for him this time.' As Lily turned to go, Katie broached the subject that had been in her mind for some time.

'Lily, why don't you have a word with Father Murphy? He might be able to put in a word for you at the housing department. He might even be able to give you some advice about how to deal with Charlie.'

Lily stopped dead, her hand on the door lintel. She said solemnly,

'Katie, I owe you a lot. You have done so much for me and I appreciate it. I really do. But please don't ask me to do that. You know I couldn't. We have had this talk before and you know how I feel about the church and the clergy.'

Katie nodded resignedly and Lily left for work.

It was true. Katie had often tried to get Lily to go to see Father Murphy. In Katie's eyes, he was a good man who would do his best to be sympathetic and to help, but Lily did not believe her. She remembered only too well the time her mother and father had dragged her to see the parish priest, Father Kelly, he was then. He told her that God would never forgive someone who married outside the church, and to a seventeen-year-old girl, this was very alarming. He did not put the fear of God into her, as her parents seemed to hope he might, but he certainly put the fear of the Catholic Clergy into her, and she never recovered. In the honeymoon months of her marriage, Lily had embraced the Church of Scotland, which was Charlie's church. It was very different and once she got over the newness of it all, she actually enjoyed going there and she made a lot of friends. But when she privately tried to seek help when her troubles began, she found the minister to be utterly useless. She continued to attend, though, because of the friends she'd made and for the sake of the children. When the children grew away from religion, so did she, and it had been many years since she'd been inside any kind of church. Lily had come to the conclusion that there isn't any divine intervention. We are on our own down here. No use asking God to help. He either can't, or isn't listening.

Katie, good Christian that she was, remained hopeful. She knew in her heart that Lily would find God again.

CHAPTER 9

It Would Take a Miracle.

Paddy was booked to do a double shift on Saturday. He had agreed to do it because he knew the extra money would come in handy, but he was not looking forward to it. Rangers and Celtic, rival Glasgow football teams, known locally as the 'Old Firm', were playing an important league match at Ibrox stadium, and that would mean that by noon the train would fill up with football supporters. Along with the genuine fans, there would be a fair amount that was no more than hooligans, looking for trouble.

Joe Gillan was the driver, and the day went badly for both of them from the start. They were already a few minutes late when they left St Enoch at nine-fifteen. They got to Hillington East. Paddy jumped on to the platform to hurry passengers on and off the train in an effort to make up the lost time. He was immediately approached by an old man asking for help.

'It's the Mrs, you see son. She needs to get to the other side,' he said, pointing across to the opposite platform. 'I came with her to the station, but I can't climb those steep stairs. I've got a bad heart, so could you maybe see that she gets safely over? She's got bad arthritis, and her hands can't grip the handrails.'

Paddy looked around for any available station staff, but there was none. He looked back at the old man and then at his even older looking wife, who was smiling at him from under-neath a little red hat and the bushiest grey eyebrows that Paddy had ever seen on a woman. She was very small and slightly bent, reminding him of a little garden gnome.

'Of course I'll take you across,' he said. 'Wait here a minute.'

He hurried to the front of the train and explained his mercy mission to Joe, who shook his head and said in an annoyed voice, 'Hurry up then, Paddy. This is all we need. We're late enough as it is!'

Paddy set out to slowly climb the stairs of the bridge, his aged burden hanging on to his arm as if her life depended on him.

'Thanks very much, son,' the old man called after them, lifting his arm to wave. That wave never stopped. He continued to wave all the time. He waved when they got to the top of the first flight. He waved as they made their careful progress along the bridge. He waved as they painstakingly descended the other side, one slow step at a time.

The old woman talked in a breathless whisper all the way, explaining that she was going to see her daughter, who would meet her at Mount Florida. At the last step Paddy was on the lookout for any loose stones or cracked paving that might trip the old dear up. He was just telling her, 'Take it easy now, you're nearly there,' when his own toe caught the inside of his trouser leg and down he went, bringing the old lady down on top of him. The fall was so fast that at first neither of them realised what had actually happened. There was a confused rolling about and a very surprised look on both their faces.

People came running to help and they were lifted on to their feet by several strong hands.

'Whaur's ma handbag?' The old lady's bewildered voice could be heard among the melee of other questions:

'Are you okay?'

'What happened?'

'Do you need an ambulance?'

It was soon established that neither was badly hurt.

'I'm so sorry. It was my fault. I tripped on my trousers. Are you all right, lady?' Paddy asked anxiously.

The woman took a few tentative steps and declared she was fine.

'The fall has stretched my old bones and loosened them a bit. I feel even better than I did when we set out, but I'm sorry, I seem to have used you as a cushion.'

Paddy grinned and said he'd hurt nothing but his dignity. Someone passed the old girl her handbag. Station staff appeared at last to take over, and Paddy was glad to say goodbye and leave her in their capable hands. He crossed the bridge running, to return to his train. The old man was still waving, and he called across to his wife, 'Are you sure you're okay?'

'I'm fine,' she shouted back. 'Watch this.' She strutted a few steps along the very edge of the platform, made an exaggerated turn and strutted back again, swaggering for all the world like a cat-walk model.

'I'm cured,' she called out. 'The fall has cured the arthritis in my knees! Look!'

Her husband said 'I'm glad you're okay. But you did look funny.' He started to laugh. So did she. The last thing Paddy saw as his train pulled out, now fifteen minutes late, was the two old people splitting their sides laughing at each other from opposite platforms. He had never before seen old people laugh so heartily and it was the strangest thing. He continued to stare until they were out of sight.

Arriving at West Kilbride, another setback occurred. Paddy was anxious to get any passengers on or off the train as quickly as possible to make up for lost time. Just when all the doors were closed, a woman, loaded down with parcels and bags, came running from the ticket office. Paddy held a door open and called out,

'C'mon, c'mon. You're just in time.'

The woman hurried along and almost tripped into the compartment. When Paddy went to close the door after her, she stopped him and looking aghast, she pointed down at the gap between the wheels and the wall of the platform.

'My shoe! My shoe has fallen off! It's down there.'

Paddy looked, and there it was: a black patent leather high-heeled shoe, lying forlornly on the track. He groaned inwardly. *Oh, God. As if we weren't late enough already!* But outwardly he smiled cheerily.

'Don't worry, I'll get the train to roll forward and we'll get it out.'

He closed the door on her and signalled to Joe to roll forward and stop short. This was an unofficial signal, but it was used regularly for just such an emergency. The train would move forward until the fallen object was exposed, allowing the guard room to jump down and retrieve it. This Paddy did as soon as the shoe was easy to reach, but consternation spread over his face when the train kept going. He was left standing in the middle of the track holding a ladies size five shoe, the owner of which was leaning out of the window, watching in gathering panic as she moved further and further away from her footwear. Joe had obviously misread the signal and the train was now heading towards Fairlie without a guard, and with a shoe-less lady on board. Paddy had to think quickly. He jumped back up to ground level and ran into the ticket office.

'Stephen, get me a taxi quickly,' he said, and then explained what had happened. 'You'd better phone ahead to Fairlie and get them to detain the train till I get there.'

'Well, I'll do my best to contact them, Paddy, but if it's that wee fellow Echo who's on duty, he might not answer the phone.'

'What do you mean?' Paddy asked. 'Why would he not answer the phone?'

'He might not be there, -eh- at this minute,' came the puzzling reply.

'How can he be on duty and yet not be there? I don't understand.'

'He should be there by the time the train is due, I'm sure, so I'll get him then.'

The taxi tooted and Paddy went out to it, shoe in hand.

'Where to, pal?' the driver asked, looking askance at the shoe in Paddy's hand.

'Fairlie! Fast!' said Paddy, his backside already disappearing into the back seat of the car.

'Are ye looking for a bag to match yer shoe? Ah know just the shop. It caters for boys like you.'

Paddy ignored this. 'Just get me to Fairlie station in a hurry! I've got to catch up with the train; there's a lady in one of the coaches and this is her shoe.'

'Are you sure you're chasing the right kind of coach? Is it no' the kind that changes into a pumpkin you're looking for?' He could see the man smirking, in the rear view mirror, his face contorted as he tried not to laugh.

'Oh aye, - a comedian!' Paddy thought. 'And you must be one of the ugly sisters!'

They could see the waiting train when they screeched into the station yard at Fairlie. Joe was furious. 'What the hell happened to you?' he growled.

'I'll tell you in a minute. Let me give this back to the passenger who lost it first.'

'Well get a bloody move on. Nae mair good deeds, Paddy! We're running twenty minutes late. Other traffic is being held up because of us.'

Paddy had to run to the back carriage and return the fateful lost property to its owner, who was delighted to be properly shod again and was full of praise for the wonders of modern travel and the splendid service provided.

Paddy joined Joe in the cabin and tried to explain all that had happened. An argument ensued for a while about the signal given, and how it was interpreted, but as they sped on, Joe was able to calm down a bit. When the time was right, Paddy ventured to ask him if he knew what Stephen at West Kilbride meant when he said that Echo might not be there if he was on duty.

'Ach, it's a well-known secret. Echo and Dougie work opposite shifts at Fairlie. Have done for years now. The pair o' them get up to all sorts of dodges. Not so much on a Saturday when it's busier, but on a Sunday, few trains stop at Fairlie so they spend all day in the Ashcroft Hotel.'

'You're joking!'

'Naw, it's true. First they open up the office, then they lift a few blank tickets and bring the inkpad and the date stamp with them to the bar at the Ashy. The locals all know where to find them and they go to the hotel for their tickets. They'll ask for a return to Paisley, or a single to Dalry or whatever, and Echo or Dougie will take the money and stamp them a ticket right there in the bar.'

'God in Heaven!' said an incredulous Paddy. 'I wouldn't mind a job like that. How do they get away with it?'

'I've no idea. They get away wi' murder. I remember one time that the two of them decided to brew their own beer in the station outhouse. They started to collect all the screw-top bottles they could lay their hands on. They collected hundreds of bottles and stacked them till they were six feet high in the cupboard in the storeroom. Then they gave up the idea of brewing beer and forgot all about the bottles. Some time afterwards, Dougie was on duty when he got a visit from the area supervisor. It was yon Fred Thomson, you remember him? Well, he says to Dougie, "You haven't swept out the waiting room, have you Douglas? It's really dusty and could do with a good sweep."

"Oh, right, Mr Thomson. It's just that there's no head on the brush. I meant to put in an order for a new head." Dougie said.

"That's easily fixed," said Thorson. "I'm sure there's a spare head kept in the storeroom."

And before Dougie could think up another excuse, Thomson was in the storeroom heading straight for the cupboard. Hundreds of glass bottles tumbled out when he opened the door. They slid everywhere, rattling and rolling into every corner.

"What on earth is all this?" he asked Dougie.

"Oh, er, Echo and me, we were saving them. The passengers leave them lying around and we thought we'd collect the deposits."

"Hm," said old Thomson. "The passengers, eh?" He must have been very well aware that Fairlie was lucky to get thirty or forty passengers in any one week, but all he said to Dougie was to clean up the mess and clear out the cupboard. He picked up a new broom head that had fallen out of the cupboard along with the bottles.

"You can use this," he said.

Dougie told me that himself,' Joe ended his tale.

⚜ ⚜

Duncan Brewer was running late too. He was going to the game at Ibrox and it had taken him ages to find his Rangers scarf. This he blamed on 'that damned home help' whom he suspected was a Celtic fan, and had hidden his scarf in the bottom of the ottoman on purpose. Davey McCally knocked loudly on the door.

'Are ye there, Dunky?'

'Come on in, Davey.'

'All set?'

'Aye, just about. The beer is on the kitchen table. Will ye see to it?'

Davey tied a large bag on to the back of Duncan's wheel-chair and put a dozen bottles of McEwan's pale ale in it.

'Right. We're off.'

They trundled down the path and covered the short distance to the station singing football ditties and cursing when the chair got stuck on some obstacle. They met up with a few mates at the station. There were some Celtic fans there too, but they kept themselves apart. If the match had been a cup final, there would probably have been some Football Specials, separate trains for the rival fans, stopping at alternate stations to keep them apart, but today they shared the same train.

Duncan was hoisted up into the guardsvan, and there was Paddy Preston grinning at him. Davey and his mates jumped in too and sat on top of any sack or box they could find.

'How've you been, Dunky? You're looking well.'

'We're going to the game,' Duncan said unnecessarily.

'Naw!' Paddy said, looking at the blue and white scarves. 'I thought you were going to church, maybe.'

'What are you doing in a guardsvan? I thought you'd be a manager by now. Were ye not station manager last time I saw ye?'

'I was. But I wanted my old job back.'

'You're mad. Have ye seen the mob that just got on? It'll be trouble on the way back, whoever wins.'

'Well, I'll hide in the guardsvan then, like I'm doing now, until they're all gone.'

'We're going to Central Station. We'll be picked up and taken to Ibrox from there. We're hoping to get the six-twenty home again,' said Davey.

'I'll be on it. I'm working a doubler.' Paddy told them.

'Good. I'll keep you a bottle of beer.'

Paddy went of to perform some duties and he didn't see Duncan or Davey again until they got off.

'See you later then, Dunky. May the best team win.'

'Aye, we know who that will be then, don't we?' He waved his scarf in the air.

∽❀∾ ∽❀∾

The stadium was filled to capacity. Davey was allowed to stay with Duncan by the side of the pitch where all the other wheelchairs and invalid cars were accommodated. Their friends took their share of the beer and went into the terraces, arranging to meet up in the station later for the journey home.

'The smell o' thae pies is making me hungry. I'll away and get us some. Do you want a hot drink? Bovril, maybe?' Davey was looking hungrily at the rows of food shacks.

'Naw. The beer'll do.'

Davey got back with an armful of pies, sausage rolls and hot dogs just as the teams emerged from the tunnel. The roar was deafening.

The game got underway. Duncan was enjoying himself. He liked nothing better than watching his team play. He consumed two pies and the same amount of hot dogs. He shouted insults and advice at the players on the pitch, but it was not a good game. The first half was hard and physical. Play was stopped more than once because of horrendous fouls. At one point a Celtic player was rolling on the ground, squirming agonisingly, after a tackle from the opposite side. The medics ran on. In a couple of minutes the player was up on his feet and running off to resume play.

'Oh aye. That's the magic sponge in use again. Did ye see that? Not a thing wrong with him! Just trying for a foul!'

'Do you not know? That's Holy Water they've got on that sponge. The lame shall walk again!'

Davey's sarcasm drew a laugh from Duncan.

The fans became more aggressive at what they perceived to be the injustices of the referee's decisions. The only commonality they shared was that the ref was a dope. At half-time, they chanted and goaded each other continuously, all through the interval.

'I'll away to the toilet,' Davey said

'Here. Before you go. Empty this for me, will ye?' Duncan produced a dark glass bottle from under his blanket.

Davey's face puckered in disgust. 'Aw. Aw. Dunky! My God! Have ye no shame?'

But he emptied it on the grass nearby and returned it to Dunky, wiping his hands on his trouser legs with a disdainful shudder before going away to relieve his own bladder.

Dunky read his programme. On the terraces, they were liquoring up.

The second half brought more of the same. The fans became frustrated, as the game never got into a good flow. Too many stops, too many fouls. The atmosphere became more menacing and Duncan noticed it. He shivered once or twice.

Then the catastrophe. Ten minutes before the end of play with still no score, the Rangers centre forward was on the ball, running towards the penalty area. The Celtic centre-half ploughed into his legs and brought him down in the box. The Rangers fans were delirious, seeing the chance for victory.

'PENALTY! PENALTY!' they screamed.

There was a palpable hush at the Celtic end.

To the astonishment of all the spectators, the referee

awarded, not a penalty, but a *Free kick*. A low drone that quickly became an angry rumble rose from the crowd. Then all hell broke loose. Rangers fans went berserk. Bottles started flying out on to the field. Suddenly there was an invasion of the pitch as raging fans tried to get at the referee to tear him to pieces. The referee was cornered on one end of the pitch, surrounded by the players. Within seconds, the match was abandoned. Pandemonium reigned. Police moved in. Bottles continued to rain down from the terraces, whizzing past the heads of the people in the invalid area.

'C'mon Dunky. We're getting out of here!' Davey pushed Duncan as quickly as he could along the perimeter towards the exit. St John's Ambulance men were helping to vacate the invalids. Suddenly Duncan slumped sideways and began to slide off the chair. Davey stopped and went to help him straighten up.

'What's wrong, Dunky?'

But Duncan was unconscious.

'Dunky. Dunky!' cried Davey. Then he noticed a beer bottle, caught in at Duncan's shoulder and a large blood-like mark was appearing as he watched, on Duncan's temple.

'Help! Help us. Over here!' Davey yelled against the uproar that was going on around them. He grabbed two ambulance men who were about to run past them on to the field with a stretcher.

'Please! My mate, he's been hit!'

They stopped, took one look at Duncan and immediately transferred him on to the stretcher, where they had him in an ambulance in minutes. Davey ran alongside the stretcher, leaving the wheelchair and the beer. Fighting fans were battling through the streets now as crowds spilled out of the stadium and impeded the ambulance. Shop windows were being smashed all around, and police, some on horseback, were giving chase and making arrests. Press photographers were snapping away, hopeful of the chance of getting '*the*' picture. All this Davey was only partially aware of as he sat with his friend in the ambulance.

They placed an oxygen mask over Duncan's face and Davey held his hand.

'Speak to me, Dunky. Speak to me! Say something!'

But Duncan Brewer never spoke again. He became the fulfilling part of his own prophecy when he was pronounced dead on arrival at Glasgow's Royal Infirmary.

⌘⌘ ⌘⌘

Lily made her way wearily through the crush of people to platform six at Glasgow Central. It had been a long hard day and she was exhausted. Lack of sleep, and worry about her situation had made concentration difficult. Or was it just that the customers had been particularly trying today? She had spent her lunch hour looking at flats to rent among the tenements of Glasgow's east end and this had left her badly depressed. She'd seen two places in Parkhead; one was four flights up and smelled as if some drunk had died there and had not been discovered for weeks. The second was directly above a betting shop and the noise from the punters listening to the Saturday race meetings filtered up through the floorboards along with the cigarette smoke and the bad language. She was actually wondering if she should consider it. At least she'd have a place of her own, and she could find somewhere else eventually. The trouble was, the terms were that she had to lease it for a year. Could she stand a year in this dump? It was nearer her work. She would only have to step outside to get a bus into the centre of town – a ten-minute journey. A sudden raucous roar from below the floorboards had made her jump.

'No doubt that's the winner of the 12:45 at Haydock,' laughed the woman who was showing the flat. 'You won't have to go far to collect your winnings.'

That did it for Lily. She was on the bus back to work before the roar had died down.

And to crown it all, there had been trouble at the Ibrox football game and trains had been delayed and cancelled because of vandalism and rowdy behaviour. Crowds of football fans were milling about the station, adding their hordes to the everyday commuters waiting to travel. The police were alert to pounce on spasmodic incidents of brawling that broke out, and though these were quickly quelled, it was all very intimidating and added to her depressed state of mind. When her train finally came in she was thankful to get a seat and sank down on it. Some poor souls, she knew from experience, would have to stand all the way. She spent most of the journey unobtrusively flicking fish scales off her fingers. No matter how many times you washed your hands, the scales still stuck. She was sick of the sight of fish. And the smell of it. She must stink of the stuff. Maybe everybody else can smell it too. She lifted the lapel of her coat up to her nose and sniffed. Fish. The smell of it seemed to fill her nostrils. There must be something better than this, surely. Half an idea that she should look for some other kind of work began to form in her tired brain. She dozed.

It took forty minutes to get to her stop and when she got out, she heard someone call her name. It was Eddie. He was out of uniform and had come to the station specially to meet her.

'I've been thinking about your problem,' he said, 'and I've got an idea, if you're interested.'

She smiled, probably her first smile of the day. Imagine him thinking of her and her problems! She raised her eyebrows questioningly. 'Okay, I'm listening.'

Commuters were pushing past them on their way out.

'Well, have you ever thought about becoming a lodger, while you're still looking for a place of your own?'

No, that thought had never even occurred to her.

'I know of a lady by the name of Martha McLaughlin who takes in lodgers. I thought about her when we talked about finding a place for you, but I decided I'd better check it out first before I mention it - see if she had any vacancies, like, you know? I didn't want to raise any false hopes. She lives in Uddingston, next door to my sister. It turns out she has a room for rent. I could take you to see it if you're interested. Here's her address and phone number.'

He handed her a piece of paper. Lily's face lit up.

'Eddie, that's a great idea. You've no idea the hovels I've seen. All wanting a King's ransom! I'll talk it over with———.' Her voice trailed off. She was looking past Eddie, over his shoulder. The station was empty now except for one unwelcome face that was approaching her right now.

'Oh no!' she whispered.

'Oh, aye. This is what you get up to, is it?' said Charlie Dunne. 'Did you think I wouldn't find ye?'

Something, maybe terror, clouded Lily's face. She said quickly, 'Eddie this is my husband, Charlie Dunne. Please excuse me while I talk to him. Thank you for your idea. We'll talk later.'

She started to walk forward, pulling at Charlie's sleeve for him to follow. Charlie stood, immovable, pushing his forearm in a windmill motion, up out of her grasp.

'No, no. There's no need for privacy,' he said. 'You've not been too careful about your privacy lately anyway, so I've been hearing.'

Lily's face turned bright red. 'Look, it's no good your coming here, Charlie,' she said. 'There is no way under the sun I'll ever go back with you. It's over between us.'

'Ha! That's a laugh! You think I've come to take you back? Not on your Nellie! I don't want you back and if this is your new fella,' he jerked a thumb disdainfully in Eddie's direction, 'he's welcome to you. I just wanted you to know that I can find you wherever you go. You can never hide from me.'

'Who told you where I was?'

'I think I'll just keep *you* guessin' for a change,' he smirked.

Eddie was clenching and unclenching his fists, uncertain what to do. He did not want to embarrass Lily, or add any more to her discomfiture, but this lout should not get away with humiliating her like that. He was just about to intervene when Charlie leaned forward.

'And I wanted to give you this,' he said, and put a small package into her hands. 'I wanted to make sure you got this.' He started to walk away. 'Remember, I can come back into your life any time I like.'

Lily and Eddie were left standing alone. She was shaking and said with as much composure as she could, 'I have to get home.' Her voice was faint.

'Of course. Take my arm, I'll walk with you.'

She was grateful for his support and for his company, because her legs felt like jelly and she was convinced that Charlie would jump out at her at the foot of the hill. She told this to Eddie and he nodded silently, but his face was grim.

∽◌∾ ∽◌∾

'Have you seen him?' Katie was busy at the cooker and had only half glanced at her sister when she heard her come in. 'He didn't show up here today.'

'Yes. He was there at he station.' Lily sounded as if she had no breath in her lungs.

Katie stopped what she was doing and focussed on Lily's face.

'Oh. Oh. You've seen him, then?'

'Yes. He gave me this.' Lily put the packet on the dresser.

'What's in it?'

'I don't know.'

'Aren't you going to open it?'

'Later. I'm too tired right now. That smells good.'

The gigot chops were sizzling away and Katie was stirring the sauce. The fragrance of fresh mint filled the air. A bowl of mashed potatoes was steaming on the table.

'I've just realised I'm starving. I was house hunting again at lunch time and I didn't have time to eat.'

'Sit down. This'll be ready in a minute. Tell me about Charlie.'

Lily put her elbows on the table and rubbed her hands over her face.

'He was his usual ugly self. He said he didn't want me back; he just wanted me to know that I could never hide from him and that he'd find me no matter where I went. Which doesn't make sense. Why would he want to find me if he doesn't want me back?'

'To frighten you, Aunt Lily. To make you think he has some power over you that will last forever,' Jamsie said, coming into the kitchen. 'Let me go and look for him. I'll show him what he'll find if he comes near you again!'

'No, Jamsie. Please! You know we've been over this.'

Jamsie sat at the table and picked up his knife and fork.

'I hope I don't meet him then, because I can't make any promises.'

After the meal they all sat back, satisfied.

'Katie, those chops were done to a 'T'. And the sauce was delicious, thank you.'

'Right, ma. Great meal,' and Jamsie disappeared. Well, there was washing up to be done, wasn't there?

'Oh, I have some news for you.' Lily tried to keep her tone light. 'Eddie McKenna gave me the address of a woman who takes in boarders. What do you think of that idea?'

'Well, if you're only going to stay there until you get a place of your own, you may just as well stay here.'

'It might be the answer, Katie. Jamsie should have his own room back. I'm not unaware of how difficult this has been for him.'

Katie looked doubtful.

'Tell you what, Kate. It can't do any harm to check it out. You can come with me. Won't hurt to take a look, eh?'

'Hm.'

⚜⚜

Neither Paddy Preston nor Joe Gillan got to work their double shift to its conclusion. Fighting football fans wrecked the carriages and the train was put out of commission. The violence was particularly bad because it wasn't just the seats the hooligans wanted to rip apart. Anyone who came near them was threatened with broken bottles and abusive language. At Dalry, police were waiting to arrest the trouble-makers and to escort innocent commuters to waiting buses where they would be driven home in safety. It was the worst case of violence both Paddy and Joe had ever encountered and each vowed they would never work a train carrying football fans again. They felt lucky to have survived un-scathed. Several trains were decommissioned, they heard later, and they were only two among many rail men to be sent home. Joe was bussed along with the other passengers to Saltcoats and Paddy was driven back to St Enoch's to collect his car.

Agnes was glad to see him home. She had heard about the violence on the news and that one person had been killed. He told her about his nightmare day from start to finish, especially that final journey. He ended by saying, 'I'm glad Davey McCally and Duncan Brewer missed the train. They must have decided to stay out of harms way in

some pub somewhere until the worst was over. Wise decision.'

Agnes could see how shaken Paddy was by the days events,
so she waited until he'd washed and eaten before saying quietly
in his ear, 'It's arrived. It's in the bedroom.'

'You're joking! It wasn't due to come till Monday. Do the
kids know?'

'No I covered it with a candlewick, but they've never even
been in the room.'

'Do you think we should set it up now?'

'I don't see why not, since it's here already. Besides, I'm
dying to see it myself.'

'Okay, let's tell them.'

They went into the living room. The boys were squabbling
over whose turn it was on a board game. Debbie's head and
shoulders had disappeared into the space left by the pulled-
back sliding doors under the window seat. This was where
she kept her dolls and their furniture and she could spend
hours with her head in there, hearing nothing and oblivious to
what was going on around her. Unfortunately, the rest of the
family could not be oblivious to her, because they were
obliged to step over her backside and legs, stretched out on the
carpet behind her.

'Right, kids. Listen. Tommy and Danny, stop fighting.
Debbie come over here and sit down.' Nobody heard a
word.

'Mum and I have got a surprise for you.' They heard *that*.
Suddenly, three fidgety kids were all ears. Debbie backed out
of the cupboard on her elbows. The boys knelt up to listen,
though they continued to make faces at one another, signifying
that the fight was not over and would resume when mum and
dad were preoccupied again.

'We feel that you've been through a lot lately when we

thought we'd move house and then we decided that we wouldn't, and you've been very good, not straying far from home since Tommy got lost, so we decided to get us all a present. A family present.'

'What is it?'

'Wait here.'

Agnes and Paddy carried it in together and the kids went wild.

'It's a T.V. We've got a T.V. I don't believe it!'

'Mum, Dad, thank you. Thank you.'

There were hugs and kisses and shrieks of delight. They jumped about while Paddy read instructions and footered about with cables and connections for the already fitted outside aerial. Tommy clapped his hands and said, 'Now I won't need to go to wee Petey's to see Champion the Wonder Horse or Skippy the Bush Kangaroo.'

Paddy looked up at him from the floor where he was squatting, fiddling with a knob.

'How come wee Petey Miller's got a telly in his house? I thought his dad was idle.'

'My pal Laura Bradshaw's got a telly' offered Debbie.

'Dad,' Danny said, 'we're the only ones who *don't* have a telly. Even Jesse Rogers has got a telly.'

'*What*? They've got a telly! And he had the cheek to cast aspersions on me because I bought a wee car to get to my work in! I wish I'd known that then.'

Paddy was attaching a plug with a screwdriver.

'Hurry up Dad!' The cries were impatient now. Finally Paddy had it tuned and they could hear voices. Gradually Richard Chamberlain's face appeared.

'It's Doctor Kildare!' shouted the kids. 'Hurrah, hurrah!'

'It's wonderful,' said Agnes, 'like a miracle. These people are Americans and we can see them here, in our own home.' The kids danced about, cheering.

'Sh! Stop the noise,' said Agnes. 'You'll have Granny Park complaining.'

They all sat on the couch, squeezing up to make room for each other and watched the T.V. all night until the dot went out.

Debbie rubbed her eyes sleepily. 'Wait till I tell Laura Bradshaw!'

'Wait till I tell wee Petey!' said Tommy.

'Wait till I get the licence!' said Paddy

❧❦ ❧❦

It didn't take Eddie long to find Charlie Dunne after he left Lily at her house. There he was, in the first pub down from the station. Dead easy! Eddie McKenna was not confrontational. By nature he was a shy, quiet man. But he had a strong sense of what was right and what was wrong, and every now and then in his life, he had been forced to act on it. This, he told himself now, was one of those times. Something was very wrong here. That man, Dunne, was a wife beater who was terrorising Lily and getting away with it.

Although the pub was busy, Charlie was drinking alone. Eddie went up behind him and tapped him on the shoulder. Charlie turned his head and studied him for a moment through narrowed eyes, then a look of recognition passed across his face.

'Oh aye. The boyfriend!'

'You're good at it, aren't you?' Eddie said quietly into his ear.

'Good at what?'

'Good at frightening women. But so far, you've failed to frighten me. But then, I'm a man and I suppose that makes me way out of your league. And hitting a woman, you're good at that, too. Let's see how good you are at hitting a man. Or do you only do women and children?'

'I never hit my children. Did that bitch tell you I did? She's lying.'

'Outside, Dunne. Now.'

Charlie was already regretting his mistake. He wished he'd gone with Lily when she tried to pull him aside, but he had acted the smart aleck instead. He should never have used such threatening talk in front of a witness. That was a stupid thing to have done. He began to feel uncomfortable, and he reluctantly followed Eddie out of the side door into the alley. Eddie was feeling a bit fearful himself but his anger and sense of justice drove him to finish what he was about to start.

As soon as they were outside Charlie said, 'Look Jimmy, I didn't mean what I said. It's been months since she buggered off, and by the time I found her I was so mad —'

WHACK!

He never saw it coming. The force of Eddie's punch, landing right in the middle of his face, sent him hurtling backwards and left him sprawling against empty beer kegs a full six feet away. Eddie stood waiting, fists clenched, expecting Dunne to struggle to his feet and come at him. But Charlie Dunne, the cowardly bully who knew how to throw his weight around when he confronted his wife, just lay there holding his bleeding nose.

'My nose! You've broken my nose! I'll have you for this, you bastard!'

'Well, come on then. Here I am.' Eddie was sidestepping about, rotating his fists.

Charlie moaned and coughed but he did not get up; he stayed where he was, balancing on one elbow amongst the empty beer kegs, cowering like a whipped mongrel.

'I thought so. You can only hit women.' Eddie strode forward and bent to look Charlie in the eye. 'Don't ever come anywhere near Lily again or *I'll* be the one to find *you*. *You'll* be the one who has nowhere to hide. Got that?'

He left him, lying in the lane, spluttering and complaining.

A minute passed and Charlie struggled to his feet and

looked around him for the bonnet he always wore. Fixing it shakily on his thinning head of hair, he called down the darkened alleyway.

'I'll be in Lanark. That's where to find me. I'll no' be hiding from anyone, me! Lanark, see! I'm getting the last train there tonight.'

But no one heard him. Eddie was already turning the key in his front door two streets away.

∽∾∾ ∽∾∾

On Sunday, Lily waited until Katie had gone to Mass before she opened the parcel that Charlie had given her. She wanted to open it privately because she had no idea how she might react to whatever was in it. But when she shook the contents out on to the bed, she didn't react at all. The numbness engendered by anything Charlie said or did must have become a habit. There was a little box containing a pair of not very expensive cufflinks that she had given to him at Christmas one year; and a fountain pen, still boxed and unused; another present to him from her. Scattered around these on the bedspread were the torn pieces of their one and only wedding photo, taken in a side room at Lanark Registry Office, twenty-five years ago. After a minute, relief flooded through her as she pushed these things around on the bed-mat with her forefinger. Slowly she came to realise the significance of this gesture by Charlie. It was an ending. He was saying that he was as glad to be rid of her as she was of him. She was actually glad to see the mutilated jigsaw that was once their wedding photo. That photo symbolised her greatest mistake and she felt no remorse at its destruction, only a sense of freedom. She could only hope that Charlie, back in Lanark now, was making his own life and feeling the same sense of freedom. Lily thought about Eddie's kindness and decided to see her lawyer again, this time to sue for divorce on account of Charlie's cruelty. She was no longer afraid of what people might get to know about the state of her disastrous marriage or what they might think of her. She wanted to be free and she knew that the cruelty card would speed up the process. She gathered up everything from the bedspread, took it all to the dustbin, banged the lid down on it and decided to wash her hair.

CHAPTER 10

Maybe It Comes in Fours

The local bus stopped at the bottom of the street. Julie Gillan stepped from it laden with shopping and slowly plodded homewards. She used her foot to kick open the garden gate and then, edging her way sideways through it to accommodate the four bulging shopping bags that were hanging from her sagging arms, she turned to walk up the path when she suddenly froze in horror. The front door, the doorstep, and halfway down the front path was all covered in coloured chalk drawings. Comical little faces with curly hair looked up at her from the path, and square houses with square windows and smoking chimneys were scrawled all over the place, along with hearts in 'Glorious Technicolor' that had initials inside proclaiming who loved who. The kids had been playing with chalk again! 'I'll kill them!' was her first thought. She recognised her eldest child's handiwork and by the looks of it, she'd given her younger sister Holly free reign with the chalk too! Julie had no time for this nonsense today. Joe would be back from the funeral at Kilwinning soon and he might have several people with him, because no one knew if Duncan's family had made any arrangements for mourners. She'd left the kids in the charge of Isabel next door and had gone to the shops. Along with a stock of her usual groceries, she had had to buy some cold meat for sandwiches and some cake and biscuits so that she could give anyone who came a cup of tea and a bite to eat, and now she'd have to clean this mess up before anyone saw it. She was already tired, and her heart began to feel as heavy as the bags she was carrying.

She made her way into the kitchen calling out 'Catherine! Catherine!' Then she added under her breath, 'Little madam, wait till I get my hands on you!'

But Katie Gillan's namesake was not in the house. There was some spilled sugar scattered on the draining board. Biscuit crumbs on the table and a couple of buttery knives in the sink showed that the culprit had entertained friends regally and had gone off to practice her graffiti somewhere else.

Julie removed her coat with difficulty because her fingers were still stiffly curled into the shape of the shopping bag handles. She sat at the table and tenderly rubbed each hand in turn until she could move her fingers without pain, then she reached across and tilted the biscuit tin towards her, but – surprise, surprise - it was empty. Not a jammy dodger or a garibaldi to be seen. She re-filled the tin with the biscuits she'd just carried home and, a cup of strong tea and two Jaffa Cakes later, she had put the shopping away, and had filled a bucket with hot soapy water and was outside tackling the job of removing the chalk marks before any visitors arrived.

She busied herself with the scrubber, her thoughts on Duncan and the terrible violence that had caused his death at the football match. Poor Duncan! Who would have thought it? After all that he'd been through, battling to make some kind of life for himself since that terrible accident that took the bottom parts of his legs off six years ago. To be struck down while innocently attending a football match, well, it just didn't bear thinking about! How easily and how suddenly a life can be snuffed out! Her own husband could have been a victim that day too, she knew. He could easily have been caught up in the violence of those rampaging thugs on his train. It was a wonder he got home safe, if not exactly sound, because he was certainly extremely shaken up that day. Later, when they discovered that Duncan was the fatality that had been reported on the news, there had been horror and absolute shock for those who knew him; for Joe and Paddy, who had seen him only a short time before it happened, but especially for Davey McCally who took it really bad. Poor Davey! And poor, poor Duncan!

Two boys appeared and leant over the gate, watching her backside shift to and fro as she scrubbed away, oblivious. They looked at each other, mischief brewing.

'Hey, Mrs Gillan, you've missed a bit!' The voice sounded behind her and at the same time a tuft of muddied grass landed with a plop on the pristine doorstep. Julie whizzed round just in time to see the two giggling youngsters, half hidden by the garden hedge, running off in the direction of the swing park. She screwed up her eyes and caught sight of a shock of telltale red hair.

'Your mam will hear from me, Wee Fella Gow! I know it's you!' she shouted after them.

Exasperated, she lifted the clump of mud and threw it into the rose bed.

'No respect!' she mumbled angrily. She finished her work and carried the metal pail inside, to slosh the contents down the sink.

Wee Fella Gow, along with Bobby Tippney, his partner in crime, ran through the swing park squawking in mock terror.

'She'll tell your ma.' Bobby said.

'Who cares? She's an old bat. I'll tell mah ma it wasnae us. She'll believe me.'

They met Peem Murphy and went off to play football, forgetting all about Julie Gillan. Julie Gillan, who really had no intentions of reporting her son's misconduct to Mrs Gow, forgot about all about them too. For a while.

∽✦∾ ∽✦∾

Joe came back from the funeral with only his brother Dan and Paddy Preston. They were all in a very sombre mood. It had been an incredibly sad affair. Duncan's elderly parents had been patently distraught during the brief service. His father had had to be helped along the aisle to his seat because his legs had gone from under him and his mother had been so overcome with grief that she fainted and was unable to go to the graveside. On route to the cemetery, the cortege slowed to a halt on the bridge near the station. Duncan's two sisters emerged from the front car and placed a small posy of flowers on the parapet. This poignant moment was explained in hushed whispers to those who did not know, that the bridge was almost directly above the spot where Duncan's accident had occurred six years before. He had been crossing the railway just when the points were being set in the signal box a mile up the line. He never talked about it afterwards, so no one knew for sure just how or why it happened the way it did, but it seems his foot got caught in the heel of the point and was trapped and the oncoming train could not be stopped. Davey McCally joined the sisters and placed a blue and white Rangers rosette beside the flowers. He suddenly crumpled to his knees and cried inconsolably. It was a wee while before they could get him back in the car.

On reaching the gates of the cemetery, they saw that football dignitaries and players from both Rangers and Celtic clubs were present. Later, one of the Rangers' players placed a large wreath of blue and white flowers on the new grave. It was a proud moment for all Duncan's friends and the tears on their faces showed that they knew Duncan would have been thrilled to know that.

All of this, they recounted to Julie as she passed round the sandwiches. She could see that they were extremely affected by the whole thing.

'It'll be on the telly,' Dan said. 'The T.V. cameras were there.'

Duncan's death had indeed made the front pages. News coverage of the violence that had erupted at last Saturday's match at Ibrox had been nationwide. Various persons had been interviewed. Local people who knew Duncan only by sight vied to offer their opinion, and gave it verbosely, some even managing to get their picture in the paper. There were calls for a ban on alcohol at football matches, and more police presence. Duncan, who had struggled on his own with the minimum of help over the last six years, had suddenly, on his death, become something of a local hero. A pure saint, they said! So it was not surprising that T.V. stations would cover the funeral in the hopeful expectation of capturing any grief stricken outbursts, or an unguarded emotional comment about the behaviour of fans of either persuasion, this ensuring good copy for T.V. and newspapers alike.

When it was time, they turned on the T.V. to watch the local news and the mood lightened a little at the unfamiliar sight of themselves on telly.

'Ho, look at you, man!' Dan nudged Paddy. 'You look like a car salesman in that suit.' They laughed, because he did.

'I didnae realise I was so fat,' said Joe. 'I look like two people from the back.'

They had another beer and some more Victoria sponge cake and when the sad coverage finished, Dan and Paddy got up to leave.

'Thanks for the tea, Julie. We're off now. See you at the union meeting on Monday, Joe?'

'Aye, lads. See you then. Cheerio.'

Julie and Joe were left alone and more mundane topics came up. Just in case Joe was left in any doubt about the kind of day she'd had, Julie told him all about the mess the house was in when she got back from the shops. She also told him about the chalk she'd had to wash off and how that obnoxious kid, Wee Fella Gow and his just as cheeky pal Bobby Tippney didn't help by chucking muck at her. Joe listened with only half an ear. Eventually, he asked, 'Where are the kids?'

'Out playing. I warned them to keep away till the visitors had gone.'

'It's time they were in. I'll go and get them.' He took his cigarettes and lighter with him. Julie hated him smoking indoors.

He found them playing in someone's garden further down the street. They demurred and begged for a few extra minutes and complained that they were always the first to be called in but came along when Joe said sternly, 'No.'

'We've got to go in now. See ye tomorra!' they mumbled to their friends, and followed Joe reluctantly.

A constant banging sound penetrated Joe's brain, and he turned to see Wee Fella Gow battering away at a neighbour's rose tree with a large stick. He had the ever-faithful Bobby Tippney in tow.

'Hey, you! Leave that tree alone. You're a menace in this area, you. You're never happy unless you're destroying something. Get away home to your own street.'

Wee Fella Gow stared at Joe, defiance on his face.

'Get away, yerself. It's none of your business, it's no' your tree!' he replied.

Joe grabbed the stick from him and tossed it aside.

'That's my pole. Gies it back.'

'If I was your da, I'd break it over your back, you cheeky young monkey. Get going!'

149

Wee Fella Gow went, but not before raising his fingers in a rude sign. Joe's kids had remained dumbstruck through this exchange, but Holly now spoke.

'He's bad, isn't he dad?' They had reached home.

'No. He's not bad, princess. He's just a silly boy. Come on, get inside kids.'

It had been a bad day from start to finish.

∽⳾∼ ∽⳾∼

The union meeting, one of many being held nationwide to find out the concerns of the train drivers on the new stock being introduced, was about to start. The main hall of the Labour Party Rooms was filled with swirling smoke and the loud noise of very vocal men. Everyone had plenty to say on how the railways could be better run. Many were of the opinion that there should be no more staff reductions or payoffs, no more branch line closures, no extra cost to the commuter, and above all, there should be a substantial pay rise for everyone. If this was unachievable, they said, it was all management's fault. However, when the meeting was called to order, it became clear that there was a genuine concern among them over the long-term future of the railways and their jobs.

The first speaker reminded the men that the railways were running at a loss. They were losing money hand over fist to new haulage companies that were transporting freight, once in the sole domain of the railways, by the greatly improved road systems. The government, he said, was spending much more money on building motorways and improving highways than it spent on the struggling rail network. Passengers too, were deserting rail travel in their droves in favour of cars. The recent drastic cuts, such as line closures and staff pruning, were all part of the big modernisation plan, implemented to combat this new competition from the popular new motorways. Steam engines could no longer compete.

They were dirty, outdated and cost a fortune to maintain. Steam was being phased out altogether, they knew, and the new electric diesels and non-diesel electric trains, already introduced in many areas, were the way forward.

Someone made the point that morale was low, as well as wages. The introduction of faster cleaner trains, he was told, was designed to woo the people and freight back, and when the railways became profitable again, wages would rise. A voice called out that Dr. Beeching, the author of this fantastic scheme, hadn't waited for profits to rise, and he had demanded the magnificent sum of twenty eight thousand pounds a year from the railways just so he could sack hundreds of people, and nearly ten years down the line, (no pun intended,) he still hadn't managed to stop the rot. There was a general babble of angry agreement. It was accepted that wages were certainly low and this was a main concern and was debated fiercely.

Joe Gillan motioned to speak and was recognised by the chair. He voiced his concern about safety. In the past, he said, when a man became a steam locomotive driver it was only after years of training and preparing. They first served their time cleaning the engine, and then they might become a footplate man or a fireman long before they were allowed to drive a train. Now they are taking drivers from steam trains and putting them overnight in charge of a diesel with no training whatsoever. This is ludicrous, he said. There was a vast difference between a steam locomotive and a diesel engine. The two were entirely different. This has to be addressed before a major accident occurred. He expressed himself so eloquently that there was an immediate hush. His mates, impressed, and nodding approvingly, burst into applause.

A lot more was said on that and other subjects and the meeting concluded with the promise that the points raised would be carried to the Railway Board and the men would be notified of the outcome. Outside, Joe was surrounded by his colleagues and praised for voicing their concerns so ably, and some said he should become a union representative. He laughed and said that Julie would have something to say about that, but he was pleased none the less.

✧✧ ✧✧

Joe didn't take too long to decide that he would not make a good union man. It was all very well to stand up at a union meeting and say his piece among fellow members, but he knew he lacked the real negotiating skills that would be required in an argumentative tussle with managers. Anyway he worked long enough hours as it was. He could agree with Julie there. She was always complaining that they never had enough time together. On the other hand, she read too many o' thae woman's magazines, right enough! Filled her head with 'We need to communicate' and 'Don't leather the kids. They need to express themselves.' If she doesn't take care, we'll end up wi' a couple o' Wee Fella Gows on our hands.

He started back-shift a few days later. He looked his engine over from end to end, running his hand knowledgably along the full length of the newly cleaned bodywork, before climbing aboard. This old girl was being phased out and was destined for the scrap heap next month and Joe felt strangely melancholy at that thought. This confused him a little, because he thought he was one of those who were glad to see the back of the old steam locos. He'd had his fill of the gloom, ash and smoke that was part of the general filth that steam maintenance produced. Besides, they were costing a fortune to run, requiring lots of manpower to produce steam-power. At the end of today, it would take as many six people to put this old girl to bed. They would have to flatten the fire and clean the firebox out. All the hot ash that got sucked along the boiler tubes and ended up in the smoke box would need to be cleaned out, and then every nut and bolt and valve would be greased and oiled and checked. Messy, dirty work. Who in there right minds would miss that? And yet some would, he knew.

He inspected the tender and shook his head at the poor quality of the coal.

'That'll never get us up the Girvan bank!' he thought.

That was another reason why steam had to go. The mining industry, especially in Scotland, was suffering badly, and over-mined coal seams and mechanised mining were no longer producing the size and quality of coal needed. Great big chunks that held the heat; that was what was needed to keep an engine like this steamed up for miles, not the dross they were supplied with nowadays.

'It's a good job we'll have a banker, then.' Davey McCally answered. He was fireman today and he climbed up beside Joe and immediately filled a large wooden box with some choice bits from the coal box.

'Reedlerye Farm,' he said. Joe nodded.

The journey began. With the help of a banker, they made it up the Girvan bank in spite of the fine rain and some light leaf fall that made adhesion difficult. Barrhill behind them, they were on route to Stranraer.

On the return journey, Joe halted at Reedlerye Farm. A woman was waving at them from the field. She had a basket of vegetables in one hand and two empty tin buckets at her feet.

'Can ye spare a couple o' rakes o' coal, son?' she called up to Davey.

'I've got them here for you, Mrs Drummond,' he said. He jumped down and brought up the buckets.

'These are the best we've got,' he said, filling the buckets with the coal he'd set aside as he spoke. 'The coal's been terrible lately.'

'Not to me. I'm glad o' it, son.'

Davey was fifty-five years old and smiled inwardly at being addressed as 'son.' When he handed her the buckets, she offered him the basket. It contained a couple of stones of potatoes and a few turnips.

'Oh ya beauty! Tatties an' Tumchies!' Davey said gleefully. He emptied the vegetables into the now empty box and tossed the basket back out to Mrs Drummond.

'How's Fred?' Joe shouted.

'Fair to middling. He's just about managing to get dressed and sit in his armchair. It's his breathing that worries me. I'll tell him you were asking. Thanks for the coal. I'm right sick o' wood smoke. And the heat doesn't last as long as the coal, and anyway, Fred's past chopping wood now. I'm getting no' bad at it myself,' she added proudly.

'We'll drop off another couple of rakes tomorrow, Mrs D. Same time.'

She waved them away and they watched her trek across the field to the farm cottage.

Davey turned his attention to the box of vegetables.

'There's five tumchies. Do you want me to halve one and we'll take two and a half each?'

'Naw, naw. One will be enough for me. You can take the rest. Julie and me like a bit o' turnip, but the kids won't eat it. Too well looked after, that's their problem. Shove in a few o' thae Ayrshires as well. There's nuthin' beats a good Ayrshire tattie.'

'O.K. I'll divide the rest among my lot when I get home. That's the worst of living within a craw's cry of each other. They'll eat ye out o' house and home in no time!'

Davey's family was grown now and all had their own homes

in the same street as their parents. The street was called Carr Street, but the locals called it McCally Street. Some people actually thought that that was the real name of the street and the postman happily delivered letters addressed to McCally Street without batting an eye.

As the light faded, they sped towards Saltcoats and home. Saltcoats' signal box loomed large and red signals were displayed. This was usual and Joe stopped for a few minutes to allow the Glasgow bound express from Ayr to pass. Turning his head to the right, he was dismayed to see a gang of boys dancing about on top of the coal ree, and chucking the biggest boulders of coal all over the sleepers and into the bushes beyond. He blew the horn and they looked across at him.

'Get away from there. You're on Railway property and I'll keep sounding this horn until the police come.'

'Aw Naw,' the familiar voice of Wee Fella Gow said loudly. 'It's old Gillan. He knows me an' he'll tell ma da, that's for sure.'

'Wee Fella Gow. I might have known! Get off that coal and stop squandering it.'

He sounded the horn again and this time he attracted the attention of the signalman, who shouted at the boys. They jumped off the coal stack, laughing and shouting abuse back to the railwaymen, and disappeared under a gap between the bottom of the fence and the ground that only a dog or a youngster could negotiate. Their voices could still be heard in the night air until the express train thundered by and drowned out everything.

Joe was indignant as he discussed the incident with Davey. 'I wouldn't mind if they were sneaking in to steal coal that would be put to good use, but to brazenly throw the coal about, just to waste it, for the fun of it, that's sheer vandalism. There's no excuse for that.'

It never occurred to either man that they'd stolen a couple of pailfuls themselves today. But they had given that away to help a sick man and his hard-working wife. That, apparently, came under 'acceptable.'

'If you know that lad, you'd better tell his dad. It's too dangerous for them to be anywhere near a railway. If they'd ventured on to the track, that express train would have made mincemeat of the lot of them,' said Davey.

Early the following day, Joe made a point of mentioning the incident to Wee Fella Gow's dad. Mr Gow, to his credit, took the story very seriously and promised to have a word with his errant son. 'Not that I expect it to do any good,' he said dispassionately. 'Can't get him to listen to a word I say. Can't tober him, no way! He's always in some sort of trouble, that boy.'

✧✧ ✧✧

Julie started to speak to him when he clattered through the back door some time later carrying little Joey's bike.

'Just wait till you read this –' she began, but Joe interrupted.

'Look what I found outside in the street,' he growled angrily. 'Our Joey's new bike! I warned him that he had to take care of it. It would serve him right if somebody stole it. It's only a lucky chance that it was me who found it, otherwise someone would have made off with it. If he loses this bike, there's no way I'm replacing it! I've a good mind to ban him from using it for a week. Does he think I'm made of money?'

Julie shrugged and went into the living room miffed, and mouthing 'Nag, nag, nag!' under her breath. 'He's always whinging about something. Why can't he ever come home happy?'

Joe shoved the bike in the space under the stairs and said, 'What were you saying, love?' Totally oblivious to her mood, he was now ready to speak to her. It would never cease to amaze her. She gave up trying to be noticed for her own sake.

'Read for yourself.' She handed him a postcard and watched an incredulous smile creep over his face. It was one of those 'My New Number' type postcards, and it was from, of all people, his mum, Katie. 'Well I never! It's my mother's phone number!' he declared in disbelief. 'I'll never believe this until I actually ring her up and she answers. Look what's scrawled along the bottom – a present from Aunt Lily.' He sat down and stared at the card, reading it several times.

'She'll love that. She'll run up some bill phoning everybody she knows. Imagine the old dear being the first in the family to get a phone!' He still couldn't get over it, and chuckled away until Julie said, 'Maybe its time we got connected. Everyone's getting a phone these days.'

'I don't think so, Julie. There's a perfectly good phone box at the end of the road. We don't need one of our own. Think of the connection charges and the rental, not to mention the actual cost of the calls you make.'

'I might have known you'd be a scrooge! It would be a great convenience. Come to think of it, that's what the kids in this neighbourhood think that phone box is – a convenience! Have you ever smelled the inside of it? Last time I used it I had to hold the door open with my elbow the whole time.'

'Too convenient, that's what I think. I don't want the Railway to be able to get in touch with me too easily. Rice Krispie says that since he got the phone in, the gaffer is never off the line wanting him to take on extra shifts at a moments notice every time somebody doesn't turn up for work.'

'There's ways round that. You don't answer the phone, I'll say you're not in. Seriously, though, Joe. The phone could save our lives in an emergency.'

'We'll see. Let me think about it. C'mon, let's go and phone Ma and let her know we got her card.'

'Are you sure? Do you not think we should just send her a letter? The post is said to be very reliable. No need for us to use any new-fangled gadgets. We've been using a perfectly good postal system for years now. Wait here while I run to the post office and get stamps. I'm sure you can buy a book of Penny Blacks now.'

༄༄ ༄༄

Martha McLaughlin's house, in the Kylepark area of Uddingston, proved to be ideal for Lily. It was a six-bedroom villa with its own driveway and an enormous garden. Lily loved the place on sight, and Martha too. *She* was a sprightly seventy-four-year old with a quick tongue and a roguish sense of humour. She had been running her home as a boarding house for over thirty years. Within a week of meeting her, Lily, with Katie's approval, had moved in, and a whole new way of life opened up to her. Her new landlady fast became a new friend and they often sat up till midnight talking.

'How long have you lived here, Martha?' Lily asked one evening as they toasted their feet on the warm hearth tiles in the big kitchen.

'All my life. I was brought up here. This was my parents' home. I've never lived any where else.'

'Oh. So did your husband come to live here with you, then?'

'No, no m'dear. I've never been married. I'm *Miss* McLaughlin, really, but for some reason, people assume that I'm a widow and call me *Mrs* McLaughlin. I think it's because I look like I must be somebody's mother. I'm a sort of motherly type, don't you think? Fat, round and always doing a washing. (Well, with a boarding house to run, you've always got a washing to do, haven't you?) I couldn't be a spinster, now could I? Everybody knows that spinsters are thin, sharp-featured and keep cats. Me, I can't abide cats! Hate them. Would kill them all if I could. Her next door, your friend Eddie's sister, she hates cats too, so between us we chase them all away and keep the place clear of the sleekit creatures! Anyway, what was I saying? Oh yes, I don't bother trying to correct people any more when they call me *Mrs*. It's a waste of time. Anyway, I rather like it really. It makes me feel less vulnerable somehow, when I'm taking in new boarders, so I don't let on.'

'Your secret is safe with me.' Lily assured her, laughing. But she had suffered her first disappointment in Martha, because Lily loved cats and it had crossed her mind to maybe get a little kitten for company, now that she was settled in.

Martha gave a long yawn and said, 'I'd better get myself off to bed. I'm up at five-thirty in the morning. Mr Phillips in the end room needs his breakfast at six o'clock. I'll take up these sheets on the way.' She lifted a pile of laundry that she had ironed earlier.

'Give me that,' said Lily. 'I'll carry it up. You rake out the fire.'

'Thank you dearie. I'll be able to hang on to the banister on my way upstairs. A great luxury for a tired old body.'

On her first day off, Lily got an insight into the colossal amount of work that Martha got through in a day. She came down that morning to find Martha struggling to fold one of a pile of heavy blankets that she'd just brought in from the washing line. Lily immediately grabbed an end, and the job was done in no time.

'It's great to have another woman in the house,' smiled a grateful Martha. 'All my boarders have always been men. You're the first woman. I suppose it's because it's mostly men who leave home to find work and they are the ones in lodgings, but things are changing nowadays. The war changed everything.'

It was while they were having their 'wee settling cup', as Martha liked to call the last cup of tea before retiring, that Martha asked Lily how she might feel about giving up her job and helping her run the boarding house. She was getting on a bit now and looking after the residents in the other rooms was hard work. Lily was ecstatic about the idea. She hated her job. So a wage was agreed, a list of duties set up and time off arranged. Lily left the smelly rubber apron and the fish scales behind and became Martha McLaughlin's live in domestic help. But it was more like her home than a 'position'. Martha and Lily were just like a little family. Katie became a regular visitor and so did Lily's daughter, Barbara. Another visitor who came regularly to see how she did, was Eddie McKenna. He came every time he paid a call on his sister next door, which Martha declared he'd done more often lately than he'd ever done before.

Katie had joyous news for them one day. She was going to have a visit from her son Chris, who worked on the railway up in Aberdeen. She hadn't seen Chris and Connie or her Aberdonian grandchildren for two years. So she arranged for Joe and Dan and their families to come, and she invited Lily and Martha too. There would be a big party. She said that it was all because of the telephone that Lily had given her as a thank you present when she left to move in with Martha. She was able to get in touch more easily, and visits could be arranged there and then.

The party was a great success. Katie was jubilant for days afterwards, just remembering the joy of seeing her all grandchildren and having the chance to fuss over her boys again, all together in her house. A little later, Katie got a call from Julie to say that their new phone was connected. Joe had given in at last. They all had phones now. The Gillans were on the up, and all was right with the world. But the Gillans were no different from any other family on the face of the earth. They can have their 'ups', but they can also have their 'downs'.

∞∞ ∞∞

Between Stevenson and Ardrossan, the railway line ran alongside the seashore. Halfway between the two towns, there was a wooden bridge across the railway that linked the main road to the shore road. Wee Fella Gow sat up on the parapet trying to pull up a large cement slab out of Bobby Tipney's grubby wee hands.

'I cannae grip it,' he said to Bobby. 'Put your toe in that hole and rest it on your knee. Then I'll be able to pull it up.'

'It's piggin' heavy man, we'll never be able to get it over. Let's just throw a stone instead.'

'A stone's nae use. It'll just bounce off. C'mon. Shove hard. We've got loads of time. The train will only be leaving Largs just now, but I want to make sure we're ready. Old man Gillan will be driving it and I want to give him the fright of his life. It'll teach him to klipe on me. I got a hammering, and it's all his fault.' But the slab was heavy and they let it rest on the floor of the bridge for a while.

Wee Fella Gow was right. The train that the two malicious wee culprits were laying in wait for was pulling out of Largs at that moment. And Wee Fella Gow had done his homework. Joe Gillan was driving.

Joe had noticed a bunch of men running for the train, as he was about to set out. They had obviously been fishing and came hurrying through the ticket barrier carrying their rods and metal boxes containing their equipment and the fish they'd caught. They stumbled along the platform calling out, 'Wait! Wait!' And laughing, they all bundled in to the nearest compartment. Joe was sure it was the first class compartment and he knew that it was already occupied by two smart men in business suits. He thought no more about it until John Cummings, the conductor, put his head into the cab.

'You'll never guess what I've just done!' he said. 'Only insulted some first class passengers who are threatening to report me for my cheek.'

Joe laughed. 'What happened?'

'Ach, two smart-suited snobby guys had been in the compartment when we were about to leave Largs. Then a bunch of fishermen with rods and waders and stuff came in at the last minute and joined them.'

'Aye, I saw them.' Joe said.

'They were wet and soggy and they'd been drinking too, you could tell. Anyway I left it because I thought, 'I'll see to them at Fairlie.' But I was too busy and I didn't have time to get to the first classers, but I noticed the posh men were looking unhappy. I was going to ignore it, but at West Kilbride, I thought, 'I better check those fishermen's tickets and move them out to another compartment.'

As John related his story, a few miles away, Wee Fella Gow sent Bobby to the edge of the bridge to see if he could see the time on the town hall clock. An empty freight train trundled slowly past and the driver made a sign with his thumb to Wee Fella Gow to get down from the parapet. Wee Fella Gow pretended not to notice. Bobby came back and it was obvious that his nerve was going.

'Your dad warned you to stay off railway property,' he said, in a half-hearted attempt to dissuade Wee Fella Gow from his plan.

'I'm not on railway property; I'm on the public footbridge. Give us up that slab. The train'll be here soon.'

'Gie it a minute yet. You'll not be able to balance it for long.'

'Aye, okay.' Wee Fella Gow swung his dangling legs and waited another wee while.

Back on the train John was continuing with his story.

'I went in to the compartment and the men were all laughing and telling stories in a good-humoured way, and the smell of fish was overpowering. I said, "I'll have to check your tickets, lads. This is a first class compartment." Imagine my amazement when they all produced first class tickets, bought and paid for. "Sorry, gents," I said. "But I had to check. It's my job."

"That's okay," they said, but as I turned to go, they called me back.

"Hey, hey! Are you not going to check *their* tickets?" they said, pointing to the city gents. I was embarrassed. "Oh, yes. Of course. Tickets please, gents!" I said. It turned out that the smart-suited bastards were the stowaways, with no tickets at all. Can you believe it? I had to eject them P.D.Q.

'What?' Joe laughed. 'You're joking! The nerve of some people!'

'You should have heard the fishermen,' said John.

"You were quite happy to believe that we were the fraudsters," they said. "You were judging by appearances." And they were right, I was. "You should be reported!"

But the truth is, they were so busy laughing at the fool I'd made of myself, that I don't think they will. '

'If that don't teach us a lesson!' said Joe, laughing heartily. 'Wait till I tell Julie that.'

They were still laughing when they neared Ardrossan, unaware that Wee Fella Gow was planning his surprise.

'Right here's the train,' shouted Wee Fella Gow. 'Gimmee up the slab!'

He twisted round, but Bobby let the slab drop. Wee Fella Gow tried to grab it and lost his balance. He fell forwards. Joe saw it happen and slammed on the brakes shouting.

'CHRIST ALMIGHTY! CHRIST ALMIGHTY!'

But he knew it was already too late. He was never to forget

the look on that eleven-year-old boy's face. That tuft of brilliant red hair and cheekily freckled face, the horrified eyes staring at him through the window as he slipped from view under the front of the engine, would haunt his dreams forever.

Chapter 11

Belt Up!

'No, Katie, he hasn't changed his mind since this morning. He still doesn't want to see anyone.'

A pause while she listened. Then she continued.

'I know you're his mother. He knows that too. I did. I did try.'

Another pause, listening.

'Only half a cup of tea and a wee bit toast. No. He's hardly eaten at all since it happened.' Her voice was subdued and weary.

Listening again.

'I've tried. Believe me, I've tried. He has hardly left that room since the inquest. He won't get out of bed. He won't shave. He won't let anyone in. He won't even see the doctor anymore. I'm at my wits' end. To tell the truth, I don't know how I'm coping. It's hellish, it really is!'

Yet another pause.

'I'll tell him, but he knows, he knows. Thanks Katie. Yes, yes. The kids are fine. Well, you know what kids are! They don't fully understand. Friday? Yeah, that would be great. I'll let you know. Thanks. O.K. O.K. Cheerio.'

Julie hung up the phone, threw herself down on the couch and burst into tears. She'd spent a lot of time crying lately. Not just because of the tragedy, but also because of the affect it had had on Joe. He suffered from immediate shock at the time of the incident and to Julie, it was as if he had died too, because the man huddled in blankets on the bed upstairs certainly wasn't her Joe. He was a stranger. Someone she didn't know. She'd complained often enough that he was such a grump, but this – this was something else! Moody, taciturn, long silences, bad-tempered outbursts – then there was maudlin and weepy, greetin' intae his tea. She didn't know which was worse or how long she could cope with any of it. She'd coaxed, pleaded, cried, tried yelling back. Nothing restored her Joe to her. It was ten weeks now since the accident. And it was eight weeks since Wee Fella Gow's funeral, and she was still living with this stranger. God knows what it must be like in the Gow household, if this was what Joe was going through.

Joe refused to discuss the incident, refused all offers of help, refused food, existing only on a few mouthfuls of toast and cups of tea. He didn't want visitors –'ESPECIALLY MY MOTHER!' He ranted and raved at the kids for making the least wee bit of noise and generally spread gloom and trepidation around freely. Julie had already stopped going to the shops. Thank God for Isabel next door, who went in her stead. The last time Julie had ventured out, she couldn't get away from people asking impertinent questions:

'I hear he's taken it really bad. What's he like?'

'Is he not over it yet?'

'How is he now? No sign of any improvement?'

Or offering unsolicited advice:

'Tell him to give himself a shake. It wasn't his fault. He's got his own kids to think about.'

'He can apply for counselling, did you know? Tell him.'

'The best thing he can do is get back to work right away. It's like fallin' off a horse. The longer he leaves it, the harder it will get. He's got to get back in the saddle. Tell him!'

What the hell did Ina Pearson know about falling off a horse? She was brought up in the tenements of Clydebank! The only saddle she knew was the one on her kid's trike! Cheek! All of it! Tell him this. Tell him that. Tell them all to bugger off!

Julie drifted off into an uncomfortable dozy sleep.

The kids banged their way in from school, waking her with a start. Holly ran upstairs before Julie could stop her.

'I've made a get-well card for you, daddy. Look!' She bounced over to the bed and bent over her father who was facing the opposite wall and shoved a painted sheet of folded paper towards his face. It was still slightly damp and smelled of school. Joe twisted round and looked at it.

'That's lovely, kitten.' He said without smiling.

'I hope it makes you better.'

'It does, honey. It does. But I'm not ill, only a wee bit tired.'

Holly propped her work of art against the lamp on the bedside table and turned back to the bed. She pulled at the candlewick, which was trailing on the floor, trying to straighten it like a little mother hen.

'Beth Brennan says you're ill. She says her dad says you're going mental. What does that mean?'

Holly jumped back as Joe suddenly shouted at her.

'And who are you going to believe, eh? Me or Beth Brennan?' Joe looked so fierce all at once. 'Where's your mother? Can she not keep you lot downstairs and let me get a bit of peace? Get out of here and leave me alone!'

His brow clouded a little when he saw the horrified tears in Holly's eyes. He rubbed a hand over his stubbly chin and in a quieter voice said, 'I'm sorry, Princess. Daddy didn't mean to shout. I just need some sleep. Thanks for the card. You go back downstairs and get your tea. Leave Daddy alone just now.'

But the damage was done. Holly backed out of the room, traumatised. Her dad had never, ever shouted at her. He'd shouted at Joey. He'd shouted at Catherine. But she was his wee pet. His wee Princess. He'd never raised his voice to *her*!

She choked back the tears until she got back downstairs and then they flooded out.

'Daddy sh-shouted at m-me.' She got the words out between sobs.

'C'mere, Precious.' Julie opened her arms. 'I've tried to explain before. You have to forgive daddy. He's not himself. He's not well just now and it's making him say things he doesn't mean.'

'He – he says he *is* well. He's j-just tired.'

'I know, darlin'. But he doesn't know he's not well. That kind of tiredness is an illness. Mammy is going to get help for him.' She held Holly tightly, rocking her to and fro, her brow set in a determined line.

'*That does it!*' she thought. She pacified Holly, fed them all, and when she'd done that, she phoned her mother-in-law.

'Katie, can you come tomorrow?' She whispered down the line. 'Don't wait till Friday. We have to do something – anything. Now. I can't cope any more. It's getting to the kids and I don't know what to do. Today is just the last straw.'

She told Katie what had happened.

'I'll be there tomorrow.' Katie went away to pack a bag immediately.

Julie put the receiver back and looked at the ceiling towards Joe's room.

'Like it or not, Sunshine! Your mother's coming! And please God she can do something with you, because I sure as hell can't.'

⁓

In the Railway Club, and in the bothy, they had a whip-round for Mr and Mrs Gow. It was the least they could do. Well, it was *all* they could do, really. But when it came to discussing what they could do for Joe Gillan, that was a different matter.

'He's really spooked this time,' said Davey McCally, one day in the bothy. He was seated at the table with others, waiting for his train to come into platform four. Some were just finished their shift, while some, like Davey, were waiting for the 'off.'

'What do you mean – '*this time*'?' asked Oweny, pouring the dregs of lukewarm coffee into the discoloured plastic cup that doubled as a screw-on top for his grubby thermos.

'Well this is the third time that Joe has had a jumper.'

'You're joking! I never knew that! He's had two previous, and he's still driving? I don't think I could handle that. I'd be in the loony bin b'noo!'

The awkward silence and sideways glances that followed brought him up short to the pertinent significance of what he'd just said.

'I mean – er, -I mean –.'

'We know what you mean, Oweny. We all hope Joe'll be back at work soon.'

'Do you not remember yon man at Crookston about four years ago? Took a flier off the platform right in front of the train. Weans on the platform an' all! Well, Joe got *him*. Screaming weans and woman everywhere. Deafening, they say. Joe couldn't speak for two weeks after that one. Stuttered for weeks.' Neil Rice loved relating all the gory details. He took a long, luxurious draw on his cigarette before stubbing it out on one of the tin lids that served as the bothy's ashtrays.

Oweny racked his brain to remember. 'Aye,' he said slowly. 'I remember that.'

'Aye, but even though he couldn't speak, he was back at work within a week that time,' Ronald Eadie said.

'What about the guy just outside Polmadie, a while back?'

'Naw, that was wee Stevie Cullen that got him. He never drove a train again.'

'Can ye wonder?'

'Who was the other one that Joe got?' Nobody answered for a while.

'I cannae remember. There's getting to be so many.' Quite a few drivers had suffered this fate more than once, the railway being a common choice for many suicides.

'I think it was yon woman at Bridge Newton.'

'Oh God. I cannae take this any mair. No' when it's a woman! Can we no' change the subject?' Jim Bonar was no Neil Rice.

'We're trying to think how we can help Joe,' said Davey. 'Avoiding the subject is too easy.'

'Well, if ye ask me,' said Neil, 'I think Joe's finished this time. He's not going to drive again. The point is, he knew the wee lad, ye see! That makes it worse.'

'I suppose so. It's bad enough when it's a stranger that jumps, but a wee boy you know —. ' Oweny trailed off, ending by blowing out a long 'Phew!'

'Technically speaking, this wee lad was not a jumper. He fell. He didn't mean to fall, but the thing is, he was up to no good, it has to be said. If he had succeeded in throwing that concrete slab onto the line, he could have derailed the train. God knows how many more deaths there would have been, Joe's among them!'

They all fell silent as they digested this. Railway accidents always had the affect of drawing strong opinions from the men. The general public were mostly unaware and unconcerned at the prevalence of such occurrences. They only knew that their train was delayed and complained unceasingly and uncomprehendingly when told that there had been 'an incident' on the line that caused the delay. They continued to grumble about the poor service.

With few exceptions, railwaymen were incredibly sensitive at such times, because none were spared the emotional cost. Sooner or later, you got to share in the cleaning up that was the grisly last episode in any fatality. At no other time was their sense of comradeship so apparent. In most people's minds, fire crews, ambulance men, policemen were the heroes at the forefront when it came to dealing with human tragedy. It was their job, after all. That's why they were called 'The Emergency Services.' And they *were* heroes, no doubt about that. They were trained to deal with harrowing events. Public services, on the other hand, were left out of the equation. They had procedural training, of course, but no emotional training. Who would know that the ordinary, untrained, just-doing-his job little railwayman might take it badly and vomit his guts up when asked to hose the front (and the sides and the top and underneath) of an engine that had been targeted by a poor tragic soul, bits of whom would never make it to the inside of his coffin. Unsung heroes, they were.

'What we mustn't forget here is that that kid had bad intentions and I have only a limited amount of sympathy for him. It's the likes of him that makes our job dangerous. If he'd succeeded in throwing that slab onto the line, I'll bet he wouldnae be taking to *his* bed with the trauma of it. He'd be laughing at the trouble he'd caused.' This was Neil Rice's opinion.

Oweny was a bit shocked at this outburst; though it was not the first time he'd heard these sentiments. 'Aw, come on now Neil, I think you're being a bit harsh. The wee lad was only eleven. He would have no full understanding of the implications of his actions. It was just a kid's prank gone wrong.'

'Naw, naw. I cannae see it like that. And if I were Joe, I'd be hanged if I let a wee bugger like that lose me a day's wages, never mind ten weeks. I'd be at my work the next day! Anyway, I better be off,' he said, getting up. Neil was a guard and part of his issued equipment was a large brown leather shoulder bag in which he kept all the paraphernalia he might need: whistle, flags, rule book, Daily Record. Stuff like that. This was lying at his feet and he kicked it aside now to rise from the table.

'It's time I was away. I'll get to the toilet before I go. If Shug Hughes comes looking for me, tell him I'll be right there.' He headed for the toilet.

The men gave each other a look.

'What do ye make of him – *'If I was Joe, I'd get to ma work,"* mimicked Davey sarcastically. 'It's obvious he hasn't a clue what poor Joe is suffering.'

'Let's get him,' said Oweny, his usual devilry springing into action.

He lifted two heavy fishplates, which are used to connect long lengths of track together, from a pile that was lying in the corner and stuffed them quickly into one of the compartments in Neil's large shoulder bag, adjusting the inside flap so that they would not immediately be seen. He just had time to close the bag again before Neil came hurrying back. He hoisted the bag onto his shoulder.

'See you later, guys,' then, 'Christ, this bag gets heavier every bloody day. The older I get, the heavier it becomes. Cheerio.'

He bustled out of the door just before the others fell about laughing.

It was decided that Davey should get in touch with Dan Gillan and ask how best they might help his brother.

It was another three weeks before Neil discovered he'd been carrying around two heavy fishplates in his shoulder bag.

෴ ෴

'Ma!'

Two seconds later - 'Ma!'

Another two seconds later - 'Are ye there, ma?'

The call was faint but Agnes heard it above the wish-wash of her twin-tub. It came from outside in the backcourt.

'For God's sake! What does he want now?' she muttered. It would do no good to ignore him. He could go on for hours. She leant across the sink and lifted the window open, her head barely reaching outside.

'What is it, Danny?' she called down. 'I'm busy!'

He was standing with some of his pals, fifteen feet or so beneath the window, all of them looking up.

'Ma, can I take the mattress out of that manky old pram that's in the coal cellar? We want it up the park.'

'Yes. Take it away. What are ye asking me for? It was you who brought it here in the first place. You be back by twelve o'clock, mind! D'ye hear? I'm taking you and Tommy for a haircut.' She closed the window.

A minute later Danny banged open the door and ran along the hall to the cluttered cubbyhole where everything in the house that wasn't being used at that moment was 'tidied bye.' He rummaged noisily.

'What are you doing?' Agnes called. 'I thought you were going up the park?'

'We are, but I need some of my stuff.' His head was inside the old chest the kids used as a toy box.

'What's that you say?' Agnes had squeezed past the twin-tub in the cramped scullery and was in the hall, coming towards him now.

'Tosh, Meeksie and Gavin and me are going to play at cavalrymen. I need a saddle, so I want something to tie the pram mattress on to the horse in the swing park.' He clattered toys about noisily in his search. Three boys were standing on the landing, staring through the open door, waiting for him.

'Guys!' called Danny. 'Come and help me carry this stuff.'

The boys looked at Agnes. She nodded resignedly and they

hurried forward into the house to help Danny with his haul. This consisted of a cowboy hat, two guns, two holsters and Debbie's skipping rope among other paraphernalia that might come in useful to a cavalryman.

'Make sure you bring all that back. You better not leave it lying up the park. You'll be sent right back up for it, if you do,' Agnes said, returning to the scullery and her washing. 'You be back in time for the barber's, now. I'm warning you!'

'Aye. Aye. I hear ye, ma. I won't be late.' Danny was impatient to be off. Straightening up, he caught sight of a leather belt dangling down from Paddy's railway uniform, hanging on a hook just above his head.

'The very dab!' he cried, visualising his saddle neatly strapped to his steed. He pulled the belt through the loops of Paddy's trousers and buckled it round his waist.

Agnes heard them clatter down the stairs and away, arguing about who was to be General 'Custard.' At times like these, Agnes had to admit to a grudging sympathy for Granny Park. 'It's not just your own kids you have to put up with. It's all their pals, too. If I had a choice, I wouldn't want to live beside me, either.'

The 'horse' in the swing park was nothing more than a long wooden pole with a horse's head at one end and a few iron handles secured at intervals along it so that several kids could hold on as they sat astride it. It was suspended from a framework and could be moved backwards and forwards by the rider or riders pushing off the ground with their feet. It could become uncomfortable after a while and that was where Danny got the excellent idea of using the old pram mattress as a cushion. With Paddy's good leather belt securing this to the pole, he was the only one with a saddle, so he had to be General Custard, leading from the front, and with Debbie's skipping rope draped over the horse's mouth, he could even rein in his horse at will. This was as near the real thing as you could get!

A happy hour or so passed before they tired of cavalrymen and ran off to play on the rope swing across the burn, now that the big lads who'd been there all morning had moved away.

࿎ঙ࿎ ঙ࿎

Danny was in mid-swing when he heard the wee man shouting.

'Danny. You've to come at once. You're wanted. Ma's mad!'

'Oh, crikey!' Danny scuffed his shoes hard on the gravely dirt under the tree. 'I forgot the time. I'm for it.' He came to a sharp halt and disentangled himself from the knotted rope, stumbling over some half hidden roots at the base of the tree.

'Give us a hand, guys! I've got to carry all this stuff back home.'

'No way!' came a chorus. 'If we leave the rope swing, we'll never get it again. That gang by the roundabout is just waiting to snatch it when we go.'

'Aw, come on guys! I cannae carry all this by myself!'

'Get yer wee brother to help. We're staying!'

Danny knew he didn't have time to argue and enlisted wee man's help with –

'Right wee man, let's get this stuff home!'

Tommy lifted one of the guns and put the cowboy hat on his head while Danny gathered up the mattress and whatever else he could carry. Wee man was swinging his father's leather belt around his head.

'Get the Skipping rope wee man!' Danny ordered. Wee man did as he was told.

They made for the track that led towards the road. On the way home, it started to rain, sparsely at first, but with those large, heavy drops that herald a real downpour. They picked up the pace and began to run, Tommy levelling his gun and shooting at imaginary enemies along the way. He transferred his gun to the other hand to get a better aim at a crow's nest high above. Unnoticed, the leather belt fell to the ground just outside Mrs Katie Gillan's front gate. The rain came down heavier and just as they got inside Hatton Close, the deluge started fast and furious. They carried their burdens up the stairs to the first floor, the sound of the rain thundering in their ears from the glass skylight on the roof.

'Wow! We made it just in time. I hope Tosh, Meeksie and Gavin get soaked. It will serve them right!' Danny was laughing, but stopped abruptly when Agnes suddenly opened the door just as he reached for the handle. He closed his eyes and waited for the tirade.

Instead, his mother asked anxiously, 'Are you wet?'

His eyes opened, slowly and suspiciously. 'Naw, only a wee bit. We got here before it came down heavy.'

'Thank God for that! Put that stuff away and get your hands washed. There's an egg sandwich for you both on the table. Do you want milk with it, or tea?'

'What about the barber's?'

'Well we can't go out in that rain. It's just as well you were late, boy. If you'd been home in time to eat your lunch and get ready, we'd have been caught right in it. We'd be half way to the barber's right now, soaked to the skin.' She ruffled their curly mops. 'So forget the haircuts. You can continue to look like wee scruffs for a day or two yet. I just hope the Social doesn't catch sight of you; they'll take you into care.'

Danny let out a low whistle when he and the wee man shared the sink.

'I don't want a piece on egg,' wee man said.

'When we get back in there, you eat it and shut up,' said Danny. 'I wouldnae push ma luck, if I was you.'

ക⁓ ക⁓

Jamsie held the net curtain back and stared out at the rain.

'It's still torrenting down out there, ma,' he said. 'You couldn't possibly go out in it. The street's like a river and there's a lake forming under the bridge already. You're going to miss your train.'

Katie tried again to click her suitcase shut. 'I'll get the next one. Julie's not expecting me till tea time so I've got loads of time. Here, Jamsie! See if you can get this case to stay shut. It keeps clicking open again.'

'What have ye got in here, ma? It's bulging! And it's a gey old case. It's time you had a new one.'

'What for? Where do I ever go that I need a case? This was your father's case and a great servant it's been. I use it to take that big eiderdown of yours to the laundry, and I store things in it all the time. It's no' just taking up space.' What Katie meant was, she hides the Christmas presents in it every year, but she didn't want to reveal that. Then she added quietly, 'We used it when your dad went into hospital.'

'Aye, I remember.' Jamsie used brute force and managed to get the case to stay shut.

'It'll not be so heavy coming back. I've got presents for the kids in it. They could do with cheering up, I'm sure. I've got a good warm cardigan for Julie, too. She always looks frozen, that girl. I got it in Grafton's this morning.'

Jamsie eyed the case with suspicion. 'I'm not happy about the clasps on that thing. Have you not got anything else you could use? I could tie some strong string round it.'

Katie was aghast. 'You'll do no such thing! I'm not travelling to Saltcoats looking like a tattie hawker!'

Jamsie laughed and gave her a hug. 'You're priceless, ma!' he said. 'What will you look like if the case falls open in the middle of Central Station?'

'Oh, don't even *say* that, Jamsie. I'd be mortified. Do you think it might?'

Jamsie picked up the case and gave it a good shake. 'Seems okay. I think it'll hold.'

Katie went to the window again. Barely discernible under the dark sky, two small figures scurried past, holding their sodden jackets over their heads against the pelting rain. 'There goes wee Tosh McIness and Scott Meek. They're drenched right through!'

A third figure followed a little way behind. Gavin Daly.

'Their mothers will have some washing to do!' said Katie, always conscious of the chores woman have to face through no fault of their own.

She came away from the window and sat down. After a while, there was a sudden brightness as strong sunlight unexpectedly filled the room.

'I don't believe it! The rain has stopped. Look at that sky! It's bright and blue and not a cloud to be seen.'

It was true. That old Scottish phenomenon, the weather, had changed in the blinking of an eye. Steam was already rising from the pavement outside. As quickly as it had begun, the rain had disappeared and a beautiful summer's day returned.

'Right, ma. Let's get going!'

Katie donned her light raincoat and affixed a jaunty straw hat to her head with a pearl hatpin. 'All set.'

They locked the door behind them and walked down the path to the street, where Jamsie spotted the leather belt lying by the gate.

'Here, ma, look at this. It's a good strong leather strap. Just what we need for your suitcase! Give me a minute.'

He darted back to the house and gave the belt a good drying with an old towelling floor cloth. Within a few minutes, Mrs Gillan had boarded her train for Glasgow Central where she would get her connection for Saltcoats. Jamsie stood by the window to wave her off. 'Tell Joe I'm thinking of him! I hope he's on the mend soon. It's a terrible thing to have to live through. Give me a call when you get there.'

Katie settled down happily in her seat, perfectly safe in the knowledge that her old suitcase would not burst open now. Paddy Preston's good leather belt was securely buckled around it.

❧❧ ❧❧

Paddy was sifting through the clothes on the coat hooks with one hand. The other hand was clutching the waist of his work trousers tightly.

'Aggie, have you seen my belt!'

'What belt?'

'What do you mean, *What Belt?* My work belt, of course! The one with the Texas Star buckle that your brother sent me from America! It's the only belt I've got, for heaven's sake!'

'It should be there, with your work clothes.'

'Well I can't find it. Where could it have got to?'

He looked behind the toy box in case it had fallen down there, then into the bedroom, ransacking through drawers and wardrobes and looking under the bed. Back in the living room, he lifted cushions and shifted magazines. Agnes came to help, asking the usual questions that are always answered with other questions and eventually lead to exasperation.

'Was it not on your trousers?'

'Does it look like it?'

'Where did you leave it?'

'If I knew that I would go and get it, wouldn't I?'

'Did you leave it at work?'

'And what would have kept my trousers up on the way home?'

'Could it be in the car?'

'What would I take my belt off in the car for?'

'Did you look on the hooks in the cubby-hole?'

179

'Well of course I did. Where do you think I hang it up every night?'

'When did you see it last? Could one of the kids have taken it?'

'I hope not. They're for it if they did. They should know by now not to touch any of my work clothes.'

Paddy gave up. 'I cannae waste any more time on it; I'll be late. What can I use, Agnes?'

'You'll have to wear the old braces. Luckily those old trousers still have the buttons for them.'

Braces it was, and Paddy left for work making dire predictions as to what the culprit who took his belt was going to suffer when discovered.

๛๛ ๛๛

Catherine gave a twirl, glancing at her reflection on the blank T.V screen. 'Thank you for the pyjamas, Gran. They're great! I always wanted a pair of Baby Dolls.'

'You're welcome darlin'. Well, the girl in the shop told me they were all the rage, and I have to agree, you look good in them. They certainly will be a lot cooler in this fine weather.' Katie replied.

'Joey, what do you say to your Granny for the lovely pyjamas?'

Joey went over nervously and planted a quick kiss on Katie's cheek, then he retreated across the room to place his back against the wall, and stare at her from what he considered a safe distance. Gran Gillan didn't fool him when she was all smiles and presents. He had a good memory, and he could still feel that skelp on the bum she'd given him for climbing on the neighbour's wall, last time *they'd* visited *her*, when uncle Chris was home from Aberdeen. In front of all his cousins, too! You never knew with Gran Gillan. Keep your back to the wall while she's here, that was his advice, if anyone was interested!

180

He watched disgustedly as sneaky wee Holly, (well she was everybody's wee pet, her, wasn't she?) knelt up on Katie's lap and hung her arms around her neck.

'Thank you for the jammies, Gran.' They rubbed noses and laughed. Then it was mum's turn. 'Night, night, mum.' Kisses all round, and three pyjama clad children headed upstairs.

'Say goodnight to dad, kids, before you go to bed.'

'Okay.'

Julie listened for a while at the bottom of the stairs. She could hear the babble of voices. 'We're here to say goodnight.' 'Look at my new jim-jams, dad.' Then Joe's voice. 'Who? Your Gran? When did she arrive?'

'A wee while ago. She brought us books and sweets as well.'

There were the usual muffled sounds as the kids finally went to their own room.

'He'll be wanting a cup of tea soon,' Julie told Katie.

'Right. I'll get a tray ready,' Katie said.

'No, no. I'll get it,' Julie began, but Katie silenced her.

'You will go and sit down. Leave this to me. You brought me here to help, and I'm going to start right now. No time like the present!'

She quietly collected a few things from the bathroom and then busied herself in the kitchen. Soon Joe's voice called down. 'Julie.'

Katie held her finger to her lips and lifted the tray she'd got ready. She disappeared upstairs and Julie went into the living room to await the outcome.

Katie pushed open the bedroom door with her backside and turning, carried the tray into the room.

'Ma!'

'Yes, Ma! Julie's hagged to death, so I've brought your tray up.'

'The kids told me you were here. You didn't need to come all this way, ma. I'm not ill or anything. I just need a rest.'

'Well, you've had a rest, Joseph. It's your wife who needs a rest now.' She dumped the tray down as she spoke and Joe stared at it.

'What's this?'

On the tray was a mug of hot water, a razor, shaving soap, shaving brush and a comb.

'Where's my toast?'

'No toast till you're cleaned up. You look a mess. Use that mirror there!' She pointed to the dressing table. 'And then get yourself into the bathroom. The water's hot and there's plenty of soap and shampoo in there. I've checked. No tea till you've done it.' She was suddenly over at the window and had pushed the curtains aside in a second. 'And this room could do with a right good airing.'

'That's not Julie's fault. I've been in here all the time.'

'Aye. Smells like it too! It's a beautiful evening outside, and you're shut up in here like it's ten below zero. Let some air in, for goodness sake!' She hoisted the window sash up to its full limit, and a fresh warm breeze fluttered in. 'Come downstairs for your supper when you're ready. Julie's off duty now, and I'm too old to be climbing stairs.' She went out, closing the door behind her.

'What did he say?' Julie wanted to know.

'The truth is, I didn't really give him time to say anything at all,' Katie said. 'I had the element of surprise, but I have no idea where to go from here if he doesn't move. We'll just take it one step at a time, eh?'

Upstairs Joe looked at the hot water and ran his hand over his stubbly chin. He waited a moment, then got up and went to the window, intending to slam it shut and return to bed. 'I'm not ready to be bossed about in my own house!' he declared petulantly. But fresh clean air was filling the room and he could smell the sea. The balmy breeze brought back memories of playing on the beach with the kids. He leant his head against the windowpane and stared out. He could hear the sounds of music coming from a house somewhere down the street, and the sound of children laughing. Suddenly he thought that there were people out there having a life – getting on with their lives. But Wee Fella Gow was not there. His wee life was over, and he, Joe Gillan had snuffed it out. Wee Fella Gow's face swam before his eyes again. He sat on the bed and cried. He had not cried since he was a kiddie. It felt strange. He did not cry for long. Suddenly he took all the shaving stuff with him into the bathroom and locked the door. Downstairs, the two women heard the sound of water gushing through the pipes as Joe filled the bath. They looked at each other hopefully.

An hour later Joe Gillan, wet hair combed back, clean-shaven and smelling a mixture of Colgate, Vosene and Imperial Leather, walked into the kitchen and filled the kettle. 'Emmdy want a cup of tea?' he asked.

༺༻ ༺༻

The mood was dark at 10c Hatton Close. The boys were waiting for punishment to be pronounced. Paddy was delivering a long lecture on the evils of removing other people's property without permission. The accused were seated together on the couch, giving all the appearance of listening penitently, but occasionally seizing the opportunity to glower at each other, daggers drawn, whenever Paddy's head was turned. The garbled tale that had emerged when questioned about the disappearance of Paddy's belt, had been so obscure that Paddy gave up trying to find out who was to blame and decided they were both culpable.

Danny had blamed Tommy because he was the last one to have the belt. Tommy was at pains to point out that if Danny hadn't taken it out of the house in the first place, he would never have touched it. He'd only been trying to help. But he lacked the vocabulary of his older brother and was unable to explain his part in the matter properly. Earlier, they had been ordered to retrace their steps all the way back to the swing park, but had returned empty-handed.

In full throttle, Paddy informed them that not being able to find his belt had made him late for work, and as a result, lots of passengers were held up too. (A white lie, this. Paddy was never late for work. But it might do the boys good to be aware that lots of other people could have been affected by the results of their misdeed. Maybe he could engender a sense of responsibility in them.) He also explained that their uncle Jimmy in America had sent him the buckle on that belt and that that was a big loss to him. He enlarged upon the indignity of having to wear braces in the meantime, like an old man. This brought puzzled looks, as they had always been under the impression that their father *was* an old man. Well, maybe no' as old as Pa McGhee downstairs, but *nearly* old. Paddy cleared his throat. 'Okay. No riding your bikes for a week, and threepence each deducted from your pocket money on Friday.'

There was a deep sigh from the couch, signifying that it could have been worse. At least it wasn't a leathering. Well, of course it couldn't be a leathering – he had no belt, had he?

'And your mother tells me you're slow to do your chores. Let me hear one more complaint on that score and you'll have me to answer to.'

Minutes later the boys were sitting on the outside stairs in the close.

'That was all your fault,' said wee man. 'You got me into trouble.'

'Don't blame me. You were the last one to have dad's belt. You must have dropped it on the way home.'

'I was only sent to get you. I didn't need to help you at all.'

'And a fat lot of help you were! Just look at what happened! We both got our pocket money docked and our bikes confiscated. So don't try and wriggle out o' it, wee man. You lost the belt, not me.'

Danny got up and headed for the street in search of older playmates. Wee brothers could be such a pain. Tommy stayed on the steps pondering the injustice of it all. He glowered mutinously at Danny's disappearing head.

'I'll get him,' he brooded darkly.

It was wee man's turn to fill the coalscuttle. This task was performed every evening on a rota basis, and was always delayed until Agnes had mentioned it at least three times, whereupon arguments about whose turn it was, and who did it last night, would take another half-hour or so, until Agnes would lose patience and grab one of them by the scruff of the neck and yell, 'It's your turn. Get the coal in NOW!' The cellars were located at the far end of the backcourt, alongside a high brick wall that separated their court from the next one. There was no lighting so you had to carry a torch at night. It was dark and scary, especially when you were on your own and it was always wee man's aim to get the task over as quickly as possible. It was while he filled the scuttle that an idea occurred to him. He knew just what to do to get his own back on his big brother. Job done, he dragged the heavy scuttle laboriously up each step, one at a time, and deposited it noisily by the front door, clanging the lid down fiercely. Then he went into the house and made a great display of washing his hands at the kitchen sink while saying loudly, 'That's the coal up, Ma!'

Agnes was reading the paper and said absently, 'Right son, that's good.'

This was not enough for wee man. He said again loudly, 'Ma, that's me got the coal up.'

'Right son.' Agnes still seemed disinterested.

'I think we need a clean towel now. I've got this one all dirty.' Wee man had his reasons for making sure that Agnes would remember whose turn it was to get the coal tomorrow. Annoyed, she clicked her tongue and got up and looked at the towel.

'What have I told you about washing your hands *clean* before you dry them?'

Wee man knew his work was done.

Next evening, Agnes made the call for more coal. 'The scuttle's empty. Who's to get the coal tonight?'

'I don't know. I think it was me who got it last night,' Danny answered, playing the usual delaying game.

Agnes thought about it. 'No, it was Tommy. I distinctly remember. I had to get him a clean towel. So you get the coal and no nonsense!'

While this encounter was taking place, Tommy quickly sneaked away, and putting a torch in his pocket, he made his way down to the coal cellar and crept inside, closing the door on himself. He groped his way to the far corner and sat high up on the coals and waited. He knew there must be spiders all around but he disdained them for once, thinking only of sweet revenge.

Then came the sound of footsteps. He could hear the coals-cuttle creaking on its handle as Danny swung it to and fro. The door opened and Danny put the scuttle inside. Tommy, unseen, waited quietly until Danny had stooped into the cellar and had started lifting a lump of coal. Tommy pulled what he hoped was a fiercely ugly face, placed the torch under his chin and suddenly switched it on letting out a blood-curdling roar at the same time. Danny's heart stopped and he gasped in terror at the contorted illuminated face that had suddenly appeared in the darkness, and his breath left him; then he shrieked in fright and abandoning the scuttle, he fled from the cellar, screaming like a girl, all the way up to the house.

Tommy collapsed on the coals and laughed and laughed until his eyes streamed and his stomach ached. A minute later Paddy was at the cellar door. 'Come here you!' he said, grabbing hold of Tommy's arm and dragging him towards the close. Tommy knew there would be a heavy price to pay, and he tried hard to stop laughing, but only partially succeeded, letting out bursts of mirth every few seconds all the way upstairs. He could see that his father was angry and that he was in trouble again, but oh, it was worth it. Did ye see his face? Another laugh exploded at the memory. Granny Park's door opened a crack. Reaching his own house, he was pushed roughly inside. Tommy glanced up at Paddy and saw that his lips were tight shut but that the corners of his mouth were turned up slightly. Paddy made his face grim, but his eyes were misting over and he hoped that Tommy didn't notice that his shoulders shook slightly. 'The wee bugger,' thought Paddy. 'He's learnin' fast. I didn't know he had it in him.'

Agnes was holding out a clean pair of trousers and a sobbing Danny was holding onto her outstretched arms, stepping into them. Debbie stood by the table watching silently. This was too much for Tommy. 'Did ye pee yer pants? Ha, ha, ha!' The laughter erupted again. Wee man could never have hoped for a better result. He held his belly and rolled on the floor.

'Get up! Get up!' Agnes shouted angrily. 'Look at your brother's face. You could have killed him with such a fright. It's no laughing matter.'

Danny was indeed chalk-white and was still shivering with shock. Agnes put a blanket around him and led him to the couch. Tommy was a little chastened and said, 'Well it serves him right. He got me into trouble when I was only trying to help him. We're even now.'

'Even? *Even?*' Agnes shrieked the words. 'What am I rearing? You! No pocket money for the rest of the summer holidays and no T.V. for two weeks!'

Wee man's mouth fell open. 'That's not fair!'

'Not a word! Not another word from you. Do you hear?' Agnes bent to tuck Danny's blanket around him. Over her head, Danny, already recovering, smirked slyly at wee man. Agnes fussed about. 'Paddy, take Tommy into the room and see to him. I'll make Danny a cup of weak tea.'

In the bedroom, Tommy got his second lecture of the week and took it like a man. By the time Paddy was finished, he had promised never to give anybody such a fright again. He admitted that it was dangerous as well as unkind. He said he would tell Danny he was sorry and indeed, he was, because the loss of pocket money and T.V. really hurt.

For days afterwards, though, he only had to think of his brother's face at that moment of sweet revenge, and he would laugh out loud. All in all, he began to feel that some pocket money and a few missed T.V. programmes were a small price to pay for the laughs alone. And anyway, maybe he could renegotiate later when things had cooled down.

CHAPTER 12

You Won't Get Me;
I'm Part of The Union.

Katie's legs were aching. She had just returned from a long walk on the beach with the kids, and she flopped onto the sofa with barely enough strength to pick up the copy of the People's Friend that was lying there. She had been amazed at the energy of those three children. No wonder Julie was permanently exhausted. They had chased each other over sand dunes and had run splashing into the cold Atlantic Ocean till they were knee deep, the bottom of their clothing getting soaking wet. Then they scampered towards the cement stairs that led up from the sands, dragging Granny by the hand.

'C'mon Gran! You promised us chips and ice cream. There's a great place just over here!'

So they tucked into chip butties and raspberry ice creams in the Sandcastle café and, recharged, they made Katie play Crazy Golf for over an hour. On returning home, they scoffed crisps and biscuits and then disappeared out to play. Katie was grateful at last for some peace and quiet. Her eyes got weary as she flicked the pages of the People's Friend and she was just nodding off when Julie's voice spoke anxiously from the kitchen where she was rummaging through drawers.

'Katie, have you seen Joe's box of pills? He's shakin' like a leaf up there and he says he needs the tablets the doctor left him.'

She closed cupboard doors and opened others. Katie's eyes blinked open and she got up stiffly from the sofa.

'What's the matter with Joe? Is he not getting up today? I thought he was over all that.'

'He's been all right for the last couple of days, but he says he's not feeling well today and he needs his medication. He's shivering. I might need to call the doctor.'

'Right!' declared Katie in a decisive voice. 'Just as I thought! It's those dam pills that's making him ill!'

'How can that be? He hasn't had any for two days. He needs them now so they can make him better.'

'I'll explain later. Let me go up to him.' First, she went back into the living room and searched through the magazine rack for something.

Katie entered the bedroom to find Joe in a terrible state. He was huddled under the blankets, trembling. He couldn't even raise his head when he saw her.

He said shakily, 'Ma. I'm sorry. I can't talk to you just now. I feel really ill. Please go downstairs till Julie can find my pills. I'll be all right then.'

Instead of leaving, Katie came and sat by the bed.

'She won't find your pills, Joe,' she said quietly. 'I threw them away.'

Joe sat bolt upright. 'YOU WHAT?'

'I threw them away. It's the pills that are keeping you in this depressed state. I've been reading about it in here.' She held a newspaper up. 'The doctor's been giving you a drug called Valium, and the latest research says it is very addictive. If you take the pills for a long enough time, your body gets so used to them that you won't be able to function without them.'

'But that's exactly why I need them, Ma! I can't cope without them. That's why I've been prescribed them! Why did you throw them away?'

'Because I want you to get well. Truly well. I want the old Joe back. You're not yourself. You're a walking Zombie. The pills might be helping you forget the horrors you've seen, but they are dulling your real personality. They are hiding the real Joe.'

'You don't understand, Ma. I know you mean well, but you don't know what it's like. So what if I'm a little bit sedated? There's no harm in it. I can get the same way with a couple of pints. It's all very well if you can face up to the nightmares! I can't. I mean, you may be right about the Valium, but I am not *addicted*, Ma. I've only been taking them for ten weeks. It takes months before it becomes that kind of a problem. But every time I try to sleep, I see that Wee Fella's face again. I haven't told you about it because...because...! I can't live with it, Ma. It was awful!'

'I don't want to distress you any further, Joe, but don't you think it might help to talk a wee bit about it?'

'No way! I'll see it forever and I don't want to tell any of you because once I do, you'll not be able to get rid of it either. Don't you see? That wee boy's face was horrified. It was as if, in the two seconds before he died, he was appealing to me "Please stop the train! Please stop the train! I didn't mean to fall!" But I couldn't stop the bloody train! What a lot of kids, and a lot of adults too, don't understand is that you can't bring 125 tons of steel to a stop like it was a dodgem car. I feel I'm to blame. I was the very last person he ever saw, and I let him down! I couldn't help him.'

Katie heard this with her head bent.

'Joe, I can only vaguely understand what must have happened that day. I know you suffered greatly and are still suffering. But this was not your fault. Actions bring consequences, Joe. And even the very young suffer the consequences of their own actions. Sometimes they can learn from it, and sometimes, like in this case, the consequences are fatal and it's too late for that person to learn. But somebody can learn the lesson of it Joe, and you can. It's too late for that wee lad. But you can learn that you were not to blame. His actions were to blame and that's the truth. Don't let the consequences of *his* actions fall on you. I could never begin to know how you can get rid of it. Maybe you never will. Not totally, anyway. But you've got a life to live Joe. Here, today. You can teach your kids about actions and consequences. You know about that now, first hand.

I know that in your heart of hearts you want to get back to the old Joe. You would never have made the effort you did the other day if that was not the case. Will you let us help you? Will you try? Please, Joe! Here, read that. It will explain it all better than I can.' She put the newspaper article on the bed. 'There's two ways to tackle this problem. You can wean yourself off the tablets by slowly taking less and less each day, which will take ages and might not work in the end because there is always the possibility that you'll just take a tablet every time you feel rough, or you can do what is called 'cold turkey' and stop them, dead. It's harder but it's quicker. I would like to help you do the latter. I want to see you well before I go home.'

'You really don't know what you're asking, Ma...' Joe's tired voice trailed off. He half raised his hand in a helpless gesture and let his arm fall back on to the bed again.

'I'm not ready for this kind of fight yet,' he said, his voice a mere whisper.

'Oh, yes you are, and we start right now! We are all in this fight with you, Joe. Me, Julie, your brothers and your kids. Even your workmates. No more pills! The fighting Gillans are on the warpath again, eh?' She made an attempt at a smile.

She leant forward and cupped Joe's haggard face in her hands, staring into his eyes.

'Joe, Joe, Joe. My son Joseph. I know you're in there and I know you can fight this. Please come back! We need you Joe!'

Katie and the lost Joe hugged each other and they both cried.

⚜ ⚜

It took three full weeks of hell before he had it licked. Once Julie got on board with Katie's help plan, she had a hard fight too. Joe had told her to trust Katie; that Katie was right and they had to do what she said. He told Julie that no matter how much he pleaded, she was not to get him any more pills. But only two hours later, he was crying and begging her to phone the doctor for a prescription. Julie couldn't take it, and ran out of the room, sobbing. It became the toughest three weeks of their lives, even more harrowing than that awful inquest and the dark days that followed. At one point they had had to lock all the doors and hide the keys, so determined was Joe that he was going to go out and get the pills himself. If it hadn't been for Dan arriving at that moment with Davey McCally, Julie did not know how it might have ended. Dan and Davey took Joe for a long walk along the seafront and then to the pub for a pint. It was good for Joe and made him feel like his old self for a while.

One blustery day, Joe awoke to find his head was clear, his hands were not shaking and he was hungry for some bacon and eggs. He got up and went to the window, looking out on to the back garden.

'My God! That grass needs cutting,' he said. And in that moment, he knew the nightmare was over. He hadn't given a toss for anything these last few weeks, least of all household chores. But he saw that the grass was overgrown and he cared.

He cared. He would cut the grass this very day! He was O.K. now. He was Joe.

❦ ❦

Jamsie met his mother at the station. He lifted the suitcase and said, 'It doesn't feel much lighter. I thought you said you'd be leaving lots of stuff behind.'

'Well, I did, but Julie and I took the train into Largs, just for a run. There were some lovely shops, so I picked up a few bargains.'

'Typical! Where's the leather strap that was round it?'

'I left it with Joe. Joe says it was a fine belt.'

'What? That soggy old strap!'

'Actually, it dried out really nice. And Joe says the buckle is a good quality one. It is the Lone Star, from the state of Texas. Joe says somebody will be very sorry they lost it. He asked me where I got it and I told him.'

'Joe says! Joe says! I'm glad to hear that 'Joe says' anything at all! When I last phoned him, I could hardly get two words out of him.'

'Oh Jamsie, don't be like that! He's been through the mill, that lad! But he's fine now. A real Gillan! He starts work again on Monday, and after what he's been through, I think he's a hero. Julie's like a cat with two tails, she's so pleased to get him out from under her feet. Anyway, what's been happening here?'

Jamsie suddenly felt the need to put the case down and change it over to his other hand. 'Oh, nothing,' he said, without looking up.

Something in his voice made his mother looked round at him, her eyes narrowing suspiciously.

'Nothing, eh? Hm!' was all she said.

❦ ❦

'They tell me Joe Gillan is starting back to work today,' said Paddy. He was bent over to tie his shoelaces.

When he straightened Agnes said, 'Aye, so I heard. I was speaking to Mrs Gillan on Saturday. She's been away at Salt-coats for over a month, you know. I was asking for Joe. She says he's still a bit fragile, but he's definitely on the mend.'

'Right, I'm away, Aggie. I'll be back around three-thirty.'

'Tell Joe I wish him well.' Agnes had never actually met Joe, but because he worked with Paddy so often and his mother lived in the town, she felt she knew him well.

It was still very early so she went back to bed and read a book for a little while. She must have nodded off and woke up two hours later when Debbie crept in beside her.

'I think you should let wee man watch T.V. now mum. He looks so miserable trying to read his book at the table and stretching his neck to try and see the telly from behind the recess.'

'Aye, maybe you're right. He can start watching tonight. He's been punished enough. But he has to learn that life isn't always fair, and he can't make it fair by taking it out on other people.'

Debbie gave Agnes a hug and went out of the room, leaving Agnes thinking that it was nice to see Debbie so concerned about her wee brother. She got up and reached for her dressing gown. It was then she heard the whisper.

'Did you ask her?'

'Yes.'

'What did she say?'

'She said "Aye." '

'Remember that's two tubes of Smarties you owe me.'

'Aye, okay. As soon as I get my pocket money back, I'll buy them. But the deal was one tube of Smarties for the T.V. and one for getting my pocket money back. Did you ask her about that?'

'Naw, wee man. One thing at a time! You're always pushing it, you! So I want two tubes up front, or the deal's off.'

'That's not fair!'

'You need to learn that life isn't always fair, wee man.'

∽≈∾ ∽≈∾

Joe slinked quietly towards the lockers in the bothy at Glasgow Central station. He hoped to slip back into his routine unnoticed, with no fuss and no questions asked. It was a forlorn hope. As soon as he was spotted, he got the equivalent of an actor's standing ovation, the noise of the applause being heard so clearly from outside that it brought even more of the guys inside to add to the back-slapping and well-wishing. When he eventually got down to platform thirteen, Paddy laughed at his discomfiture.

'What are you laughin' at?' Joe asked him. 'I've only returned from sick leave, not single-handedly saved the Railways from the Beeching Axe!'

'It's your face! You look as if you've been caught with your trousers down.'

'Talking of that….' Joe put his kit bag on the ground to pull out a brown paper bag, which he proffered towards Paddy. 'How on earth have you been managing to keep yours up?'

Paddy tore open the bag. It was now Joe's turn to laugh at the look on *Paddy's* face. It was an expression of sheer bewilderment, because there in his hand was his good leather belt, complete with the Lone Star buckle.

'How did you get this? I gave it up for lost weeks ago!'

'Never you mind,' said Joe, feeling the need to enjoy himself by keeping some of the mystery to himself. 'I recognised it as soon as I saw it. You wear it every bloody day, man! And you've boasted about it often enough!'

'Still fits!' Paddy said, buckling the belt around his waist. Immediately, his demeanour changed. In discarding the old braces, he seemed to throw off that 'old man' persona that had been dogging him lately. Having his smart leather belt around his waist made him feel trendy and young again.

'Look at me,' he boasted. 'I feel like a new man.'

'That makes two of us.' Joe said.

༄ ༄

Katie Gillan had noticed some subtle changes in Jamsie since her return. She couldn't quite put her finger on it, but he was different. He went out more often after work, not just at weekends, and stayed out later. 'If I know the signs,' she told Lily, who'd dropped in one morning for a cuppa, 'he's got a girl-friend. I mean, a serious girlfriend, not just one of the usual flirts that he and his mates hang around with up by the café.'

Her intuition proved to be right. 'Ma,' Jamsie said one morning, 'I was wondering if I could bring a friend over on Thursday? Only for a few minutes, before we catch the train to Glasgow. We're going to the pictures.'

'What's her name?'

He smiled. 'What makes you think it's a 'she'? It might be a mate of mine.'

Katie lifted an eyebrow and gave her son a quizzical look.

'If it was a 'he', you wouldn't ask, you'd just walk in with him like you do all the time with your pals.'

'Her name is Teresa, but we all call her Terry. Isn't that a great name for a girl?'

It was obvious she was talking to a man in love.

'I would prefer Teresa, myself, if it was *my* name. Where did you meet her?'

'It was when you were away. I met her on the bus going to Crossmyloof Ice Rink.'

'Oh, she's a skater, then?'

'She's absolutely brilliant at skating. She's won medals for it,' he informed her proudly. Katie was impressed. She'd never been near a skating rink in her life and it sounded very exotic to her.

'Well, why don't you invite her to have her tea here before you go?'

'Great, ma! That's what I hoped you'd say. You'll like Terry. She's a friend of Lizzie Crilly's. It was Lizzie who introduced us.'

Immediately the bubble burst, and a red warning light blazed suddenly in Katie's head. Katie had never liked Lizzie Crilly. Far too forward by half, and you could hear that coarse laugh of hers a mile away. Always cracking chewing gum in the most vulgar way, and the clothes she wears….! Oh, my God! What is Jamsie getting mixed up with?

'I can tell he's smitten with her. I haven't even met her yet, but I have this awful dread. I just know that she'll be a brazen hussy. What am I going to do?' she asked Lily when the two of them were shopping together next day. 'Do you think you could come on Thursday and look her over with me, so that we can discuss her when she's gone, and you can help me to devise a plan to separate her from Jamsie?'

'I'll come if you want, Katie, but I never knew anyone like you for crossing bridges too soon. Wait till you meet her first. You might like her.'

'A friend of Lizzie Crilly's? Are ye joking? Pigs'll fly!'

Pigs flew. No doubt about it, they flew. Teresa Briody was ushered shyly into Katie's front room on Thursday and stood for a moment under the scrutiny of her boyfriend's mother and aunt, before moving forward, her hand held out.

'Mrs Gillan, I'm Terry. Thank you for inviting me.' Her voice was self-assured and polite, her gaze direct and unabashed, and in that first moment, as Katie shook the soft little hand held out to her, she was unashamedly smitten too.

The girl was elegantly dressed and held a pair of soft kid gloves along with a very chic handbag in her other hand. She had gleaming long reddish blonde hair and her slightly freckled skin was flawless. How on earth this sweet little vision could in any way be connected with the harsh brash loud-mouthed Lizzie Crilly, Katie was at a loss to understand.

It was Katie who suddenly felt that Jamsie looked a little ragged, and she wished she had insisted on ironing that shabby looking polo-neck shirt that he had opted to wear, instead of letting him iron it himself. Teresa was introduced to Lily who was also captivated by her warm smile and clear blue eyes. The little tea party passed successfully, the only frown appearing on Jamsie's brow when his mother, for some unknown reason, kept referring to him as James, instead of the familiar nickname he was more used too. But it didn't put him out too much, and he couldn't have been more aware of the ladies needs during the meal, or a more attentive listener to all the small talk he would have found so boring a short time ago.

The sisters waved the couple off and watched them cross the road hand in hand towards the station.

'Well, if that don't beat all!' Katie said, still flushed with pride and excitement. 'What do you think of her Lily? I thought she was charming.'

'She is delightful. I don't know what you were worried about. She's not a bit like Lizzie Crilly.'

'Lizzie Crilly? What's she got to do with it? And Worried? Worried? I wasn't the least bit worried. I brought Jamsie up, remember, and his brothers before him. Give me credit for knowing he'd have good sense when it comes to women.'

'Don't you mean *James*?' Lily said mockingly, turning away from the window. Under her breath she muttered, 'Give me strength!'

Part Three

Little children listen to me.
Do not play where you should not be.
Don't play games on the railway track.
If you're hit by a train, you'll never come back.

M.C.

CHAPTER 13

The Last Chocolate Éclair.
Four Years Later

It was late November and Katie studied her face in the mirror above the fireplace, moving the skin about roughly with her hand and critically surveying the wrinkles she found. She put her hands on either side of her face and stretched the skin towards her ears. She looked as if she was in a wind tunnel. That looks better she thought. If only I could keep it that way with Kirby grips. She removed her hands and the skin returned to its usual position.

'Who is this old biddy?' she asked her reflection. 'Who are you? You're not me! Where did I go?'

She lifted the photograph of her dead husband Dan down from the mantelpiece and sat in a nearby armchair, staring at it in maudlin mood.

'Well Dan, at least that's one hardship you won't have to face. Growing old! It's demoralising! When I moved here to this new council house four years ago, I thought that life would be easier - hot water on tap, a washing machine, my own back garden - all the things you wanted for us but never lived to see. But life just got hectic! They've knocked down the old tenement where we lived, you know. It's making way for a brand new health centre. God knows when they'll start work on it! It won't stop me getting old, though. It'd take a good doctor for that, eh? Between you and me, Dan, I sometimes get the feeling that I'll soon be joining you. Old and alone! Yes, it's finally happened; I'm alone in the house now. Jamsie got married in September. You would have been proud of him and his new wife. She's a bonnie girl is Teresa, (or Terry, as Jamsie calls her, though I find it hard to think of her as that.) A good head on her shoulders too! She'll need that, married to our Jamsie. They've moved to a rented flat in a tenement in Motherwell. The area is due for development soon, so they hope to get a council house out of it. Probably one of these new high-rise flats. Tower blocks, they're called. But they're so happy I don't think they'd notice if they lived in a mud hut. All in all, I've made a good job of the boys and I'm satisfied, though it was never easy!'

Katie's eyes dimmed with unaccustomed tears. 'What on earth is wrong with me, today?' she declared, surprised and not a little irritated. 'I'm greeting like a Christmas card! That's not like me at all. You know me, Dan. Not much time for tears! I was strict with the lads. I had to be. I was their only parent after you'd gone. I wanted to raise them right for you and see them settled, and I've done that. I think it's just that, now that my job is done, I'm giving in to exhaustion.

It's been an exhausting four years, I can tell you! What with moving in here and the hassle of emptying the old house, and I'd hardly got settled when Lily came to stay for a while, and what with trying to sort out her problems with that horrible Charlie Dunne, and keeping a tight rein on her when it comes to this new 'romance' of hers! Then there was Joe's illness to be seen to – he's fine now, but I couldn't have him losing his voice again, like before. In fact, I'm pretty sure it would have been his *mind* this time, not just his voice. And Jamsie's wedding took a lot out of me. But what a wedding it was! The Gillans were all united for it. Lily was there with Eddie, and Martha McLaughlin. Lily's daughter Barbara came, with her fiancé, Douglas. The reception was held in a posh Glasgow

hotel. Teresa's parents are comfortably off, you know, and
insisted on paying for everything, (though Jamsie paid for all
the transport and the band,) so I helped in all the practical
ways, like sewing bridesmaids dresses and the like, and doing a
bit of decorating at their flat. Always was able to turn my hand
to anything! That's one thing I'm not shy to say I'm proud of!
A bit of hard work never hurt anyone. But what am I wasting
time talking to a photo for? Lily will be here soon and I had
better get on.'

She got up and dabbed at her eyes with the corner of her
apron. She kissed the glass frame lightly, and replaced the
photograph on the mantelpiece, but avoided looking again at
the old woman in the mirror.

Lily arrived with great news. She held her Decree Absolute
in her hands and jumped up and down. 'It's over! It's over at
last, Katie! I'm free! Now Eddie and I can get married.'

She caught a look on her sister's face. 'Are you not happy for
me? Katie, you're not going all righteous on me, are you? You
know that Eddie and I planned to marry as soon as my divorce
came through.'

'Of course I'm very happy for you. And as for going all
righteous…..!' She knew Lily was referring to an earlier
conversation about getting married in a registry office. Katie
had been disappointed at this, because it was hard for her to see
that as a 'Blessed and Holy union,' like Jamsie and Terry's
wedding, but she was determined to try her best not to make
waves. It was none of her business, after all.

'If there's one thing I've learned, it's to live and let live. I
can't be the judge of you, Lily. Even though I view things
differently, yours is a difficult position, and I don't know the
answers to the complex problems of life any more than the
next person. Your first marriage was a disaster, but you were
only seventeen. We were all so naïve in those days, not like

youngsters today. They've got it all worked out; the whole world at their feet, so to say that because of that one mistake you should never be able to try again and be happy, seems a bit harsh to me.'

Lily looked closely at Katie. 'Are you all right, Kate. You look a bit peaky.'

'I'm awful tired, Lily. I've been on the trot since seven this morning. I'm getting too old for all this housework.'

'Och, away! You're only fifty-eight.'

'Fifty-nine, but you're welcome to chop a year off if you like. You'd think I'd have nothing much to do now that Jamsie has gone. I don't know where all the work comes from!'

'It comes from *you*, Katie. *You* go and find it. *You* bring it in. You need a wee change, that's all. A day out! What say you and I have a day in town next week? We'll get our hair done and do some Christmas shopping and have our tea out. We could even go to the pictures. There's nothing stopping us. What about it? I'll make the appointments for Thursday, okay?'

'Hmm.'

❧❧ ❧❧

It was to be Paddy's birthday on December the nineteenth. Agnes had no idea what to get him. She leafed through catalogues at home and stared uninspired into shop windows when she was out.

'I'll need to go into Glasgow,' she told herself. 'Maybe I'll hit on an idea there.' Agnes loved Glasgow, but she hated being there on her own. It was always busy and bustling and the heavy traffic made her nervous. She would need some company, and an excuse to cover up the real reason for the trip. She could say she was doing some Christmas shopping, but Paddy would insist on running her in by car on his day off. Besides, they always did Christmas shopping together, and this year all the kids' toys had been ordered locally, so there was not much to left to do. She had a good look through the kids' wardrobes. Tommy's school shoes were a wee bit scuffed and his best trousers had been patched, though very cleverly, so nothing was as yet in a desperate state. She could really hold off till the January sales, but she seized her excuse.

'I'm going to keep Wee Man off school on Thursday,' she told Paddy. 'I'll take him into Glasgow for some new clothes. He hasn't a decent pair of trousers to his name and he could be doing with new shoes for his Christmas party.'

'Do you need to keep him off school? Why don't you go on Saturday? I could run you.'

'There's only three more Saturdays till Christmas. The shops will be mobbed and the queues will be a mile long everywhere. I could get it done in half the time if I go on Thursday.'

'Okay, I suppose you know best.'

Agnes wished she could have asked her sister to go with her into town, but since Sadie Crilly 'got religion' as they say, she was a pure waste of space. Sadie would not have approved of buying a birthday present.

'Only Pagans and Heathens celebrated birthdays in the Bible,' she had told Agnes once. Agnes, who was not particularly religious herself, had replied, 'Well, I celebrate the gift of life, and to my mind, it's nice to tell someone you are glad they were born.'

Agnes loved her sister, who lived only a few streets away, and she missed her. Well, she missed the girl that Sadie used to be. Happy, laughing and full of surprises, so unpredictable that you never knew what she would say or do next. But now she was dull company, always watching her behaviour in case she might do or say something wrong, never trusting herself in any company other than that of her newfound 'Christian' brethren, in case she would be led astray, off the path of 'righteousness' that she was now on. She was past talking to and it worried Agnes no end. And hurt her too. They sort of avoided seeing one another, each feeling uncomfortable in the other's presence.

'Such a shame; I feel that I've lost my sister, that I should be in mourning.' Agnes thought ruefully. ' Ach, cheer up, old girl. Sadie's counted herself out, so it'll have to be the wee man, then.'

⦿⦿⦿ ⦿⦿⦿

The weather had turned really cold by Thursday, and Agnes was already regretting her decision to take Tommy with her. She looked at the wee figure beside her on the platform, shoulders hunched against the biting wind. She leant down and straightened the woollen balaclava over his fringe and pulled the collar of his trench coat up around his neck. She was not comfortable that she had used some deceit to get her own way.

'I'm sorry son, I should have let you go to school today as usual,' she said, a little guiltily. 'It's too cold to be travelling and the truth is, you could get new shoes any time. It didn't have to be today. You'd be far better off in your warm classroom.' Tommy looked at her as if she was daft.

'I'd much rather be here, Ma. We might see Dad at Central Station. He says we're to look out for him. And you promised we'd see the lights in George Square and do Lewis's windows.'

It had become a tradition with Glasgow folk to view the lights in George Square and Buchanan Street and to 'do' Lewis's windows. Lewis's was a large department store in Argyll Street and their annual window display was the event of the year for Glasgow shoppers. Each window formed a chapter of a special Christmas Fairy story, culminating in a happy ending at the last window. This is what Tommy would suffer any amount of chilly discomfort to see. He stood happily beside his mum, watching his breath make a little cloud in front of his face every time he breathed out.

Just as the train pulled in, Mrs Gillan and her sister Lily appeared and hurriedly made for a compartment further down the platform. Agnes didn't see them again until the train arrived at Glasgow. They all waited together at the ticket barrier for the crowd to thin out.

'Hello, Mrs Preston. I'm just saying to Lily, it's really cold today. The chill hits you as soon as you step off the train.' Katie said.

'I know. I'm beginning to wish I hadn't bothered to leave home. The cold water pipes were frozen at our house this morning. We had to fill the kettle from the hot water tap.' Lily said, shivering.

Agnes could only agree. 'It's amazing how quickly the weather can turn. How did Jamsie's wedding go, Mrs Gillan? I heard that his bride was beautiful.'

'She was, Mrs Preston. Beautiful! I must bring the photos round for you to see. They are all in colour, you know.'

'My Goodness! I would certainly love to see them.'

Katie leaned over. 'Hello, Tommy. Not at school today?'

Tommy shook his head bashfully.

'I'm taking him for new shoes. The shops are so crowded on a Saturday. – Oh, here we go, it's our turn. Bye.'

They moved through the barrier. 'See you later, Mrs Preston.'

They went their separate ways.

∽⊕∾ ∽⊕∾

It took Agnes longer than she had anticipated to get Tommy fixed up with new trousers and new shoes. The shops were busier than she had expected and there were queues everywhere.

'It's just as well we came today. If this is what it's like on a weekday, Heaven knows what it will be like on a Saturday.'

In the shoe shop, Tommy was spoilt for choice. Glasgow

shops had so much more to offer. He 'hmm'-ed and 'haa'-ed and stomped up and down in pair after pair of shoes until at length Agnes cried out, 'Those are the ones! They'll do! They fit, they're sturdy and they're the right price. Wrap those up!' she ordered the salesgirl.

She took Tommy for some lunch at the restaurant on Lewis's fourth floor. Tommy loved it, and tucked into fish and chips and when he'd eaten it all, was allowed to choose a cake from the three-tiered cake stand to have with his glass of milk. This proved to be more difficult for him than deciding on a pair of shoes. There was a currant slice, a fern cake, an iced ginger cake, a cream cookie and a chocolate éclair. All of them his declared favourite! How on earth was a boy to choose? However, in the end, he chose the éclair and re-minded Agnes that they had not yet seen the lights or Lewis's window display. She watched indulgently as cream and choco-late icing appeared around his mouth and was secretly glad of the stolen time she was having with her youngest child. *Life is so busy,* she thought. *You never really take the time to get to know your kids. He's a great wee lad. Quite patient, really, for a boy his age. He must take that after his Dad. I've got no patience whatso-ever.*

The patient lad had to be taken to the Ladies' room later, to have his hands and face washed, an indignity still deemed to be worth it, on account of the treats still to come.

Agnes had still not begun her search for Paddy's birthday present and it was nearly three o'clock. When they stepped outside onto Argyll Street, she was surprised at how dark it had become. It had been raining; a rain heavily mixed with snowflakes, and a light fog was beginning to descend.

'We'll do the windows now,' she told Tommy. 'It's dark enough. They always look better when it's dark.'

The pavements glistened, black with melted sleet and rain-water, yet cheerfully reflecting the bright colours of the Christmas illuminations all around. It was freezing cold. But that hadn't stopped the crowds coming in their droves to do their Christmas shopping and to 'do' Lewis's windows. They moved slowly, as the people inched their way past the eight large plate glass windows, gazing and gasping at the beautiful winter wonderland scenes depicted within. Tommy, now eight years of age, was still young enough to be entranced.

෴ ෴

Lily and Katie had high tea in Fuller's. Katie could not resist the occasional glance at her new hair-do in the mirrors that were all around.

'You look great,' Lily said. 'Years younger.'

'I wish I'd had it done like this for the wedding.' Katie was moving her head about, looking through her eyes sideways.

Lily resisted the impulse to say 'I told you so.' She had begged Katie to get her hair cut and coloured for the wedding, but Katie had laughed at the very idea. (No point in putting on airs just because Teresa's parents are well off, was her attitude at the time.)

Now she realised the beautifully beneficial effects of a new look. She touched the hair over her ears and patted it. It felt hard because of the hair lacquer, but at least it was keeping its shape.

'You look great too,' she told Lily, and meant it.

'I'm experimenting with styles for my big day.'

'What's my colour called, again?'

'Rich Mahogany. Mine is Amber Glow.'

Katie looked once more in the mirror, a self-conscious smile curling her lip. '*Rich Mahogany*,' she said, derisively.

They giggled like girls and ordered another pot of tea, ate another scone each, and went out onto a drizzly dark

Buchanan Street. The coloured lights looked fuzzy through the fog, which had thickened considerably while they were indoors.

'Lily, I think we should just get home now. We'll give the pictures a miss. I don't think we should stay out late in this fog.'

'Aye, it's quite eerie, not being able to see ahead. I've had enough too. Let's get home.' They turned into Gordon Street and then the station.

～～～

After 'doing' the lights in George Square, Agnes took Tommy to Buchanan Street and the posher shops. No expense would be spared, if only she could hit on the right thing for Paddy. A fruitless search ensued and by four o'clock she was no further forward, and she began to think of getting the train home, her quest unfulfilled. She decided to have a last look in at Lewis's. She hadn't tried the basement. Maybe she could get him some tools, or something. The basement was full of vendors doing floorshows for their products. Crowds were gathered round all the stands, and Tommy became transfixed by a glove puppet being manipulated on a toy stand. They stood for a while, and the Wee Man laughed at the antics and the jokes. He was invited to stroke the puppet's head. The puppeteer made it growl and Tommy jumped back, startled. People laughed, and then Tommy had to shake its hand. It wouldn't let go and Tommy became part of the act. It was while Tommy was engrossed in this adventure that Agnes's attention was caught by something in the next stand. She told Tommy to stay where he was while she went over to investigate. She jostled her way to the front and discovered the very thing for Paddy. A Car Radio. All frequencies, all stations, full instructions inside. So simple, the man was saying, that a trained monkey could install it. And a money-back Lewis's guarantee! Who could pass up such a bargain? Agnes had her purse at the ready. It was parcelled up for her and she returned to Tommy triumphant and glowing. Mission accomplished!

Wee Man and the puppet were by now great friends. It was obvious that he'd fallen for this cheap piece of hairy cloth, so in an indulgent mood, and because he had been such a good boy all day, Agnes bought it for him. This meant, of course, that she had to buy a jigsaw for Danny, and a book of cardboard cutout dressing up dolls for Debbie. She could not return to Hatton Close with a glove puppet for Tommy and not have something for the other two. Every mother knows that!

In the station, Wee Man kept looking around for Paddy. 'I think we've missed him, son,' Agnes said. They waited outside the barrier for their train to come in, watching the board. Mrs Gillan and Lily were standing further along. They were talking to a young girl. When Katie saw Agnes she moved towards her bringing the others with her.

'Mrs Preston,' she said. 'Let me introduce you to my daughter-in-law. This is Teresa.' They shook hands and engaged in some small talk. It transpired that Teresa was in town for rehearsals for the Christmas Ice Show at the Kelvin Hall. She was playing Cinderella. Mrs Preston was suitably impressed and said she would definitely buy tickets to see the show this year. The children would love it. She was delighted to learn that Teresa was such a good skater, and realised she was speaking to a celebrity of some note as she now recognised Teresa's face on the many posters advertising the Ice Show that she'd seen around the town. Teresa explained that rehearsals had been cut short to let people get home in case the fog worsened. Jamsie would be surprised, she said, to see her home at teatime for once. Agnes nodded and laughed and complimented both the older ladies on their hair, and was wondering what to say next when she heard her name being called.

'Daddy!' Tommy cried in delight. Agnes excused herself

and went to meet Paddy, who lifted the Wee Man up in his arms.

'Dad, look what I've got.' He held the bag open so that Paddy could look inside. 'It's a hairy green monster and if you press him he growls.'

'That's great, Wee Man.' Paddy looked at the parcels Agnes was carrying. 'You've been on a spending spree, I take it. I hope you didn't run up any bills in Goldberg's.'

'I haven't been anywhere near Goldberg's. Just some stuff for the wee man and some bits and bobs that we need. I'll show you when I get home.'

'Dad, we've got presents for Danny and Debbie.'

'That's good, Wee Man.' And to Agnes, over his head, 'I'm glad you're going home now. The fog is causing delays although the trains are still running. I've only got one more run to do to Paisley and then I'll be home.'

'Dad, I was in a floorshow,' Wee Man was saying.

'Tell me all about it later, Wee Man. I've got to go.'

He kissed them both and they waved until he disappeared up the concourse in the direction of platform thirteen.

At platform six, the barriers opened and people made their way towards the train bound for Motherwell, stopping at Rutherglen, Cambuslang, Uddingston and 'stations in between.' Tommy insisted on travelling way up the platform to the front carriage. Agnes was only glad to get a seat. She nodded to Darren McKean, the butcher's son, on his way home from Glasgow University. His sister Rhona and her friend, John Anderson, were squeezed in beside him. Lily Dunne, Mrs Gillan and her daughter-in-law were seated on the long seats by the door. The train got busier and people had to stand. Into the journey, Agnes occupied herself by trying to guess what was in the parcels that people were carrying. Tommy asked if he could open his bag and play with the green hairy monster. Agnes nodded and her eyes closed. She held her bags tightly against her chest, resting them on her lap.

Somewhere near Newton it happened. There was no sign, no warning, no screeching of brakes. Just a shuddering, thundering, deafening bang, then darkness. erybody was flung about as if they weighed no more than a tea towel. There was a terrible clanging sound that seemed to last for ever. Agnes felt herself being thrown into the air and she seemed to be hanging upside down. She could feel bodies sliding past her. She tried to shout out Tommy's name, but she didn't have a voice. Blood was rushing to her head. She tried to get the right way up, but she was jammed tight. She couldn't move and she could see nothing. It was pitch black. There were some screams and then there was silence. An eerie, smelly, smoky silence. Then, in the darkness, came the sound of cries for help. There were muffled sobs, and even the sound of men crying. Names were being called out. 'Jim. Neil. Are you okay?' and 'I can't see. I can't see!' and 'Jean, Jean. Where are you?' and 'Oh my God! Oh my God. Help us, Help us.'

Sometimes there was an answer, 'I'm over here. I'm okay, but I can't seem to move.' Sometimes there was no answer, and the calling got frantic and the screams started again.

But Agnes heard nothing. She had slipped into unconsciousness.

꘏꘏ ꘏꘏

A few yards away on the side of the track, Katie Gillan opened her eyes. There was a whirring sound in her ears, like a wheel spinning round and round, but she couldn't see what was causing it. There seemed to be a light flashing somewhere, and men's voices shouting. It was dark so it must be nighttime.

'Who's that shouting at this time of night, waking people

up?' she thought. 'I hope it's not Jamsie. No, no. It couldn't be Jamsie. He doesn't live here anymore.'

She looked up and could see what looked like twisted metal. Tangled, twisted metal hanging down. 'What on earth is that twisted metal doing there?' she asked aloud. It's supposed to be Mahogany. Rich Mahogany.'

Then she said, 'Oh God. It's a dream. A nightmare. Please God, let me wake up now. I can't move. I hate these kind of dreams when you can't move and you can't wake up. What's that? Is it wet? I think I'm wet. Surely I haven't wet the bed?' Katie closed her eyes.

CHAPTER 14

In Time.

There were many times in the next few months when Katie wished her eyes had never opened again. She cried many times into her pillow. 'Why did I survive? Why me? I was ready to go. I should have gone. I should be with Dan now. I've had a good life; my family don't depend on me for anything. Why? Why?'

When she'd emerged from the coma, she was in Law Hospital and it was twenty-two days after the tragedy. Already some of the funerals had taken place. Throughout that time, the family had come and held her hands and talked to her, willing her to pull through, but it was days before they could tell her that nine people had died and thirty-six were seriously injured, herself among the latter. They broke the news slowly, by degrees, gently easing her way into the full horror of what they knew and what they'd been trying to cope with. And eventually she got hold of a newspaper in the dayroom and read the names of the deceased for herself, as if she didn't already know, but she wouldn't really believe anything until she saw it in black and white. There they were in alphabetical order:

John Anderson. (20)   Rhona McKean. (18)
Lily Anne Dunne. (49)   Thomas Patrick Preston. (8)
James Garrity. (34)   Dennis Robertson. (72)
Teresa May Gillan. (22)   Joseph Robertson. (50)
Darren G. McKean. (19)

The list went on, but Katie had read enough. Names jumped out at her from the page. Until she read that list, she was still stupidly hoping that she was imagining all this. That she wasn't really in hospital and that she'd awake to find it was all a bad dream. But this made it real. She could not pretend any longer. The pain of her injuries was easier to bear than the pain of this reality. She wished she'd never read the bloody paper. She wished......she wished.....!

Her grief knew no bounds. Who should she mourn the most? Her lovely sister Lily? Her sweet and talented daughter-in-law of only a few months, Terry? That dear little child, Tommy Preston? Who could she comfort? Her son Jamsie, a widower at twenty three? Who can guide me through this Hell? Oh, God! Oh, God! Is there even a God, now? That's another question. Could she comfort Eddie McKenna, or the Prestons? She wished with all her heart that she had not survived, because this...this.... Living hell of a nightmare was worse than death. She would never, ever get over this. It was too much to bear.

She looked at the list again and read her sister's name aloud. Her eyes travelled down the page. She couldn't bear to see the number eight next to wee Tommy Preston's name. 'He's only a baby. Dear God, only a baby!' She vomited several times, but couldn't stop, even though her stomach hurt when she did so.

Jamsie came to visit and she couldn't bear to look him in the eye. The lines on his face told a story she'd rather not know. He told her with a dull voice and dull eyes not to worry, to get better. She was convinced he was really saying, 'Why are you here? Why did you, a woman who is nearly sixty, survive? Why could it not have been my darling, beautiful, talented wife that survived?' The truth is, Jamsie felt none of those things. He felt nothing. He would never feel anything again. He was so dead, he might as well have died in the crash with Terry.

People. People were a nuisance. They said stupid things. They meant well, Jamsie knew, but he wished they would all go away. They said things like, 'You're young, Jamsie. In time you'll get over this.' In time. Middle-aged people. Old people. They all said it – 'In Time.' Had they lived so long and learned nothing about grief? Jamsie had. He'd learned now, at twenty-three years of age, that no amount of time would ever help him. He saw time as an enemy now, stretching endlessly before him as he carried his pain through an empty life.

People. They said things like, 'You've got your whole life ahead of you. You're young enough to meet someone new one day, and you'll be happy again.' Now, that was a corker, that one! A pure corker! If only he could *feel*, he would have been angry enough at that one to punch whoever said it. Instead, he had looked at the 'well-wisher' in a detached way. He didn't speak, but inside he was yelling. 'Do you think my wife was like an old shirt that got damaged in the wash? Throw it out and get a new one! Is that what you'd do? That one died, so marry another! Maybe pretty wives were for sale in the shops in packs of two. YOU STUPID BITCH! You can't just go out and buy a new one! This was a PERSON! An irreplaceable PERSON! A living, breathing, *adorable HUMAN BEING.*'

He did have the sense to realise though, that up until this happened, he wouldn't have had a clue what to say to a bereaved person either. He would probably have been just as insensitive, just as clumsy. Well, he knew now, didn't he? He could be a really compassionate, understanding person now. If he wanted. Not at all like the thoughtless, happy-go-lucky, ecstatic newly wed he was four weeks ago. Yeah, he'd lost a wife, but, hey, he'd learned a valuable life-lesson in the process. Look folks, a very empathetic, sympathetic, well-rounded individual! Now, if you look at it that way.....!

❧❧ ❧❧

Had there had been a funeral? Paddy wasn't sure. He was trying to remember. He turned his head on the pillow and
thought there must have been, because the house had been
full of flowers, which had all gone now, leaving just a heady
perfume. He racked his brain. Yes, there had been a little
white coffin. He was sure he'd seen that. But something had
happened. He didn't know what, because he couldn't remember. The only thing he knew for certain was that there
was a pain. Dire, dreadful, God-awful pain, somewhere deep
in his chest and there was no pill for it. He drifted back into
oblivion. It had been a very strong sedative.

Along the hall, the living room was still full of people. Relatives, friends, neighbours, maybe about sixteen in all, and yet it
was so quiet. No one spoke, because nobody wanted to say
anything. Every platitude had been said and every one of them
sounded hollow. The silence was only broken when a new
arrival appeared, or when someone took their leave, and even
then everyone spoke in hushed whispers.

'It's good of you to come.' Paddy's sister Margaret was
saying.

'I've brought some biscuits.'

'Thank you.'

'How is he now?'

'He took it so bad. Threw himself on the coffin. Had to be
dragged off. I think I was actually glad that Agnes wasn't there.
Then they might have helped each other to bear up, but somehow, I have the feeling they would both have reacted the same.
The doctor was here earlier and gave him an injection.'

'Where are the children? I mean, the other two, Danny and
Debbie? Who's looking after them?'

'They're with Sadie at the moment.'

'Can I get you a cup of tea?'

'No, no. Please don't trouble. I only came to pay my respects.'

'I've left a wee cake in the kitchen. It's not much, but it's the least…you know?'

'Does Agnes know the funeral was today?'

Whispered questions, whispered answers. Paddy, awake again, heard the quiet hissing. Whisper, whisper, whisper.

'What are they whispering for? Do they think that by whispering the pain will lessen? Like when someone has a hangover and they say, "Don't shout. It makes it worse." '

Since the tragedy, while Agnes lay in hospital, Paddy could not rest. His dreams were filled with the memory of a sweet little boy who was wearing a fluffy green glove puppet when they lifted him from the wreckage. He wore it still, in his grave. Paddy made sure of that. Why hadn't he listened to him at the station? Tommy had wanted to tell him something about a floorshow and Paddy had not had time to hear it. He had plenty of time to badger Agnes though, about the money she had been spending!

'I want that moment back!' he screamed silently, time and again. Sometimes his grief turned to hot anger and he threw things about. Pots, plates, shoes, anything, and when he became aware of the noise he was making, he shouted even more loudly, 'and just let Granny Park complain! If that decrepit old biddy as much as mentions the word noise I'll…I'll…' He struck his palm with a fist. 'Always complaining about him, she was. Never gave the kid a moment's peace! "He's been shouting in the close again, Mr Preston. Can ye not get him to stop? The echo makes it twice as loud." "He's been trailing in dirt again, Mr Preston. I've had to sweep the landing three times today." Well, he'll not go shouting in the close any more, and he won't be trailing in any more dirt. That's one less kid she'll have to put up with! She'll be happy about that.'

In this, he wronged the decrepit old biddy. She had her own torturous conscience to contend with. She sat hiding in her home, terrified of meeting Paddy or facing Agnes when she eventually got home, (please God,) having no idea what she could say. Too late, she had come to appreciate that she actually liked those kids, and wee Tommy in particular, but there was no good saying that now. Not after all the earache she'd persisted in doling out to them.

For the first time in her lonely life, Jean Park realised that she should have been more tolerant, kinder even. She had been so spoiled by her easy life, having neither chick nor child to care for, that she had not understood how to live and let live. She attended the wee lad's funeral, but had kept well back from the bereaved Paddy and his relatives. She had never in all her life witnessed anything so painful. When the minister asked the packed congregation to pray for the wee lad's mother, so ill that she could not attend her own son's internment, there was not a soul who did not openly weep, including herself. And when Mr Preston threw himself on that wee white coffin, well——.

≪≫ ≪≫

At visiting time next day, Paddy leant over and kissed Agnes's cheek. She opened her eyes. Danny and Debbie stood at the bottom of the bed. They had been warned what to expect; that their mother would be hooked up to lots of wires and would not be able to move. They were not to be alarmed. The machines and gadgets were there to make her better. She lay facing upwards, only her eyes moving.

'Did you lay him to rest? Is my baby really gone?'
He squeezed her hand tightly. 'Yes.'

'I wanted to be there. I should have been there. Why did you not wait? I begged you to wait until I could be there!' Tears ran sideways from her eyes and soaked her ears.

'Aggie love, you will be in hospital for a long time yet. We could not delay the funeral indefinitely.'

'You don't understand. I needed to be there…'

'Aggie, sh..sh.. The kids are here!'

Agnes became aware of them standing at the foot of the bed. They were holding hands, pale and frightened.

'C'mere babies,' she said. She wanted to hold out her arms and hug them, but she couldn't move. They crept forward and each kissed her gently on the cheek.

'Come nearer where I can see you. I wish I could hug you. You know that, don't you?'

'Never mind, Mammy. We'll hug you.'

They all hugged and their tears mingled.

All at once, Paddy seemed to remember something. 'I've got a surprise for you. Look - it's Jimmy.'

A large figure appeared and leaned his face above her head. Her brother Jimmy, all the way from Texas. He hadn't been home on a visit for six years. More hugs and tears.

'Were you here for the funeral?'

'Of course I was, and Annie too. We got here late on Monday.' He sounded so American.

'It's so good to see you, Jimmy. I've missed you.'

The children cheered up a bit when Agnes smiled. Maybe uncle Jimmy's visit would do her good.

It did do her some good, and in the days to come, she showed slow but steady improvement. Physically, that is. Emotionally, it was another story.

Agnes didn't want to feel better. She didn't want the pain of her injuries to go away. She deserved every agonising ache and more. She had wanted so much to be at her baby's funeral. The doctors had said it was impossible; she was unfit to be moved. She pleaded with Paddy to delay the funeral. She *should* be there. If anyone deserved to witness that event, *she* did. She deserved to suffer every heartbreaking moment of that day, because she had *caused* it. She was a bad mother. She had kept Tommy off school for no good reason. He should have been safe at school. Instead, she had brought him into Glasgow on a train journey in the fog. She did it. Her deceit, her duplicity had killed her own son. She should have been dragged to that funeral and been made to witness it all. She deserved to live with the memory of it all her life. Tears had gone now. Tears were of no use whatsoever. 'Cry all you want,' she told herself. 'You can't bring him back. Cry. Cry.'

She couldn't cry. How false it would be of her to cry. They say a good cry can release the tension and give relief. 'Then cry, I won't. I don't deserve relief. If it wasn't for Paddy and the kids, I'd curl in a ball and stay like that for ever.'

Paddy's birthday had come and gone unnoticed. Christmas and New Year had passed in a haze of plaster cast applications and physiotherapy sessions for Agnes. Progress was slow because her morale was low, the doctors said.

'C'mon, Mrs Preston,' an exasperated nurse had tried to encourage her at one such session. 'You have to try harder. Anyone would think you didn't want to get better!'

Agnes only stared at her with hollow eyes.

In spite of everything, time did pass and people's broken bodies recovered. One by one, those injured in the crash went home from the hospitals that held them. Katie Gillan got home at the end of January and towards the middle of March, it was Agnes's turn. Returning to 'normal' life was the hardest thing of all, harder then any hospital routine. For both women, the world as they had known it had changed forever. Large empty holes had appeared in their hearts and no operation could fix that.

Agnes and Paddy skirted gingerly around each other, their relationship under a strain. They said very little, especially about the tragedy. Debbie and Danny seemed to catch this subdued atmosphere, and played quietly when indoors, reading or doing jigsaws, not watching much television. Watching television was a 'normal' activity and was seldom indulged in. Maybe when things got back to normal, they would be livelier, like they used to be. But who would turn on this 'normal' switch? It was as if some electricity had failed somewhere in their lives, and there were no electricians to reconnect the supply.

For the sake of the children, Paddy and Agnes tried to be normal. They watched T.V, and once or twice, one or other of them actually forgot themselves in the programme and would laugh out loud. Then a guilty silence followed as each wondered how on earth they could laugh when this awful thing had occurred. Surely laughter could never be allowed again? Not when little Tommy was......not with little Tommy......!

They muddled on with their lives, and the weeks passed. It was mid summer before the inevitable happened. The laying of blame. It all started over something very trivial. Debbie had gone to play at Laura Bradshaw's house and had, Agnes said, been told to be back in time for tea at five-thirty. It was now nearly seven, the others had eaten and there was still no sign of Debbie. Agnes tried to stay away from the window, but kept returning, searching the street below for her daughter's fair head. Irrationally, she began to panic.

'Danny, go at once to Laura Bradshaw's house and tell Debbie to come home immediately. She should know better than to be so late.'
Danny was making great headway with a difficult jigsaw and was reluctant to leave it.

'Mam, there's no need to worry. You know Laura Bradshaw's got visitors from America, don't you? Debbie's probably stayed on to have her tea there. She's absolutely besotted with one of Laura's American cousins.'

'Besotted, is she? I'll give her besotted. You go and get her now.'

Danny went, clumping huffily towards the door and muttering about how unfair his life was. Paddy asked, 'Did you definitely tell her to be back by five-thirty?'

'Of course I did. Anyway, she knows we have our tea at six.'

'It's just that she knows you are bound to worry, and if you'd given her a time, it's not like her to be late.'

'What are you saying? Are you saying I didn't tell her when to be back?'

'Aggie, don't be so sensitive. I'm only saying that maybe you didn't stress the time, assuming that she'd know to be back in time for tea.'

'I know what I said, Paddy.'

'Aye well, we don't always know if what you say is what you mean.'

Guilt was so embedded in Agnes's heart, that she immediately assumed this might be a reference to the day they never mentioned. The day she was responsible for her son being in the wrong place at the wrong time.

'What do you mean by that, Paddy? Do you think I tell lies?'

He looked straight at her and raised his eyebrows questioningly. He was thinking of the change in her nowadays. The uncomfortable, stinted conversations she had with everyone now that confused him and today he was tired of making allowances for her grief and the fact that she was still convalescent. 'I don't know, Ag. I don't know anything anymore. I don't know why you just can't be straight with people. Maybe if you had......' He stopped himself, but not in time.

A dark silence descended on both of them, like a cold shower. They stood very still.

A moment more he waited, and then he walked from the room and Agnes heard him leave the house. It was the first time he had ever walked out on her. She felt suddenly faint, and gripped the edge of the table, a growing discomfort in the pit of her stomach.

Debbie came home with Danny a few minutes later, protesting.

'Mam! I was having such a great time at Laura's. Mrs Bradshaw let me have my tea with them, so it's okay, I've eaten. And Laura's cousins are so cute. They are called Tony and Freddy. You should hear how they talk! Quite different from our uncle Jimmy in Texas. They're from Denver, Colorado. Isn't that so exciting! Please let me go back. Can I Mam? Please!'

Agnes nodded, defeated. 'You can stay until nine, okay? Nine. Do you hear?' She had to call the last word after her, as Debbie had skipped to the door, hurrying excitedly away. 'Yes, mum. Thanks, mum.'

She went to the window and watched her young daughter skip happily along the street.

Cute, eh? American boys! Well, maybe the child could do with a diversion considering all they'd been through. She was twelve years old, after all. Agnes remembered being twelve.

Paddy returned much later. He smelled of beer. He offered a mumbled apology, which Agnes accepted quietly, but he never said the words she really wanted to hear. Words like,

It was never you're fault.

How could you know what would happen?

I'm glad you survived.

I'm glad you are here and that I didn't lose both of you.

We are hurting so badly, but it will get better.

We have to realise that it could have been even worse. It could have been the two of you.

That's what she wanted to hear. That's what she needed to hear, but Paddy had no way of knowing this, because she had never mentioned her secret quest to get him a special birthday present, though she had explained that Tommy really hadn't needed new trousers or new shoes, and that she'd brought him along with her that day just to have some company.

∽◌∾ ∽◌∾

It was a few weeks before Paddy got a clearer insight into what was going on inside his wife's head. A 'Personal Property' office had been set up for relatives and survivors to claim belongings that had been gathered from the wreckage. Agnes and Paddy had never been, but now it was time to do it. They went together, hand in hand, to look along the rows of trestle tables where all that had been salvaged had been respectfully laid out. She recognised her parcels immediately. That stupid, stupid car radio had survived without a dent. *WITHOUT A DENT*! In perfect working order! She couldn't bear to look at the thing. The thing she'd cheated Tommy out of his life to buy. She wept bitterly at the box of 'Boyproof' shoes, child size twelve, which had never made it to the Christmas party. It was the first time she had cried. And Paddy let her.

When the presence of the car radio was explained to Paddy, he began to understand the extent of the guilt Agnes was carrying. Back in the car, before he started up the engine, Paddy looked at Agnes's and his own eyes filled. He gripped the steering wheel and, staring straight ahead, he said, 'Ag, it was not your fault. Do not feel that. I used to hear my mother say that after every death there is always the If Only. We have to understand that.' He paused and choked out his own If Only.

'He tried to tell me about his puppet show and I didn't have time to listen. Tell me later, I said. Later. There was no later.

That was it. That was my last chance to listen to him, ever! I wake up some nights screaming in my head because I want to know what he wanted to say. I'll never know now. It's too late. Too late.'

The last two words disappeared into a choking sound and Paddy wept too while Agnes pressed her head against his.

∽∾∾ ∽∾∾

When the inquest into the disaster finally got under way, it transpired that a freight train, carrying empty coal wagons had somehow been crossing the main passenger line at the wrong time. The drivers of both trains had survived the impact and were able, after a time, to clarify what had been mystifying officials. The front carriage of the passenger train was almost completely mangled, having suffered the full brunt of the impact. The intricate details of the how and the why meant nothing to the Gillans or the Prestons. No published facts or figures were ever going to include the only news they would love to hear; that the death toll had been miscounted and that Tommy and Lily and Terry were unaccountably safe and well and had been in a hospital somewhere, suffering from amnesia. Even though the bodies had been positively identified and the funerals had taken place, it was still hard to believe that all this had actually happened, and it was the easiest thing in the world to imagine there had been a colossal mistake somewhere and the nightmare could be over. For a little while, Agnes actually believed this might happen, and then she knew it wouldn't. The long hard slog through the Great Healer, – Time, began at last.

∽∾∾ ∽∾∾

The car radio was installed and Paddy was proud of himself. He carried out all his own repairs, and realised he was good at car maintenance. He decided to enrol in classes at night school to learn more, and swapped shifts accordingly. In no time at all, local people came to him for help in fixing their cars and he was kept pretty busy.

When they broke the news of Lily's death to Eddie, his heart actually stopped beating. His body went limp and the only thing he was aware of was the pain. He rallied, of course, but not fully. He receded into his lonely world again, the world he inhabited before Lily came. Was God punishing him because he'd actually fallen in love with Lily before her marriage ended? Nobody knew that. He hadn't even told Lily until her divorce was all but final. Whatever the reason, the brief interlude where he thought that life held more for him was over. He would never open his heart again. It was not worth all the pain. He would learn his lesson this time. To care was to invite pain and hurt.

⚜ ⚜

The boy who had been the amusing and genial life and soul of every party, Jamsie Gillan, and who had broken a score of hearts when he married Terry Briody, began to drink in pubs he'd never set foot in before. He became aggressive and quarrelsome, finding any excuse to have a punch-up with anyone who crossed his path. It added to his mother's pain that he spent more than one night in the local police station in the months following the tragedy.

Katie spent hours on her knees before the Lady altar in the chapel, her lips silently mouthing prayers to the movement of her rosary beads as they slipped through her fingers, trying to find consolation in the belief that God knows best. He must know best, mustn't He? After all, if He was the Architect of Man's sojourn on earth, if He was the Great Providence, the great and loving Heavenly Father, who gave no one any reason, but implied, through his ministers on earth, that he had one, then this suffering, this uncertainty, must all be worthwhile, must all be for *something!*

Katie decided she would hang on to her faith a little longer. Maybe God would send her hope again. She would be a good Christian and take it all uncomplainingly.

Children continued to laugh and play games in the street, Danny and Debbie among them, behaving like the others, running, jumping and shouting.

Sparky followed Paddy everywhere whenever he could. Man and dog were often seen walking together, either going to or coming from the cemetery. Dogs were not allowed in the cemetery, but Paddy was never asked to leave the little grave where the doggie lay quietly and waited until Paddy was ready to move on.

∽◌♁∾ ∽◌♁∾

Most visibly affected by Lily's tragic death had been old Martha McLaughlin. Lily's daughter Barbara came with Eddie McKenna to collect some of Lily's things, and Martha tried to make tea but her mind was just a muddle and she couldn't remember where anything was.

'I don't know how I'm going to manage without her,' she said for the fourth time, dabbing at her reddened eyes with the hem of her pinny. "I came to depend on her so much. And our life here had changed. There are no boarders now, which is just as well. I couldn't cope on my own anyway. But I don't want boarders back. I want Lily back.'

Eddie, who's own heart felt like lead said, 'Course you'll manage. 'Course you will!'

'She was like a daughter to me. She was the daughter I never had.' This was true. Lily had found in Martha the mother figure she had lost so young; someone to listen to her problems and make comments and offer solutions, just like a mother would. They had quickly discovered that they shared the same sense of humour and laughed at the same things. Although Martha was now nearly eighty, she had loved pouring over fashion magazines with Lily, as she planned her wedding outfit. Lily had settled in so easily, she had become part of the house and Martha had been content to hand over the reins to her. She could relax at last. She knew now that she could not go back to the hard work on her own.

'Can't do it any more. Can't do it. I miss her so much.' She sobbed silently and Eddie and Sadie stood by numbly, feeling every bit of her distress.

Left alone when they'd gone, Martha sat a long time by the fireplace. She rubbed her arthritic knees through her heavy denier stockings and recalled the day Eddie McKenna had come knocking on the kitchen door.

'Morning, Martha. Can I speak to you for a minute? It's about renting a room.'

He had a deep pleasant-sounding voice, and his crinkly-eyed smile appealed to her. She showed him into the kitchen, moving a stack of towels from a chair so he could sit down.

Eddie McKenna had never gone shopping in his life. His daughter Helen attended to all that sort of stuff, and before that his sister took care of it, yet here he was, virtually shopping for a room to let for somebody he hardly even knew. He coughed lightly into his hand and fidgeted. He began.

'I wondered if you had a room to let, and if it might be available right now.'

Martha was surprised. Why would Eddie McKenna want a room? He had a perfectly good home, that he shared with his daughter and new son-in-law. Maybe they'd fallen out. If she took him in, it could be awkward, being involved in a family feud, especially with his sister living next door.

'Actually I wasn't planning to re-let again Eddie. Tell me, would it be a long term or a short term let you'd want?'

'It could be for quite a long time, I think. Maybe a year, or even longer.' Then Eddie realised that he wasn't making himself clear. 'Oh, the room is not for me. No. It's for a friend of mine. A lady. She's staying with her sister, but she wants a place of her own, even if it's only temporary.'

A lady. Martha was intrigued. 'I've never had a woman boarder before. I was not planning to have any more guests, but you've got me thinking. It might be nice to have a woman in the house.'

'You'll like this woman.' Eddie's voice could not hide his eagerness, or his eyes their sparkle.

She offered him a cup of tea, but he politely refused. By the time he left he'd arranged to bring Lily to see her.

They came next day accompanied by Katie, and soon it was all fixed.

Martha's eyes misted over. 'I had never realised just how lonely I was until Lily came,' she remembered. No brothers or sisters, no nephews or nieces, no kith, no kin, Martha had tasted the joy of Family through all of Lily's comings and goings. It was going to be doubly hard being on her own again. Why does God play these cruel tricks on people? She had thanked him time and again for Lily, yet all of a sudden she was gone. Did The Lord giveth and The Lord taketh away? It would seem so! She got up and busied herself in the kitchen. She did not like remembering. It was too painful, but how do you stop memories cascading into your mind?

What was that? Was that Lily laughing? No, no. It was just someone in the street outside. Who's that? She thought she heard Lily calling her and got up to see.

Lily's room was empty, her bed empty and still. Make-up on the dresser, a book on the bedside table. Pink fluffy mules lying in the corner mocked Martha. A sign of life, but a past life. She went to bed and took two sleeping pills.

Martha survived only a few more months. She gradually got weaker, and Katie took to staying over at her house to keep an eye on her. She died peacefully in her sleep one night while Katie held her hand.

✑✑ ✑✑

Soon after, Barbara Dunne received a surprising letter from Martha's lawyer. It seemed that Martha had made her will out in Lily's favour, leaving the house and everything in it to Lily. Should Lily predecease her, (thought to be a highly unlikely occurrence at the time,) the estate was to go to Lily's daughter Barbara Dunne. All the legalities were examined, and it appeared that Barbara was the rightful heir of what should have been her mother's property. She was now the owner of 'Quarryknowe', the lovely old property in Uddingston.

Barbara was flabbergasted. This was a totally unexpected turn of events. She went at once to her Aunt Katie to discuss it. She found Jamsie there with her. She tried to explain how she felt.

'The lawyer told me that mum had no idea that Martha had done this. Martha had arranged it all in secret and had entrusted them not to tell mum. She would have had a fit. Can you imagine it? I am absolutely stunned. I don't even know if I'm happy or not. It all seems so wrong. It's not the way it was supposed to be.'

'You be happy about it darling,' Katie said, reaching across the table and patting Barbara's arm. 'Who are we to know what life has in store? We take what comes, good and bad, and live on. We will never be able to figure things out.'

Barbara looked at Jamsie.

'Don't ask me. I don't know if you should be happy or not. I was happy and the rug was pulled from under me. I'm with ma on this. Some things happen. You can't do anything but go with it. We are all pawns in the Big Man's sick games. And when my turn comes, I'll be happy to go. I had a good life for a while. I had a happy life. But I don't want life anymore. It's not that I don't like life. It's that I don't like death. Death spoils everything, because we can't predict it and we can't prevent it. Life would be okay if it wasn't for death. There's no point in living when you only have death to look forward to, and I look forward to mine.'

Katie was shocked at these morbid revelations from the mouth of her son.

'Jamsie, son,…..' she began, but he held up his hand.

'Don't, Ma. Don't say it. Not just now!' He got up from the table and left the house.

CHAPTER 15

Katie, Back on Track.

Katie took her seat in the waiting room at the surgery, trying not to show the apprehension she was feeling. She had suffered from memory lapses and bad headaches ever since her severe head injury at the time of the accident had sent her into a month-long coma. She remembered the essential things, like who she was and where she lived, but she often forgot the names of everyday objects; words like shovel, or marmalade, or wrist watch or picture frame. She knew that the names that escaped her were just under the surface of her memory, waiting to pop into her head, but the words just wouldn't come. And as for *people's* names – well! Jamsie had once or twice laughed at her and told her she was suffering from old age ditheriness. She was secretly terrified that this might be true. These episodes of forgetfulness caused her to stay at home because she never knew when the lapses would occur, and her constant worry about them seemed to make them and the headaches worse. She seldom ventured out now, doing most of her shopping in the nearby corner shop instead of in the main street, where she once loved to trot, hoping to meet her cronies for a good old chinwag. How things had changed! She flicked through a magazine, smiling, seemingly unconcerned, at the new receptionist.

'Shouldn't be too long now, Mrs Gillan,' the woman said for the third time, and Katie nodded.

The buzzer sounded above Dr Mowatt's door.

'Right, Mrs Gillan, that's you!' the receptionist said unnecessarily, because Katie was already turning the handle and entering the surgery.

In previous years, she had been an infrequent visitor here, and it was only during her late husband's illness that Dr Mowatt became acquainted with the Gillans. Since her dismissal from hospital though, she had become a more familiar face, and Dr Mowatt was very aware of the circumstances that created this change. After a few words of greeting, she began talking right away.

'I feel that my memory has been irreparably damaged, Doctor. I cannot remember the accident at all. I remember having my hair done with Lily. I remember eating a meal somewhere, but nothing at all after that. I cannot remember boarding that train. If only I could remember what actually happened, maybe I could understand why I survived and so many others didn't. Then there is another part of me that doesn't want to remember. I don't even want my mind to think. I want to blot it all out and not even remember that Lily or Terry ever existed. Remembering is the sorest thing. So painful. And when I try to think what Jamsie must be going through, and Eddie McKenna, or even Mr McKean, who lost both his lovely children, I wish I could FORGET, FORGET, FORGET.' These last words were said loudly and with great despair, holding on to her temples, as if trying to push something into her brain, or out of it. She stared into space for a minute, trying to find words to explain the unexplainable. 'It's like I don't want to be in this time and place. I won't go out in case I meet someone who wishes I had died instead of their loved one.'

Katie realised she was crying. Fat wet blobs splashed down her face so fast she had no way of stopping them. And sobs. She could speak no more because of them. Her whole body shook, and gave way to uncontrollable gusty expirations.

Dr Mowatt came round the desk and held her hands. He said nothing until

Katie's paroxysm subsided. Exhausted, she sat quietly hiccupping, drying the incessant tears with her sodden hanky.

She started to apologise. 'I'm sorry Doctor. I did not mean to do that. I thought I was beyond tears. I have not cried since – since – '.

'Okay, Mrs Gillan, let's get you checked out.' He chatted informally while he took her blood pressure; looked again at the external wounds, healing nicely, and then he asked her a few questions.

'Right.' He was back at his side of the desk, checking through her notes. 'On the whole I am very pleased with you. Your memory lapses are certainly due to the very severe injuries you have sustained, and are a common factor in recovery stages. The good news is, they may get better, and it's possible they may even disappear in time, but I can assure you, they will not get worse. You are definitely over the worst.'

A quiet sigh from Katie indicated a slight relief of pent-up tension.

'I was afraid that I might be going senile,' she said quietly.

'No. You must not underestimate what you have been through.'

Are you joking? Katie thought, *there's hardly any chance of that!*

Dr Mowatt continued. 'Your blood pressure is slightly raised, but no cause for alarm. Easily treatable. The headaches are another matter. I believe they are migraine headaches, brought on in the first place by the accident. However, I feel that in your case, their continuance is more likely to have an emotional, rather than a physical cause. These headaches can be the result of worry and tension. I know that you are very worried about James, understandably so, and I think that this could well be the underlying cause of both the headaches and your higher blood pressure. I will give you pills for both.'

He wrote the prescription and explained how to take the medication. As Katie got up to go, he asked, 'How is James, Mrs Gillan? Is he coping any better?'

'I hardly know how to answer that question, Doctor,' Katie sighed. 'You are right. I am desperately worried about Jamsie. He is a different lad. A different person altogether, and I can't help him. He doesn't want help and he cares for nothing or no one now. He drinks too much. He's irritable all the time, and argumentative. He takes time off work, something he never did before. I'm afraid he'll lose his job and when I say so, he gets angry and tells me to mind my own business. As if he *wasn't* my business! In fact, I'm glad he has his own place because his mood can change in an instant and I'm almost afraid to speak in case it sets him off. I feel as if I am watching him – ' (she was going to say 'ride straight to hell in a handcart,' but thought better of it, in case the doctor wouldn't approve of that kind of language.) Instead, she said, ' - throw his life away. He used to be such a lovely lad. And I feel sorry for myself too, because I have no one to talk to now. There is no Lily, and I certainly can't talk to Jamsie.' She wiped her eyes all the time with her totally useless hanky.

Katie pulled on her gloves and lifted her umbrella from the chair, but the doctor came forward and taking her elbow kindly, he led her back to her seat.

'I want you to listen carefully to me now. We are in the process here of building a whole new health care programme; the new health centre is nearly finished, and soon several surgeries are going to share the benefits of specialised nursing care and new services. The groundwork has been established and is already in operation. We are now able to offer far better individual care. There is a therapist I'd like you to see. She specialises in loss of memory and other complications due to trauma and accidents. I'll make an appointment for you and you'll be notified when to attend.'

'Will I have to see her at the hospital?'

'No. You will see her here, at this surgery. A room will be made available – unless the new building will be opened for business by then. That's a possibility, because it could take a week or two to get an appointment and the new heath centre building is due to open next month.'

He paused, then continued. 'The thing is, I would really like you to mention this to James. I feel he would be greatly helped if he could meet with this therapist too – in his own time, of course. Maybe you could suggest that he comes to see me and we have a talk about it.'

Katie looked doubtful. She knew Jamsie needed help, but she would hesitate to suggest this. He might hit the roof! Then she thought of an idea. She would phone Joe, Jamsie's older brother. He could surely help.

'I'll see what I can do, Doctor,' she said. 'He doesn't take kindly to what he calls 'interference', but I'll try to broach the subject, or at least get his brother to. For my part, I think it's got to be worth a try. Thank you very much for your help, and your time today, Doctor. I feel a bit more encouraged now. Now that I know I am really over the worst.'

Katie left the surgery in raised spirits. It's amazing what just having a chat with someone can do. She would not have described herself as being 'in the pink', but she was definitely feeling much better. Learning that her memory lapses were not the onset of senility, (of which she had an absolute dread,) had uplifted her. It was such a relief to know that she was going to get help and counselling. It made her realise that she wanted to talk about all that she had been through. She wanted to tell someone how it felt to wake up in hospital and learn that you'd been there over a month and that your sister and daughter-in-law were dead. She wanted to cry on someone's shoulder and tell them all about the pain in her back and in her neck and in her shoulders – the list could go on and on. You see, she told herself, I don't have Lily to talk to now, and Jamsie, well, he couldn't bear to hear it, and no wonder!

She decided to take her newfound courage in her hands and walk into the town. Her first stop was the chemist where she collected her prescription; that done, she made her way to McKean's Butchers. Through the window she could see Roy McKean, white coated, slicing Lorne sausages from the batched block of minced meat. The bell jangled and he raised his head slightly as she stepped on to the sawdusty floor. Suddenly, he darted into the back shop, leaving his young assistant to attend to her. Katie was so taken aback and so hurt by Roy McKean's hasty retreat that she hardly heard a word that Harry the Butcher Boy said to her. She left, feeling bewildered with some pork links and half a pound of Ayrshire bacon.

Turning into Neilson Street, she bumped into Carol Lively. Carol was one of her cronies from the Woman's Guild. She gave Katie a hug and said how pleased she was to see her out and about. Katie was not used to public displays of affection; in fact, having had only sons, she was not used to any displays of affection at all. A gruff 'How are ye, Ma? Okay?' to which she always felt obliged to answer Yes, was about as loving as it got for her. She was a little overwhelmed by the kindness in Carol's greeting, and she tried to respond without bursting into those dreaded tears again. It had started to rain again and Carol sheltered Katie with her umbrella while Katie said, 'This is actually the first time I've been out on my own for a while. I'm getting tired now and was just on my way home.'

'You look shattered, Katie. C'mon into Di Giacomo's for a cup of tea. Let's get out of the rain.' Too exhausted to resist, Katie was ushered into the nearby café. This was new territory for her. She had never seen the need to buy a cup of tea in Di Giacomo's since she lived only a few hundred yards away.

Much cheaper and more comfortable just to go home and put the kettle on and her feet up. But in no time, she found herself sitting opposite Carol in a leather-lined booth, with a pot of tea and two slices of hot buttered toast in front of her. She felt weird, as if some outside force had taken over her life and was orchestrating her movements. Everything was being arranged for her and now she was eating tea and toast that she didn't think she wanted, yet she was surprised to discover that the tea was just to her taste; nice and hot. The toast was great too; pan bread. Katie made a mental note to buy some later.

Carol said, 'I often come here, especially on a Friday. I get a coffee and read the local paper. It's busy on a Friday, and you can catch all the gossip.'

So that's how she does it, thought Katie. She had often envied Carol's ability to be first at the Guild with any big news. Katie was always the last to know anything! And yet, Carol was not a gossip. Far from it! She was interested in people, and like her surname, she was lively, but she was also caring and discreet with anything she learned. Katie had known her for years, and before long she was telling Carol everything that had happened to her today. She mentioned how hurt she was at Roy McKean's behaviour.

'I know he saw me, but he just ignored me. I think it was because I survived the crash and his children didn't. I was so embarrassed. I've been a customer since he opened that shop, but I won't be going in again.'

'Katie, don't you know? Don't you know what's happened?' Carol asked softly.

Katie was puzzled. Of course she knew what happened. She'd been there, hadn't she? She'd lost – she'd lost – . She'd lost, too.

Carol continued. 'Roy McKean has never spoken a word since the accident. Not one word. He doesn't serve anybody at all. As soon as someone enters the front shop, he darts into the back. He uses his own made-up sign language to communicate with his wife and his staff. It's been the talk of the town. Tragedy on tragedy, people are saying.'

Katie was flabbergasted. Roy McKean had been the biggest blether. He never stopped talking. But she had been so quick to judge. Poor Mr McKean! What he must be suffering! Trying to run a business while coping with his double loss. Will this never go away, she wondered? She began to feel extremely tired. She had had a very emotional day and had learned so much and it wasn't even lunchtime. She told Carol that she'd have to get home. Carol walked with her to the railway bridge.

'Will we see you at the Guild on Wednesday?' she asked.

'I don't think so, Carol. I'm not ready to face people yet. I'll think about it. I will be back, but not yet.'

Carol said she understood, and gave Katie her phone number and another hug.

Over the next few days, Katie thought hard about Roy McKean and about how this terrible event had affected everyone. She remembered how Joe had developed a stutter when he was stressed. She must fight the compulsion to stay indoors and become a recluse. Maybe a wee trip to Saltcoats for a few days would help. She'd see Joe, Julie and the kids. Maybe get a chance to talk to Joe about Jamsie. Kill two birds with the one stone,eh?

She bought her ticket.

CHAPTER 16

The Not-Very Artful Dodger.
1974

As the fare-dodging drunk followed him through each carriage, hurling abuse, Paddy wondered if he should have listened to his mother all those years ago. She had begged him not to follow in his late father's footsteps by joining the railway, but to stay on at school and get good qualifications, and consequently, a 'good' job. But being the son of a railway signalman, it was already too late for Paddy. Trains and railways were in his blood. As a wee boy, he and his brothers had spent many hours in the signal box with his father during the school holidays. And unknown to his father, he often played on the wagons that lay idle overnight in the I.C.I. complex a mile away. Sometimes he would be caught by the irate night watchman and would be dragged by the elbow, home to his embarrassed parents. More often than not, though, he would outrun the watchman, and live to 'drive his trains' another day. He knew every stretch of track in the area where he grew up, and when he lay in bed at night listening to the clanking and shunting noises from the nearby marshalling yard, he could name every locomotive just by the sound it made.

But he didn't have time to think of that now as he travelled along the aisle examining people's tickets and pretending not to notice the hooligan who was following him. The other passengers seemed to find the man's antics hilarious, and Paddy hoped their laughter might help to keep things from getting out of hand, but what was he going to do about him? He was worried, and was playing for time by continuing to call for tickets and to talk to passengers, seemingly unconcerned. Abusive passengers, stroppy mothers with unruly children, teenage pranksters who though that jamming the automatic doors open with a bulky holdall was great fun, were all part of the job and Paddy was good at his job. He had learned to defuse most potentially bad situations with good humour and a generally helpful attitude, but drunks were hardest to handle because they were unpredictable. At best, they could be funny, or annoyingly amiable; at worst, they could be nasty and violent, and there were children aboard today who could become frightened if this one proved to be the latter.

It had been a tiresomely eventful day already. Holiday traffic and the extra summer excursions made this particular line very busy. The hot weather, being surprisingly seasonal for once, had caught most people out, and the heavy coats and cardigans that they had started out with were no longer necessary. Along with the hard-pressed staff, passengers had become hot and bothered, uncomfortably lugging around hastily doffed clothing with their luggage. Paddy wished, not for the first time, that the railway uniform could have a lighter, summer-weight variant.

Earlier this morning the train had ground to a halt on the way through Corkerhill. It transpired that some evil pranksters had pulled the communication cord 'for fun'. This was not a regular occurrence, but it did happen a lot more often in the holiday season. In spite of a hefty fine for improper use, every now and then, some joker, usually full of lager, would hit on the 'original' idea of causing as much inconvenience to fellow passengers as possible. *What a laugh! Let's see what happens when* ——. *But don't be seen. We don't want to*

be slapped with the fine, so don't own up, right? Kenny, you do it!
Make like you're going to the toilet, right, and pull the cord two or
three carriages up, then come back here fast. They'll never know who
did it. It'll be a blast, man! Go on, I dare ye!

Paddy was already weary of this trick, and sick of the hassle it caused. But at least he could be pragmatic about it. The
good thing was in discovering that there was no real emergency. The driver was understandably livid, but as the culprits
remained anonymous, there was not much could be done
about it. The cord was re-set and the journey continued.
Some people missed their connections and already fractious
because of the heat, sounded off at the wrong target, namely
the innocent staff at the ticket barrier.

Then there had been thirty members of a cycling club,
who'd booked tickets, but hadn't thought to pay for the trans-
portation of their bikes. Thirty bikes! These they were happily
trying to load into the guard's van when Paddy came across
them. With not one of them paid for, and none of them pre-
booked, this caused quite a problem and more delays while it
was all sorted out.

Paddy glanced now at the drunk who was tailing him and
wished for a moment that he'd had a pint or two inside himself.
This man and his wife had joined the train at Saltcoats.. Panting and gasping for breath they had barely managed to scram-
ble aboard with their luggage before the doors closed and the
train pulled away from the station.

'What did ye pick this carriage for?' breathed the man, still
panting from the exertion of dragging his heavy suitcase
halfway along the platform. 'There was a door stopped right
beside us where we stood.'

'It wisnae a smoker. Ye'll want a smoker, will ye no'?'
Breathing heavily, the woman looked around for a seat whilst
trying to catch some air back into her lungs. With one arm

lugging a heavy suitcase and the other clutching a number of carrier bags, she pointed with her chin.

'There's wan right at the end.'

They squeezed along the passageway to where two empty seats were available.

'We'd better get these cases up on the rack. It'll gie mair room.' The man grabbed the largest of the cases and struggled to raise it above his head.

'Boaby! Don't stand on the seat!' She looked round apologetically at the other passengers and shook her head in her husband's direction as if to say, *'He's not normally as badly behaved as this. I don't know what's got into him.'*

As was soon discovered, several pints of beer and maybe a few whiskies had got into him.

After a few abortive attempts in which other peoples' cardigans and coats were dislodged, replaced and generally shuffled around - *Oh, sorry pal. Wis that your anorak? I didnae see it there*, - they eventually got their suitcases up on the luggage rack above them and plonked down on the seat where they fell into a pointless argument about whose fault it was that they nearly missed the train.

'We wouldn't have had to rush so much if you hadn't disappeared just when the train was due in. Trust you!' said the woman.

'Ah needed the toilet.'

'There's toilets on the train!'

'Ah couldnae wait, I've had a' that bevvy.'

'Aye well, the train couldnae wait either. It's a good job you appeared when you did. We nearly missed it.'

'What are you moaning for, woman? We got the bloody train. God in heaven, gie's peace!' He fell into a sulky silence.

Further up the train, Paddy had begun his ticket inspection. He had been working for a time as conductor / guard in the new

Inter City trains, but today, a special day for him, he was on duty on this Class 101 DMU on the west coast route from Largs to Glasgow. It was a busy time; the end of the Glasgow Fair Holiday Fortnight and the train was packed with people returning to the city after their two weeks at the seaside. He negotiated bags and cases that were sticking out into the aisle as he made his way through, calling 'Tickets please,' eventually reaching the Saltcoats couple who suddenly appeared to be sleeping.

'Tickets please.' Paddy said. There was no response.

'Tickets, please.' Paddy said again, a little louder.
Boaby opened his eyes and drowsily indicated the luggage rack above his head.

'They're in the case.' he said, sending a beery breath in Paddy's direction and closing his eyes again.

'Well I'm afraid you'll need to get them out of the case, sir,' said Paddy.

Boaby opened his eyes once more and said angrily, 'Will ah hell! Ah'm no pulling that thing doon again. It weighs a fuckin' ton! It took all ma strength to get it up there.'

Oh God! This is all I need today, thought Paddy.

'Look, I need to see your tickets, sir. It's my job to see that everyone has paid the appropriate fare. You'll need to get your tickets out of the case.'

'Away ye go! Ah'm no rummaging through that suitcase on a crowded train. Ye can see for yersel' there's nae room to swing a fuckin' cat.'

Along the carriage, magazines and newspapers were lowered and heads turned towards the scenario as people awaited the outcome.

'Then I'll have to ask you to pay your fare again, sir,' said Paddy

'Aye, that WILL be right!'

The argument went back and forth a little while longer.

'What are you looking at?' Boaby's wife snarled suddenly at the passenger opposite, who immediately retreated behind his copy of the Sun with renewed interest in whatever was in its pages. She then turned to her husband and wagged a finger in his face.

'Look, Boaby. Get the man the tickets or gie him the money,' she said.

Boaby slouched back in his seat and folded his arms.

'*You* gie him the money,' he said.

'Ah've no' got any money. Fine ye know that! You took my last fiver at the Station Bar in Saltcoats.'

'Look, I'll tell you what I'll do,' said Paddy. 'I'll carry on through the train checking tickets and when I've finished, I'll come back to you. Either have your tickets ready for inspection or pay your fare. If not, you'll be lugging your cases along the road, O.K, pal?'

Paddy turned and walked into the next compartment calling 'Tickets please!'

He was wearing the new regulation uniform, complete with the cap emblazoned with BR's double arrowed logo. Suddenly a voice behind him said -

'Gie ye's a uniform and ye's become wee fuckin' Hitlers.'

Paddy glanced round and to his horror, there was drunken Boaby following behind. He was doing a goosestep. His right arm was stretched out in a Nazi style salute and he was holding his left forefinger under his nose to emulate a Hitler-like moustache. In this way, he followed Paddy through several carriages.

STOMP, STOMP! went the goosestep. Boaby straightened his knee out in front of him with each step and brought his heels together in a clicking sound whenever he stopped.

Paddy tried to pretend that Boaby wasn't there and carried on with his job.

'Tickets please. Any more tickets, please?'

'Give zee Gestapo your fuckin' tickets or you vill be thrown from thees train.' Boaby assumed a German accent, and STOMP, STOMP, CLICKED, behind Paddy.

Paddy checked some more tickets and moved on

'Any more tickets, please?'

'No need to be afraid, mien Frau.' Boaby bent his face into that of a bemused middle-aged woman. *''E ees only doing hees job.'*

STOMP, STOMP. CLICK!

'What time are we due in at Paisley?' a man asked Paddy, glancing sideways at Boaby and back again to Paddy. Before Paddy could reply, Boaby rushed forward and staring wildly into the man's face, arm still extended, his finger still acting as a moustache, he yelled in mock menace -

'Vee vill ask zee kwestions!'

And so it continued. Some of the passengers were speechless with laughter. They were enjoying the spectacle while Paddy pretended to be taking it all in good part and see the funny side, though inwardly he could only hope that it wouldn't turn nasty.

Paddy gave the passenger the necessary information and sighed inwardly.

'Tickets, please.'

'You heard zee Commandant! Show your teeckets. NOW!'

STOMP! STOMP!

Eventually boozy Boaby, evidently feeling that he'd made his point, stumbled back to his seat, pleased and exhausted with his own performance, and Paddy was able to continue his work.

After doing a complete ticket check, he made his way back through the train, which was now pulling into Johnstone station, about halfway to Glasgow. Paddy reached boozy Boaby's seat just as the train was slowing to a halt. It stopped right beside two railway policemen who just happened to be standing at that very spot on the platform where the window of Boaby's seat came to a stop.

'Hello Paddy. Everything all right?' one of them asked through the opened top of the window.

The panic on Boaby's face was wonderful to see. He must have assumed that somehow, Paddy had arranged for the policemen to be there, because all of a sudden, he reached into his pocket and pulled out a handful of crumpled notes and coins.

'Two singles tae Glesga,' he said.

∾∾∽ ∾∾∽

Paddy was especially relieved to know that Boaby's escapade had ended without incident, because this was his very last day on the job. At 3.45pm when his feet jumped down on to Platform 13 at Glasgow Central, Paddy Preston, one time ticket clerk, guard, signalman and lastly, conductor, would hang up his arrowed cap for the last time. When he travelled back to Ardrossan tonight to attend his farewell do at the Railway Club, he would be just an ordinary passenger. The last five years had been really tough for Paddy and Agnes. After the tragedy, the sight of a railway track filled Agnes's heart with sadness. She couldn't see a railway uniform without reliving that awful day, and she had never been on a train since. Paddy too had lost the total commitment to his job that he once had. It wasn't working for him any more, and the railway had not felt the same to him for some time.

He had finished his training and was now a fully qualified car mechanic. He and his neighbour from downstairs, Walter Samson were going into business together and were opening a car maintenance workshop.

'How do you feel about that?' someone had asked Agnes.

'I think it's great. We're both very excited about it. Now that I've passed my driving test, we travel mostly by car anyway, so it makes sense that Paddy should know how to fix cars. And he loves it, which I find most surprising of all. I don't think he'll miss the railway at all.'

Famous last words.

As Paddy emptied his locker, and made his way to the office to hand in his locker key, his thoughts returned to his old mother. I've got a proper job at last, ma, he said. I went back to school and got 'good' qualifications. I'm starting my own business. And he wondered what she would have had to say to that if she were still here.

Printed in the United Kingdom
by Lightning Source UK Ltd.
124997UK00001B/223-249/A